Also by Paige Tyler

STAT: Special Threat Assessment Team
Wolf Under Fire
Undercover Wolf

SWAT: Special Wolf Alpha Team
Hungry Like the Wolf
Wolf Trouble
In the Company of Wolves
To Love a Wolf
Wolf Unleashed
Wolf Hunt
Wolf Hunger
Wolf Rising
Wolf Instinct
Wolf Rebel
Wolf Untamed

X-Ops
Her Perfect Mate
Her Lone Wolf
Her Secret Agent (novella)
Her Wild Hero
Her Fierce Warrior
Her Rogue Alpha
Her True Match
Her Dark Half
X-Ops Exposed

ROGUE WOLF

PAIGE TYLER

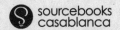
sourcebooks
casablanca

Published by Sourcebooks Casablanca, an imprint of Sourcebooks
P.O. Box 4410, Naperville, Illinois 60567-4410
(630) 961-3900
sourcebooks.com

Printed and bound in Canada.
MBP 10 9 8 7 6 5 4 3 2 1

With special thanks to my extremely patient and understanding husband. Without your help and support, I couldn't have pursued my dream job of becoming a writer. You're my sounding board, my idea man, my critique partner, and the absolute best research assistant a girl could ask for. Love you!

CHAPTER 1

Dallas, Texas

"Man, I hope they're wrong about someone dumping a body out here," Officer Connor Malone murmured as he moved through the heavily wooded area ten yards to Senior Corporal Trey Duncan's left. Fellow SWAT teammate and werewolf Corporal Trevor McCall was another ten yards beyond Connor, while Officer Hale Delaney was a bit farther out, bringing up the end of the search line. "I mean, dumping a body anywhere is sick, but this place is way too beautiful for crap like that."

Trey agreed with his blond teammate. The Trinity River Audubon Center was part nature preserve, part public park along the southern side of the county. In the distance, he could hear the drone of vehicles speeding along the Interstate 20 belt loop, but for the moment at least, the area he and his pack mates were in was quiet and tranquil.

That would all change if they found anything. In a heartbeat, a place usually known only for its slow-moving streams and mist-shrouded walking trails would immediately be overrun with cops and crime scene technicians looking for clues to help them identify the person the local papers had tagged as "the Butcher."

While the name of the latest serial killer to terrorize Dallas might not be original, it was unfortunately devastatingly accurate. Four bodies had been found over the past week and a half. Or more precisely, *parts* of four bodies had been found. In each case, the corpses—all men—had been found dumped in wooded or remote locations missing their heads and both hands. The theory was that the killer was mutilating the bodies to make it harder to identify the victims. If that was the plan, it was working, because the Dallas Police Department had yet to put a name to a single one of them.

Four bodies found with hands and heads removed was morbid and depraved enough, but unfortunately, there was more. Each victim was also missing at least one other body part—the right arm in the first case, right leg in the second, both lungs in the third, and on the body found two nights ago, several whole sections of skin had been missing. The DPD had tried to keep those details secret until they had a suspect, but somehow, it'd leaked out and the media had been running the Butcher storyline nonstop ever since.

"Did you hear what happened to make them think there's a body out here?" Hale asked as he dropped to one knee to look under some thickets near the edge of the stream that served as the leftmost boundary for this part of the search grid. Tall and muscular, he had dark-blond hair and blue eyes.

Trey could have told him there weren't any remains to be found under there. If there were, they'd be able to easily pick up the odor. But even by normal human standards, Hale's nose was bad. Compared to the other members of the pack, their fellow were-wolf couldn't smell anything at all. That's why he tended to trust his keen eyesight for everything.

"Something about an older couple out here walking their dog, I think," Trevor said as he waited patiently for Hale to finish looking under the brush. There was a time when everyone in the Pack used to rag on Hale about his nose, but now, they all felt bad for him.

"Yeah, that's it exactly," Connor said as Hale stood and rejoined their line moving through the woods. "But you missed the best part. It turns out the couple's dog ran off while they were here, and when the poor guy finally came back a few hours later, he was covered in blood. They assumed he was hurt, so they took him to the vet. When the vet figured out the dog was okay and the blood wasn't his, she ran a precipitin test, then called the PD first thing this morning when she confirmed it was human."

"No wonder Chief Leclair pushed to get so many volunteers out here searching." Trevor ran his hand through his dark hair. "If the dog was loose for hours, there's no telling where he was when he found the body. It could be miles from here."

Trey didn't comment and neither did his pack mates. They searched in silence for a while until Trevor spoke again.

"So, how'd your date go last night, Connor?"

If they had been close enough, Trey would have fist-bumped Trevor to thank him for coming up with something to talk about besides the mutilated remains they were out there looking for.

"In a word—a disaster," Connor said, tilting his head back to sniff the morning air like he'd picked up a scent. But whatever it was must not have been all that interesting because he continued, "Seriously, it was the worst date ever."

Trey was fairly sure his pack mate was exaggerating. He'd seen Connor and the nurse talking a couple weeks ago after Connor had gotten roughed up during a confrontation with a drunk man on a bulldozer. Connor hadn't been hurt—he was a frigging werewolf after all—but a reporter had seen the blood, so a trip to the hospital had been mandatory. Which meant Trey had been forced to watch her and Connor flirt for nearly an hour as she'd taken her time cleaning his injuries. There'd definitely been a spark there.

"Come on," he scoffed. "It couldn't have been that bad."

Connor snorted. "Trust me, it was worse." He sighed. "I mean, dinner went fine and there was some chemistry—not any kind of serious connection, but we clicked well enough to see where it might lead—but it all went downhill once I took her back to my place and she met Kat."

"Ah," Trey said in understanding even as Hale and Trevor did the same.

In theory, Kat was the SWAT team's feline mascot, but honestly the cat put up with the SWAT Pack simply because that's who Connor hung out with. She was definitely his cat. Hell, she even followed him on their incident calls, regardless of the danger. And forget trying to keep her and Connor separated. Trevor had tried locking her in the armory to keep Kat from going out on a barricaded active-shooter situation, and the damn cat had shown up at the scene five minutes after the SWAT team, somehow having hitched a ride with a uniformed patrol officer who had no idea she was even in his car. No one had a clue how she'd done it. Suffice it to say, Trevor was her least favorite werewolf in the Pack. The look she gave him every time she saw him would melt the paint off a car. The only reason the creature hadn't come this morning was that it was o dark thirty. Kat never got out of bed this early unless it was to watch Connor and the rest of them shower after physical training.

"What happened?" Trey asked, though he was sure he already knew. Kat had a way of letting people know what she thought of them.

"Nothing at first," Connor said. "Kat was nowhere in sight when Michelle and I got back to my place after dinner, but the moment we sat down on the couch, she jumped up and shoved her way between us, deliberately knocked the glass of wine out of Michelle's hands, then clawed her dress."

Trevor snorted. "I guess Kat didn't approve of your date."

"You think?" Connor asked dryly. "Regardless the date was over. And before you ask, Michelle and I won't be going out again."

"It's not her fault she decided to date a werewolf with a possessive cat for a pet." Trey would have said more, but a familiar scent caught his attention. He stopped and looked left, out across the slow-moving stream.

Trevor and Connor must have smelled it, too, because they both paused and sniffed the air.

"What is it?" Hale asked.

"Blood," Trevor murmured.

Hale didn't bother to try to trace the scent, but simply followed them as they ran along the bank of the stream.

"How are we going to explain ending up on the other side of the stream and well outside our search grid?" Connor asked.

"Don't worry about it," Trey told him. "I'll come up with something believable if anyone asks. Right now, just focus on finding the source of that scent."

They followed the trail for another thousand yards or so before the stream narrowed enough for them to leap across. Not that a normal human would have been able to do it, but that was simply one more lie Trey would have to come up with once the questions started.

The scent led them to a low-lying area blanketed with thickets and brush, the kind of place Trey recognized as perfect for hiding a body—even if getting it here would have been a major pain in the ass for whoever dumped it.

He and his pack mates stopped the moment they saw the body, staying far enough away to hopefully not trample any forensic evidence that might have been left behind. It helped that there was no reason for them to move closer to check for a pulse. Even from fifteen feet away, Trey's hearing told him the victim didn't have a heartbeat.

It was another one of the Butcher's victims. The man lying in the shallow grave had been partially dug up. Probably by the wandering dog. The head and hands were gone, along with another leg. It also looked like the stomach cavity had been ripped open, but that might have been the dog's doing, too. As a cop, and before that a soldier who'd seen more than his fair share of combat, Trey had seen a lot of dead bodies, but this was as bad as anything he'd ever experienced. This killer was sadistic as hell.

"What am I smelling?" Trevor asked, sniffing the air.

Trey took a whiff and realized there were two separate scents competing—and neither of them were blood. The first one was sharp, similar to a cleanser or disinfectant, but with floral notes, like perfume. The other smelled almost human, but something wasn't quite right about it. He was still trying to figure out what it was when he picked up a burnt electrical odor. While the first two scents lingered on the body, the third hovered around it. As if it belonged to whoever had carried the body and dumped it here.

Trevor must have concluded the same thing because he gave Trey a worried look. "You think we're dealing with some kind of supernatural killer?"

Trey almost groaned. That was all they needed. Serial killers were bad enough. But if this one was indeed supernatural, there might be more to the Butcher than they'd thought.

―――――――――

"How exactly did you end up finding the body on this side of the stream when you and your teammates were assigned to a grid nearly a quarter mile away from here?"

Dark hair pulled back in a neat bun, Chief Leclair regarded Trey curiously where they stood several yards away from the organized chaos that was the crime scene.

"Pure luck," he said. "We finished clearing our assigned grid when we saw some buzzards circling this area, so we decided to check it out."

Leclair continued to study him as if she somehow knew he was lying through his teeth. Trey hoped not.

"I see," she finally said in a soft, noncommittal tone before glancing down at the bottom of his tactical uniform pants. "And how did you get across the stream without getting wet?"

Trey did a double take, completely caught off guard by the question. Which is probably why she'd asked it. Damn, he and his pack mates were going to have to be careful around the chief. She was a cop through and through.

"The stream narrows quite a bit if you wander down that way," he said as casually as he could, jerking his thumb in the stream's direction. "We were able to jump across it."

Leclair didn't look like she believed that for a damn second, but at least she didn't continue grilling him about it. "I suppose we should be thankful you followed your instincts and searched this area. I doubt anyone else would have bothered to fight their way through so many thickets on a whim. Then again, it's starting to become the norm for me to find my SWAT team in places where they're not supposed to be. Fortunately, things always seem to go right when you and your teammates go off script."

With that, the chief walked away, heading toward the taped-off crime scene to talk to one of the detectives from the serial killer task force. Given that no one had approached the body yet, it was likely they were waiting for a medical examiner to arrive. Hopefully, they'd get here soon and Leclair would be too focused on that to worry about him and the other members of his pack. Because she definitely seemed suspicious right now.

"Everything okay?" Connor asked as he came up beside him. "You and the chief seemed to be having an intense conversation."

"I think we're good," Trey answered. "Though I'm pretty sure she knows I'm lying about how we found the body."

Connor blew out a breath. "I figured as much. We need to be careful around her. She's sharp."

Trey opened his mouth to agree, but the words got stuck in his throat as a blond-haired woman carrying a heavy-looking bag with the Dallas County Medical Examiner's Office emblem on the side approached the crime scene tape and walked directly over to the chief. Between the bag that she had to lug half a mile through the woods in the mid-August heat and the navy blue coveralls she was wearing over her regular clothes, complete with high rubber boots, Dr. Samantha Mills was glistening with sweat, some of the long, blond hair escaping from her messy bun.

Damn, she was the most attractive woman he'd ever seen in his life.

"You ask her out yet?" Connor asked casually.

Trey glanced at his buddy to see him wearing a knowing grin. It wasn't a secret that Trey had a thing for the assistant ME. He'd done nothing to hide it from the moment he'd first seen her at the site of the SWAT team's raid two years ago when half the Pack had fully shifted into wolves. After that, Samantha seemed to show up at every crime scene to collect forensic evidence all while looking at them sideways. Hell, just this past June, while helping them with a case, she'd openly admitted to knowing the team was playing fast and loose with the truth when it came to how they did their jobs. He and the rest of the Pack had been worried she might be onto their secret—that the DPD SWAT team was composed entirely of werewolves—but when she hadn't exposed them, they'd relaxed a little.

Now, if only Trey could figure out how to man up and ask her out when he couldn't even seem to talk to her without getting tongue-tied.

"I've been meaning to, but I haven't found the right time to approach her about it," he said.

Connor shrugged. "How about right now?"

Trey snorted. "Yeah right. She wants some guy to ask her out while she's leaning over a dead body."

"Dude, she deals with dead bodies every day, so you're going to need to come up with another excuse. You're a werewolf, not a werechicken. Just ask her to go out to dinner. What's the worst that could happen?"

Trey would have laughed at the werechicken comment if this thing he had for Samantha hadn't gone on for so long it had somehow taken on a life of its own. The thought of asking her out only to be turned down was something he didn't even want to think about. That was why he kept putting it off. He was waiting for some sign to light up and tell him to finally go for it.

But that was stupid. There wasn't going to be a sign, and if he kept waiting, the worst that could happen—*would happen*— was someone else would make a move on the beautiful, brilliant woman and he'd be left thinking about what could have been. The thought alone made Trey's gut clench.

Dammit. He was going to ask her out—today.

But as he watched her drop to a knee beside the body and lean over to study the headless corpse, he decided he'd wait until she wasn't leaning over a mutilated body.

CHAPTER 2

SAMANTHA UNLOCKED HER OFFICE AND WALKED IN, LETTING the quirkiness of the space soothe her aggravated mind and soul. With its light gray color scheme, the room was sleek and modern, like the rest of the Dallas Institute of Forensic Sciences. While the shelves filled with medical journals were fairly standard for a pathologist's office, it was the other shelving units on the far wall that defined the space. The display cases showcased her collection of antique medical devices and various other medical curiosities, including a human skull saved from a sanitarium where they'd practiced medicine that could only be labeled as barbaric. She kept it as a reminder that psychos could be found wearing all kinds of disguises…including doctor's garb.

Standing in the middle of her safe zone, she took a deep breath and let it out slowly, releasing the urge to throttle somebody.

"Briefing go that badly?"

Samantha turned to see her best friend, coworker, next-door neighbor, and all-around confidant Crystal Mullen in the doorway. Petite with brown eyes and her shoulder-length dark hair in its signature ponytail, Crystal was always there when Samantha needed to vent about something. These days, that was a lot.

When her boss, Louis Russo, said he was assigning her to the serial killer task force, Samantha had been thrilled. Okay, that sounded bad. For a nerd like her who was used to working miles behind the lines, where she barely had a clue what case she was involved in, the chance to team up with the police as they chased down a murderer, uncovering clues and questioning suspects, sounded exciting. Then she'd started going to meetings, and the shine had quickly worn off that particular apple. Now, after only a little more than a week, she dreaded every briefing she was forced to attend and their ability to frustrate her beyond all rational explanation.

"No worse than usual, which is to say horrible," Samantha admitted, moving over to her minifridge to pull out a bottle of water. She held another up to her friend, but Crystal shook her head. Crystal was a die-hard caffeine addict. Seriously, her friend would wheel around her coffee in an IV stand if Louis let her.

"Let me guess," Crystal said as she perched on the chair in front of Samantha's desk. Her friend never actually sat back in the comfortable club chair like a normal person. Probably because she had way too much caffeine in her system. "They're upset you haven't already solved the case for them."

Samantha sat down behind her desk with a sigh. "Pretty much. They didn't want to hear that I barely had time to do more than an initial assessment of the body found this morning." Opening the bottle, she took a long drink of water. "Never mind that I was able to establish an approximate time of death and confirm the amputations were accomplished with the same type of saw as the one used in the previous Butcher cases. Or that the cuts were made by the same person, based on the angle and technique involved. I even got samples collected and prepped for DNA profiling and checks against CODIS and NDIS, but that still wasn't enough for them."

"Sounds like a lot to me," Crystal said. "What else were they expecting?"

Samantha shrugged, relaxing back in her chair and lazily swiveling from side to side. "I think they're all waiting for the wow factor to kick in like all those *CSI* shows on TV. You know, where they collect and profile DNA, then a computer spits out a name before the first commercial break? They don't want to hear this killer chooses his victims specifically because they aren't in the system and that he's too meticulous to leave behind any hair, fiber, or blood evidence. And because I know the killer is a man from the size and depth of his boot prints, they think I should be able to track those boots to a specific store and found out who bought them. But I can't do that because it doesn't work that way." She sighed. "I know they're just trying to catch this guy, but so am I. But when there's no evidence, there's no evidence."

"Maybe I can find something to make the task force happy," Crystal said.

"Let's hope," Samantha replied.

Crystal was a forensic technician at the lab, working on a little bit of everything, but concentrating mostly on latent prints and tool marks. Before coming to work at the institute, Samantha never would have thought there'd be a call for someone to do that full time, but Dallas was a busy city when it came to crime. Crystal could work overtime for the rest of her life and never catch up with the backlog of cases that needed her expertise.

Samantha was about to ask Crystal if she wanted to start going over the body together when footsteps outside her office interrupted her.

"Senior Corporal Duncan," she said with a smile even as Crystal snapped her head around to see who was at the door. "Come in."

Trey and the other three officers with him from the SWAT team exchanged looks before stepping inside. Her office wasn't small by any means, but with the four very large cops in there, it suddenly seemed much harder to breathe.

Or maybe that was simply a side effect of being so close to Trey.

Samantha would be the first to admit she and Trey had been bouncing around in each other's orbits ever since she'd responded to a crime scene involving the SWAT team and found a handful of dead criminals who'd supposedly been mauled by wild coyotes in the middle of the Dallas-Fort Worth International Airport. Her experiences with the team had only gotten stranger from there. To say that they weren't quite normal was an understatement.

Okay, so maybe her intellectual curiosity wasn't the only reason she'd spent most of the past year and a half stalking Trey. With that square jaw, intense blue eyes, and perfect amount of scruff, the man *was* extremely attractive. Not to mention the fact that he looked amazing in the dark blue tactical uniform. But there was more to it than that. Simply put, there was something about him that mesmerized her every time she was around him. His presence at the Audubon center this morning had made it damn hard to focus on her work, that was for sure. Even with a headless corpse there to distract her.

The funny thing was, she wasn't surprised at all to see him and his teammates here in her office today. In fact, since hearing that it had been Trey and his fellow SWAT officers who'd actually found the body, she'd been pretty much expecting a visit from them. Just like back in mid-June, when they'd inserted themselves in the middle of that delirium drug thing…which really hadn't been a drug thing at all. When things got weird in Dallas, SWAT was going to be there.

Realizing she'd yet to make any introductions, Samantha quickly did so. Trey did the same, introducing Connor, Trevor, and Hale, though she could have easily introduced them herself since she had files on every member of the SWAT team. Crystal was well aware of Samantha's fascination with all things SWAT—and Trey in particular—so it was no surprise when her friend came up with an excuse to leave, saying she needed to start working on the body Samantha had brought in earlier.

"Normally, I'd ask what brought four of Dallas's finest down to my office," Samantha said as she moved around the side of the desk and sat on the edge to study the four men, "but since you showed up minutes after I got done briefing the task force—and you were also at the crime scene this morning—I'm assuming your visit is related to the Butcher."

Trey glanced at his teammates, who returned the look, as if saying *your call.*

"You're right. It is." Trey gave her a smile, flashing the most perfect dimples. "We're hoping you might be able to tell us a little about the case."

Samantha had to fight the urge to return his smile. Damn, when Trey put on the charm, it was scary how badly she wanted to walk over there, climb him like a sloth, and start coming up with names for their future children. But she fought off the desire. Besides, she didn't need to think about names. She had all four of them picked out a few days after meeting the hunky cop. No, she needed to play this cool and use the situation to get what she wanted.

"I really don't think I should be talking to the four of you about the Butcher case since none of you are on the task force," she said.

Trey smiled again, his eyes holding hers captive. "I know we're not on the task force, but we're asking anyway."

"And why is that?"

He crossed his arms over his broad chest, treating her to a pair of biceps she couldn't have gotten both hands around if she tried. And boy, would she like to try. "Do you remember what I said to you back in June to get you to help us with that delirium case?"

That had been two months ago, so Samantha had to really think about it to come up with what part of the conversation he was talking about. Most of her memories were of the stunningly attractive Trey Duncan practically begging for her help on that case and her feeling badly about not being able to offer up anything.

"I remember you said you needed my help because you and the rest of the SWAT team were the ones who had to deal with the people you thought were on some drug called delirium and that you needed to understand what you were up against."

Trey gave her another distracting smile. "Exactly."

"I don't understand," she said.

Samantha thought back to the delirium case. Was there some kind of connection to the current serial killer terrorizing the city?

She couldn't see how that was possible. The two men responsible for those crimes had something in their DNA that allowed them to turn people into puppets and control their minds simply by wiping their blood on their victims. Unfortunately, she hadn't been able to figure out exactly what was in their DNA, and while the Butcher might be scary as hell, she hadn't found anything to make her think he wasn't a regular human.

Unless…

"Wait a minute," she said, her mind starting to spin at a hundred miles an hour. What had she just said to herself only a few minutes ago? *When things got weird in Dallas, SWAT was going to be there.* "Are you saying the Butcher isn't a normal killer? That he's different like the men responsible for making all those people do things against their will are different?"

Another look passed between the big cops before Trevor, Connor, and Hale all seem to pass some kind of unspoken signal to Trey. Only then did he nod.

"We noticed something at the body dump this morning that makes us think the person who dragged the body there wasn't a normal human. Don't ask me to explain what that something was because I can't tell you, and you wouldn't believe me if I did. I simply need you to trust me."

Samantha almost said to hell with it. If they didn't want to tell her anything, why should she tell them anything? It was her butt on the line if her boss found out. But then she looked at Trey and realized there was no way she could say no to him. He was like her own personal brand of kryptonite.

"Okay." She leveled her gaze at Trey. "Same deal as before. I'll tell you everything I have on the Butcher, but you personally owe me a favor."

Trey's mouth edged up, the twinkle in his eyes making her a little weak in the knees. "You know, you still haven't collected on the first favor I owe you."

She smiled up at him. "Maybe I'll just keep collecting them so I can use them all at once."

He chuckled, the husky sound doing crazy things to her pulse. Beside him, she caught the smiles on his teammates' faces.

"Deal," Trey answered with a dip of his chin. "One favor for anything you have on the Butcher right now and anything you might find on him in the future."

It wasn't a shock he'd try to weasel a little extra information out of her, but she'd already made up her mind to tell him as much as she could. Partly because she had a thing for Trey and partly because she already believed there was something strange going on with this serial killer case. She had no idea what it might be, but it could explain why they had so many victims and still no serious clues about who the killer was or why he was mutilating them.

"I guess I should start by admitting we don't have a whole hell of a lot on the killer, even with all the emphasis the chief is putting on the task force," she said. "What I can tell you is that this guy is no random slasher. Most of the cuts on the bodies were professional and surgical in nature, without a single sign of hesitation or doubt. On top of that, I found signs of arteries and veins being tied off prior to some of the amputations, along with indications that some of the victims were still alive when the killer did it. Believe it or not, keeping someone alive while you dismember them is actually rather difficult."

"And sick," Trey muttered. "So what you're saying is that we're dealing with a doctor of some kind. Or at least someone who went through a good portion of medical school."

"Which means we're not talking about a small pool of potential suspects," Connor added with a frown. "Especially if we include everyone who was kicked out or dropped out of med school."

"It definitely isn't a short list," Samantha said. "Unfortunately, the situation is even more complicated than that. Like I said. *Most* of the cuts were clean and precise. But there were others, namely the ones at the neck and wrists, that were quite ragged. They were basically hack jobs."

That earned her a grimace or two from Trey and his friends.

"So what are you saying? That there are two killers working together?" Trevor asked, clearly surprised. "I never heard of serial killers teaming up."

Samantha shrugged. "Me, either. I wish I could say for sure there are two killers, but I can't. Some people on the task force think there are, while others insist it's one guy and that the less precise cuts are because he loses control and goes completely psychotic."

Trey grimaced. "Any connections between the victims yet? Or how the killer selects his targets?"

When she admitted the answer to both of those questions was no, Trey and his teammates were clearly surprised they hadn't identified any of the victims yet, much less establish a serious connection between the men.

"So far, the only thing we can say for sure about the victims is that they're all in their late twenties to midthirties, in good shape, over six feet tall, and weigh more than two hundred and thirty pounds," she said. "And before you ask, no we're not sure if this is significant in some way or simply a coincidence."

Trey and his teammates seemed more than ready to keep grilling her for information about the case, but just then, all four of them got odd looks on their faces, then turned as one to face the door. Samantha was just about to ask what the heck they were doing when she heard footsteps in the hallway. A few moments later, her boss walked in with two of her coworkers.

"Samantha." Her boss eyed Trey and his teammates curiously from behind his wire-rimmed glasses before looking at her. "We were walking by and heard you talking to someone. I didn't realize anyone from the task force was still here."

How many more people were going to try to squeeze into her

office? The room had been crowded before with the four large cops, but now it was nearly claustrophobic. "These officers aren't with the task force. They're here to tie up a few loose ends on a case from back in June." Before her boss could ask which case, she quickly made the introductions. "Officers, this is Louis Russo, the chief medical examiner. And this is Hugh Olsen and Nadia Payne, two of my fellow assistant MEs."

Her gray-haired boss immediately reached out to shake hands with Trey and his teammates as she continued with the introductions. Hugh merely nodded stiffly in greeting while Nadia offered them a cool smile. No surprise there.

While Samantha loved working with Louis, who was a brilliant pathologist, a willing mentor, and completely above the politics that sometimes made working in the ME's office a pain in the butt, she couldn't say the same about Hugh and Nadia. They were both smart and capable at their jobs, but spending so much time among the dead had made them cold and detached. Almost like they didn't know how to interact with the living anymore. The only time either of them pretended to care was when Louis was around to see it. To say they'd been pissed when Louis had assigned Samantha to the Butcher task force was putting it mildly. The way they saw it, this was the kind of case that could catapult their careers to the next level and put them directly in line for chief ME when Louis left. The fact that there were people actually dying out there thanks to this psychopath didn't seem to register with them at all. Hugh, in particular, had campaigned heavily for the assignment, and when Louis gave it to Samantha, he'd nearly exploded. Since then, he never let a chance to bash Samantha pass him by. Nadia was more circumspect about it but equally bitter. Luckily, Louis never listened to their crap.

The moment Hugh and Nadia figured out they weren't going to be able to undermine Samantha—or hear anything about the serial killer case—they both left her office, mumbling something about needing to catch up on paperwork. Louis left soon after they did, asking Samantha to stop by his office before she left for the day so they could go over whatever she had learned from the Butcher's latest victim.

Thirty seconds later, Connor, Hale, and Trevor headed for the door, too, saying they'd be waiting out by the truck. And just like that, Samantha found herself left alone with Trey. It occurred to her then that it was the first time that had ever happened.

"Not very subtle, are they?" Samantha asked with a soft laugh.

Getting to her feet, she moved closer, mesmerized by the way his presence still seemed to fill the room even with only the two of them in it. Samantha found it impossible not to stare up at him. To say he was the most gorgeous man she'd ever seen was an understatement.

"No, I guess they aren't," Trey murmured, gazing down at her, his low, sexy voice drawing her in even closer. "Sorry we chased off your coworkers like that."

"Did you hear me complaining?" she countered. "Anything that gets me out of talking to Hugh and Nadia is all good in my book."

Trey snorted, his lips curving into a smile. Samantha had an overwhelming urge to rub her face against his like a cat just so she could feel that scruff on his chiseled jaw against her skin.

"Yeah, I couldn't help but pick up on the bad vibe between you and those two," he said. "If you want to use up one of those favors, I happen to have a few friends in the federal government. I could have them sniff around their background, see if Hugh cheats on his taxes or Nadia hacks into her neighbor's Netflix account."

Samantha was too caught up in Trey's blue eyes to answer right away. Sometimes they seemed darker in color, like the sky at night. Other times, they reminded her of the sky on a sunny day. She wondered if it was possible for eyes to change color like that, to lighten and darken with one's mood. Maybe she should ask for permission to lay on his chest for a few hours to study them just to see if she was right.

But while lying atop Trey certainly sounded like fun, Samantha realized maybe she needed to start with something a little less familiar.

"If I'm going to use up one of my favors," she said softly, keenly aware of Trey leaning in even more, then closing his eyes and inhaling. Like he was trying to breathe in her scent. "It wouldn't be for snooping into either of their backgrounds."

"What would you use it on then?" he asked, lifting his gaze to hers. Oh yeah, his eyes definitely darkened a bit more, like the ocean in the middle of a storm.

Inspiration hit then, and Samantha didn't even pause to wonder if she should do it or not.

"I'd use it to have you take me out to dinner," she said before she could come to her senses and chicken out.

From the way Trey gaped, Samantha could tell she'd thrown the big cop for a loop. Fear and doubt immediately started creeping in, making her think she'd royally screwed up. Maybe Trey was one of those men who was more comfortable doing the asking instead of being asked. She didn't like to think someone who was clearly so strong and confident would be insecure over something like that. But maybe she'd read him all wrong.

"Are you asking me out on a date?" he said, and she was relieved when she saw a spark of interest there in those mesmerizing eyes. Like he suddenly found a game he unequivocally liked.

She stepped closer, smiling as his eyes darkened again. "Actually, I'm using one of my favors to have you ask me out. That way, I can be progressive and traditional at the same time. That doesn't bother you, does it?"

He grinned, his expression making her pulse skip a beat. "Definitely not. I'm a huge fan of progressive traditions. Dinner tomorrow night work for you?"

She had to force herself not to pump her fist in excitement. "It does."

"Good. Should I pick you up at your place? Say seven o'clock."

She nodded, then watched in disappointment as he turned and headed for the door. Not that seeing him from behind was a bad view or anything.

"Hey," she called before he disappeared into the hallway. "I didn't give you my address."

Trey paused long enough to give her another one of those smiles that turned her knees to Jell-O. "At the risk of sounding like a stalker, I already know where you live."

He was out the door before Samantha could say whether it made him seem like a stalker or not. But in all honesty, it wasn't like she could complain very much since she already knew where he lived, too.

CHAPTER 3

WHEN TREY GOT THE CALL FROM HIS COMMANDER/PACK alpha at five o'clock in the morning telling him to get to the McCommas Bluff Landfill, he'd assumed it was going to be another body dump. And when he'd pulled up the map on his phone and realized the landfill was only a couple miles from the Trinity River site where they'd found the body a few days ago, he'd been even more sure. So he was a little stunned when he reached the front gates of the landfill and didn't see a single member of the press or the normal collection of morbid gawkers who liked showing up at any scene that might belong to the Butcher. Trey found it hard to believe the DPD could have kept something like this quiet. No matter how hard they tried, word always seemed to get out.

He got another surprise when he reached the backside of the landfill and saw only four vehicles parked on the side of the road. Typically, there'd be a frigging parking lot full of city, county, and state emergency vehicles at a scene like this. But other than the bulldozer sitting in the muddy field across the road, this part of the landfill was essentially deserted.

Trey climbed out of his truck, immediately spotting Connor, Trevor, Hale, and their other pack mate, Zane Kendrick, standing a few yards away staring at something on the ground behind a big pile of construction scraps. He'd only taken a few steps in their direction when he caught sight of two other people he definitely hadn't expected to see here. For the first time, he began to think maybe there was something different going on.

"Corporal Duncan." Deputy Chief Hal Mason stepped forward in the dim morning light to shake Trey's hand. "I'm sorry for dragging you out of bed this early, but as you'll soon see, this isn't something that could wait." Mason oversaw the SWAT team, along with several other specialty units within the DPD. And while he was fully aware that the entire team was composed of alpha werewolves, it was rare to see him in the field. The man was high enough up on the food chain that he didn't go after bad guys himself, but low enough that he wasn't expected to show up at crime scenes purely for publicity's sake. "You already know Agent Carson," he added, motioning toward the tall, slim woman with blond hair pulled back in a neat ponytail standing beside Zane.

Yeah, Trey knew her. And Alyssa, on the other hand, had no business being at any normal DPD crime scene—publicity or not. She was Zane's mate and also an agent with STAT, aka Special Threat Assessment Team, the secretive joint FBI-CIA group that had the job of dealing with those things that went bump in the night. Things that very few humans ever had the opportunity to learn about until they were unfortunate enough to get eaten by one of them. If she was here, it couldn't be good.

Or normal.

"I'm guessing this isn't another Butcher body dump?" Trey asked as he and Mason moved over to join everyone else.

"No," the deputy chief said. "At least we don't think so."

That sounded ominous.

Trey walked around the shoulder-high pile of construction debris, slowing at the sight of a black cat sitting there all prim and proper atop a pile of bricks. The cat looked back at him, impatience clear on her furry face. If the creature could talk, Trey was pretty sure she'd be asking what took him so long to get there.

Trey threw a glance in Mason's direction to see what he thought about there being a pet at a crime scene. It said something about how jaded the deputy chief had become to the strange and unusual that he acted like the cat wasn't even there.

Pulling his attention away from the cat, Trey turned to look at whatever was on the ground that had everyone's attention, grunting when he finally caught sight of it.

"What the hell?" he murmured, stepping closer to the body lying among the rubble near a beat-up piece of plywood.

If Trey had to guess, the victim had to be in his nineties at least. Hell, for all Trey knew, the guy might even be a hundred years old. Then again, maybe the killer had left the body someplace really hot and really dry...like an oven. Because that was the only thing that might explain why the corpse looked like a mummy. The body was shirtless, the pants undone and shoved halfway down his legs to his knees. Other than being dried out and shriveled up like a raisin, the body appeared completely intact. Trey couldn't even see any visible wounds on the man.

He definitely had to agree with the deputy chief. This didn't seem like the Butcher's MO.

Pulling a pair of rubber gloves out of a cargo pocket, he slid them on, then knelt down by the body, his medic instincts demanding he figure out how this guy had ended up like this. The moment he picked up the man's wrist—and almost snapped off the hand—he realized the nearly weightless corpse wasn't just dry. It was desiccated. Peeling one eyelid back revealed nearly empty sockets. The eyes were nothing more than pea-sized kernels of hardened goo. And everything that was supposed to be behind the eyes was dried up to the point of being little more than gray dust. It was hard to even look at it without being sick.

Trey glanced at Alyssa as he straightened up and took off his gloves. "Do you think it's possible he was tortured? Like whoever did this took an old man from a retirement home and stuffed them in a ceramics kiln or something like that?"

Alyssa shook her head. "If this is like the last body we found this way, we're going to find out the victim is probably in his midtwenties or early thirties at the most."

Trey looked down at the body again, trying to understand how that could be possibly be true. He couldn't see it. "There have been others like this you said?"

"Two of them, killed about a week apart, both in Dallas," she said. "The first one was found in a garbage truck parked at the Fair Oaks Transfer Station and the second was found in the middle of the DFW landfill. Our working theory is that the killer murders them somewhere else, then uses the nearest convenient dumpster to get rid of the bodies. If that's the case, who knows how many others there are? We wouldn't have found this one if the truck hadn't accidentally dropped off this load of construction scraps in the wrong place and someone had to come out here to move it."

Trey exchanged looks with his teammates before turning his attention back to Alyssa. "If you're involved, I'm assuming you think whoever did this is some kind of supernatural."

She nodded. "Our medical examiners are still arguing over the actual cause of death. Some are going with heart failure due to rapid loss of fluids and electrolytes. Others are sticking with some vague concept that the killer sucked the life force out of these people, whatever the hell that means. Ultimately, it doesn't matter. We need to stop this thing."

"STAT has officially asked for our help on this one," Mason said.

"Unfortunately, San Antonio PD has some murders that look like ritual sacrifices that STAT wants me to take a look, and Zane is coming along for backup," Alyssa said. "Which means you'll be on your own for this."

Trey could understand why Zane would be her first and only choice for backup. If you were heading into a freaky, unknown situation, it never hurt to have a werewolf around to help. If that werewolf was your soul mate, even better.

"You sure you don't need a little more help?" Connor asked. "One of the other guys or I could go with you."

Kat didn't seem to think much of that idea if the way she

jumped off the pile of bricks and sank her claws into the leg of Connor's uniform pants was any indication. The glint in her green eyes suggested she'd shred him to pieces if he even considered going with Alyssa and Zane.

Muttering something under his breath, Connor scooped Kat up with one hand and stuck her in the SWAT SUV, where she sat on the dash, staring at him with a pissed-off look that only a cat could come up with.

There is something seriously wrong with that cat.

That thought earned Trey a long-distance glare from Kat...like she'd actually heard him thinking it.

"Thanks for the offer," Alyssa said. "But I think it'll go better with just the two of us. We'll draw less attention that way. Besides, there's a good chance this is nothing but a bunch of college students playing with some old books they dug up somewhere. If it turns into anything more, we'll call you guys."

They talked for a while longer about what kind of supernatural creature might be involved in murders that would leave a desiccated corpse until an unmarked SUV that belonged to STAT showed up. A moment later, a man and woman got out to collect the body, as well as take pictures and samples from the surrounding area.

"All my files from the previous murders are waiting for you at the SWAT compound," Alyssa said before she and Zane headed for their car. "You'll have access to STAT intel support and our medical examiners. If you need anything else, just ask and they'll get it for you."

"What about the Butcher investigation?" Trey asked Mason as his pack mate and fiancée drove off.

"I'm hoping you can work both cases," the deputy chief said. "Gage told me that you have an inside track with the medical examiner assigned to the Butcher task force. If she's willing to float you a few leads now and then, you should be able to sniff around and find something they might not recognize."

Trey scowled at Connor, having no doubt he was the pack mate who'd ratted him out to their SWAT commander/pack alpha, Gage Dixon. That was the only way the boss could have learned about the "inside track" he had with Samantha. The grin Connor gave him confirmed he was to blame.

Mason left a little while later, telling them he expected frequent updates. "And try not to do anything that attracts Chief Leclair's attention. She's already suspicious of your team."

Trey watched the deputy chief drive away, wondering how the hell the man expected them to track down what was possibly two supernatural killers when they knew next to nothing about these creatures. This was so far outside the SWAT job description it wasn't even funny.

"Okay, now that Mason's gone, tell us what happened with Samantha," Connor said, looking at him expectantly. "Did you finally ask her out or what?"

Connor and his other pack mates had been riding him nonstop about whether he'd asked her since they'd left the forensic institute yesterday. They all assumed he had, since he'd been grinning like an idiot when he came outside. After the way they'd ribbed him for the past two years, he figured he earned the right to mess with them.

"You know, it's okay if she turned you down," Hale said. "Rejection stings like a son of a bitch, especially when you're really into the person, but it happens to everyone. I've been there, so trust me, I know how you feel."

Trey snorted. "While I'd love to stand around this landfill and talk about it, in the interest of full disclosure, Samantha didn't turn me down. We're going out to dinner tonight."

Connor did a double take. "Damn. You actually asked her out?"

"What, I thought you were all about me going out with her?" Trey frowned. "In fact, you were the one pushing for me to do it the other morning. Over a dead body, no less."

Hale laughed. "Don't take this the wrong way, but we had a pool going at the compound over how long it would take before you two actually went out. Connor is pissed because he bet it'd be at least another two weeks."

Trey looked at Connor, not bothering to hide his disappointment. "Really? Two weeks?"

"Sorry." Connor shrugged. "But damn, dude. You've been dragging this out for months. At two weeks, I was actually one of the optimistic ones. Not as optimistic as Gage, who pegged you for this weekend. But at least I wasn't as bad as Trevor. He put twenty dollars on you never asking her out at all. He insisted you'd never get off your butt and do it and that Samantha would have to make the first move."

Trey didn't say anything. Because the truth was, he'd been shocked as hell when Samantha asked him out. He'd always thought he'd be doing the asking. The only reason he'd waited so long was because he genuinely *had* been worried she'd turn him down. He wasn't afraid of going up against bad guys with machine guns half as much as he was afraid of being rejected by the woman he'd been head over heels for for going on two years.

"Wait a second," Connor said, looking at him sharply. "You did ask her out, right? Not the other way around."

Trey grinned as he opened the door of his pickup. "Actually, she asked me. Though technically, she collected on one of the favors I owe her by having me ask her to dinner, so I'm not sure how you guys are going to work that out."

Climbing into the truck, he started the engine and put the vehicle in gear, chuckling as Trevor insisted he should win the bet. Trey was tempted to hang around and see which of his teammates won that argument but decided against it. If he stayed, they'd only end up ripping on him for not asking Samantha out in the first place.

CHAPTER 4

"So, does Trey know you've been stalking him?" Crystal asked as she watched Samantha try on yet another dress.

Samantha ignored her friend for the moment as she studied her reflection in the full-length mirror on the inside of the closet door, checking out the little black dress she was wearing. After going through nearly half her clothes, she'd ended up going back to her trusted LBD, throwing on a silver chain necklace and over-sized matching hoop earrings. It was the perfect blend of casual and elegant for a first date, and she probably should have simply picked it to begin with, but her head was spinning a bit.

"I have not been stalking him," Samantha insisted, most of her attention now focused on which shoes to wear. She was leaning toward the black sandals with the kitten heels, but she wanted to see if there was anything else that might work.

"Oh, right," Crystal murmured, pulling out a pair of black wedges with silver accents and handing them to her. "You've been *investigating* him. Following him around, taking pictures of him and his SWAT teammates, and snooping through his trash. Sounds more like stalking to me."

The urge to stick her tongue out at Crystal was hard to resist, but she did, because she was an adult. And sticking your tongue out at people—even if they deserved it—wasn't a very adult thing to do.

"I *have* been investigating him," she said firmly, deciding to go with Crystal's choice of shoes, then turning to check her makeup one more time in the mirror. "And don't act like you don't know why. Not after everything Trey and his teammates have been involved in."

Crystal shook her head in exasperation. "The coyote thing again?"

"It's more than that and you know it." Samantha caught her friend's eye in the mirror. "The list of unexplainable crap SWAT has been involved in boggles the mind. There was that crime boss who got all clawed up at the airport, then those Albanian mobsters who said some kind of creatures attacked them. And don't even get me started on that naked SWAT cop in the middle of a blood-spattered crime scene. Or that blood sample I thought was his. I still haven't figured out what happened to it."

Crystal rolled her eyes. "You mean the sample that came back contaminated with animal DNA?"

Samantha had been sure she'd get something useful from the sample she'd collected at the black market organ-harvesting operation, but the lab she'd sent it to claimed it was contaminated and had destroyed it. Crystal had ribbed her for months about it.

"Yes, that one," Samantha replied, ignoring the smirk on her friend's face. "Toss in the wolves that people claim to have seen running around crime scenes where SWAT just so happens to also be, the city's former chief of police trying to assassinate them, and mysterious federal agents scooping up suspects after SWAT has arrested them, and you can't tell me all that doesn't make you the least bit curious."

Crystal's dark gaze was assessing. "Sure, I'm curious. But that doesn't mean I'm willing to play games with a guy I'm interested in on the off chance I might learn a few secrets. I don't mess with other people that way."

The accusation hit a little too close to home and Samantha saw herself blush in the mirror. Her conscience had already spent the past few days berating the hell out of her for what she was doing. "It's not like that. I'm not playing games with Trey."

"Really?" Crystal asked, her expression downright dubious. "Here's a simple question then: Is this thing tonight a date or part of your investigation?"

Samantha fussed with the big, bouncy curls she'd put in the ends of her long, blond hair. "Can't it be both?" she asked after delaying as long as she could.

"No, it can't." Crystal sighed. "Look, if you're going out with Trey Duncan because he's a sexy guy and you have the hots for him, that's one thing. But if you're going to dinner with him tonight because you think it'll help you dig up all his secrets, that's another. They're mutually exclusive and it's screwed up. Not to mention something the friend I thought I knew would never do."

The air left her lungs all at once, and before she knew it, Samantha found herself sitting on the edge of her bed, Crystal down on her knees in front of her, asking if she was okay.

"Yeah." Samantha nodded even as she struggled to get over her minor panic attack. "It's just that…I don't have a clue what the hell I'm doing. Sometimes, I am so attracted to Trey that it's hard to breathe when he's around. But at the same time, I know he and the other members of his SWAT team are hiding something huge. I don't what or how coyotes and wolves play into all of it, but I know it's something big. And you know I don't deal well with secrets. So I'm stuck between wanting this thing with Trey to work out and wanting to figure out what they're hiding."

Crystal shook her head in exasperation. "And you're not worried that going for the latter will destroy any chance of the former?"

Samantha shrugged. "I'm hoping it doesn't come to that."

Frowning, Crystal opened her mouth to say something, but the ringing of the doorbell interrupted her. A glance at the clock showed that it was seven o'clock. Trey was right on time.

With a sigh, her friend stood, pulling Samantha up with her. "Well, I think you're crazy. If I had someone like Trey interested in me, I'd do everything I could to make sure he stayed that way. But if this is how you want to do things, I guess I'll just wish you luck. And hope you don't end up regretting this plan."

"I hope I don't, either," Samantha said.

"Wait a second. What do you mean, it was destroyed?" Samantha asked as the hostess at the bar and grill showed them to their booth. "Why would someone destroy your truck?"

The woman gave them a curious glance before telling them to enjoy their dinner, then leaving them to look over the menus. North of the city center in the Greenville area, the restaurant had lots of exposed wood and bare lightbulbs strung along the ceiling in a way that surprisingly worked with the decor. Samantha had never eaten there, but Trey assured her they had the best burgers and cheese fries in town. If the aromas coming from the kitchen were any indication, he was right.

Admittedly, Samantha had been amazed at how relaxed she'd been on the drive across town. After her conversation with Crystal, she'd expected to be a little tense, but within minutes of getting into his new silver Jeep Gladiator and discovering they both loved that wonderful new-car smell, it felt like they'd known each other for years. Trey had totally floored her when he said he bought the pickup because his 1990 Ford Bronco had been destroyed. Samantha knew SWAT got involved in crazy stuff, but that was a story she simply had to hear.

"You remember when those guys attacked Diego in the parking lot outside the SWAT compound back in June?" Trey asked, glancing at the menu. "The ones we thought were high on delirium?"

Samantha remembered it very well. She'd gotten there less than thirty minutes after the shootout to find four dead assailants, their bodies still warm. There'd been a lot of confusion at the time about what had happened, but she definitely remembered it had seemed like a war zone to her inexperienced eyes. In fact, one of the vehicles in the parking lot had been ripped to shreds from all the gunfire.

"Crap." She gasped, suddenly realizing the implications. "That shot-up vehicle in the lot was yours?"

Trey nodded sadly. "Yup. Diego swore he didn't pick my vehicle to hide behind on purpose, but I think he's being less than honest since he's been hounding me forever to get a new truck. Regardless, he did, and it was totally destroyed. Every window was broken, all the tires were flat, and the engine block got turned into swiss cheese. My insurance payoff barely covered the cost of towing it to the junkyard. But on the bright side, it finally got me off my butt and into a vehicle made in this century."

Samantha couldn't help laughing. How anyone could find a silver lining in having their car shot up was beyond her, but the fact that Trey could was another indication of how amazing he was. Even if he failed to mention at least one of those men who'd attacked Diego Martinez back in June had somehow ended up with their throats torn out by some kind of claws.

"Since you've eaten here before, what do you recommend?" she asked, turning her attention to the menu.

"You can't go wrong with anything they serve. It's all basic comfort food that tastes like it's homemade," he said with a smile Samantha decided she was becoming dangerously addicted to. "We definitely have to get the cheddar fries to start with because it would be criminal not to. After that, I usually go for one of their cheeseburgers, but their chicken strips and chili dogs are good, too. Sometimes I can't decide, so I end up just getting all three."

Samantha stared at him, sure he was kidding. But from the sincere expression on his face, it seemed he wasn't. "Mind giving me your secret? If I ate that much, I would be in serious trouble."

The smile on his face slipped for a second as he glanced down at the menu in his hands. "I've always had a fast metabolism."

Trey might have been wearing an untucked button-down, but Samantha had seen him in his tight uniform T-shirt more than once, so she had a pretty good idea of the kind of shape he was in, and it sure as hell had nothing to do with a fast metabolism. "Okay.

I'll share some of your cheddar fries, but I think I'll limit myself to one entrée."

When their server came over to take their order, Samantha got the classic burger with cheese and a side of guacamole along with an iced tea. She had to bite her tongue to keep from laughing as Trey ordered the chili cheddar burger with double beef patties and a full-sized bowl of chili on the side. And if that wasn't enough, he also got a large order of cheddar fries with a double serving of bacon.

"Fast metabolism, huh?" she teased after the server left.

He shrugged, his gaze locked on hers, the warmth in his eyes enough to make it feel like someone had turned up the temperature. "I'm lucky that way, I guess."

Resisting the urge to fan herself with her hand, she picked up the iced tea the server brought and took a sip. "How'd you find this place? I've driven past it at least a dozen times and never seen it."

Trey sipped his beer before answering. "SWAT got called out to a barricaded suspect near here a few years ago. We ended up spending over twelve hours waiting for our negotiator to talk the guy out of the house and this was the first restaurant we saw after packing up. We all fell in love with the burgers—and the prices. We stop by to eat anytime there's a call in this part of town."

She pictured all of those big cops in here, eating their weight in burgers and hot dogs. "I get the feeling you and your teammates spend a lot of time together outside of work."

His mouth edged up. "Yeah. Our team is like a big family. We get together at least once or twice a week in addition to the weekends. And even when we're not getting together as a pack, smaller groups of us hang out together all the time."

Samantha stared at him, wondering if she'd heard right. She opened her mouth to ask but was interrupted by the server showing up with a ridiculous plate of fries buried in melted cheese and crumbled bacon. Her mouth watered at the sight and she eagerly reached for a fry, moaning as the combination of cheddar, fried potato, and crispy bacon hit her tongue.

She was helping herself to another when she remembered what she'd been going to say before. "When you were talking about your teammates, you called them a pack."

Trey paused, a handful of cheesy fries halfway to his mouth. "I did?" he asked, the words coming out light and casual.

She nodded. "You did."

"It's just a nickname we have for the team." He shoved the fries in his mouth, then wiped his hands on his napkin before undoing a few buttons on his shirt and tugging it to the side to reveal a tattoo of a wolf head on one side of his muscular chest. As far tattoos went, it was amazing. And as far as chests went, it was spectacular. "We all have this same tattoo, so we call ourselves a pack. Goofy, I know."

Samantha laughed, telling herself that made complete sense. But if that was the case, why did she still think it was total BS?

They ate in comfortable silence for a while before curiosity got the better of her. She was tempted to dig a little more into the pack thing but decided against it. After the quick answer he'd had to her first question, he'd probably be prepared and already have a logical answer to whatever other questions she asked about his team.

"How did you end up in SWAT?" She nibbled on another cheesy fry. "Did you go straight into that when you became a cop, or did you do something else for a while first?"

"Actually, when I first moved to Dallas, I worked as a paramedic." He picked up his bottle of beer. "I was a combat medic in the army for almost six years and was sure that's what I wanted to do for a living after getting out."

She'd known he was in the army before becoming a cop because that had been in the personnel record she'd been able to put together on him. But she hadn't known he was a paramedic. "What changed your mind?"

He fell quiet for a moment, the crease in his brow making her think maybe she'd brought up something he didn't like to talk about.

"I found out that just because you can do something, it doesn't mean you want to," he said softly. "Hell, at one point, I thought I'd make a career of the army. In fact, I was only a few weeks from reenlisting when things changed."

She sipped her iced tea, not wanting to push. While she wanted to know everything she could about Trey, forcing him to talk about something that obviously upset him didn't sit well with her.

"I was in a firefight in Afghanistan," he murmured, pausing to slowly eat another fry before continuing. "I was hurt bad and my best friend was injured even worse, but somehow, we both made it out. The army wouldn't have let me re-up even if I'd wanted to—they had concerns about internal damage if I ever tried to do another airborne jump—so I got out and joined Dallas Fire and Rescue. The first time I showed up at the scene of a major car accident, every injury and death I saw in combat came back to me, and I realized I'd made a mistake. I left DFR the next day, but I still wanted to be able to help people, so I joined the DPD. I did about a year in patrol before my SWAT commander suggested I join the team."

Samantha didn't say anything as the server placed their plates of food before them. Part of her wanted to know what had happened to Trey in Afghanistan, but the other part didn't. The thought of him being hurt made it hard to breathe.

Not trusting herself to speak right then, she concentrated on biting into her burger. It was juicy and perfectly grilled with the perfect ratio of cheese to beef.

"I can understand why you wouldn't want to be a paramedic anymore, but I heard somewhere that you're one of the SWAT medics." She glanced at him as she dunked her cheeseburger in a pile of ketchup. "That means you treat your teammates' injuries, right?"

Trey looked confused for a moment and Samantha hoped she hadn't slipped up and said something she shouldn't have. "I read in the paper that you've received several commendations for using your paramedic skills to treat your teammates' injuries," she added.

He shrugged. "It's different when it's my teammates. Time has helped blur some of those old memories, too. It's not as bad as it used to be."

"I'm glad."

Samantha had never known anyone who'd been in the military, but she could imagine the atrocities Trey had seen in the army. No one should have to experience that stuff.

"You were right about this place," she added, hoping to lighten the mood. "These burgers are awesome."

As they ate, Trey talked about what it was like to be part of SWAT. While she didn't learn any deep, dark secret that might explain any of the weird crap that had gone on around the team, she learned enough to know Trey did some really dangerous stuff, he adored his job, and he loved his teammates.

His pack.

She didn't realize they'd been talking for hours until she looked around and realized that it was almost closing time. The burgers and cheddar fries were gone down to the last little nibble. Heck, there wasn't even any cheese left on the plate to scrape up. A warm sensation swirled inside as it dawned on her that she'd never been on a relaxed, effortless date in her life. And even though she'd eaten more than her share of cheese fries to go along with her burger, when Trey asked if she wanted to go for ice cream, she didn't even consider saying no.

There was an ice cream shop just a few blocks away that made fancy desserts using liquid nitrogen. The place looked like a lab, complete with billowing steam coming out of the high-tech mixers. There were so many flavors on the menu and toppings to go with them that it was difficult to choose, but she and Trey finally decided on double scoop waffles cones with cheesecake-flavored ice cream mixed with pieces of Oreo cookies.

As they sat on a bench in front of the shop, eating ice cream, Trey told her about his family and growing up on a soybean farm in North Dakota. From the warmth in his voice, it was obvious he loved the wide-open spaces and working the farm with his family, but he admitted the idea of becoming a farmer like his parents, brothers, and sisters hadn't been something he wanted to do.

"That's why I joined the army," he added. "I wanted to see some more of the world, and once I did, there was no way I could go back. I mean, I go back to visit my family on the holidays, and they've come down here to visit me a few times. But it's hard for them to get away from the farm for long, so I mostly make the trek to see them."

She smiled. It was nice to hear he was close with his family. "I can understand not wanting to move back to North Dakota after traveling around the world for six years in the army, but what brought you to Dallas? Were you stationed in Texas when you got out of the military?"

Trey didn't answer and when the silence continued to stretch out, Samantha got the feeling he wasn't comfortable discussing it. Maybe it was too personal. Or maybe he'd finally caught on to the fact that they had spent the whole night talking about him. She hadn't necessarily intended to do that, but whenever he'd posed a question about her background, she found herself steering the conversation back to him.

"You don't have to tell me why you settled in Dallas if you don't want to," she said softly, finishing up her cone and realizing that his was long gone. "I get that some things are too personal to talk about on a first date."

"Yeah, I guess they are." His mouth curved into a small smile. "Is that your way of asking me out on another date? You must be eager to use up your second favor."

Samantha laughed, relieved she hadn't messed anything up beyond repair. "Do I need to use a favor to go out with you again?"

She hoped that wasn't the case. And not merely because she still wanted to learn whatever it was he was hiding from her. The truth was, there was something special about this man. Something that attracted her to him like the proverbial moth to a flame. And she desperately wanted to know why that was.

"No, you don't need to use another favor to get a second date," he murmured, his gaze becoming more heated by the second. "You just need to say yes."

"Yes," she said without hesitation.

Then Trey was slipping a hand into her hair and tugging her closer on the bench, his very warm mouth coming down on hers. The kiss stayed casual and chaste for all of two seconds before his tongue slipped between her lips. She couldn't stop the moan that came out. He tasted delectable. And it had nothing to do with ice cream or what they'd had for dinner. There was simply something there she couldn't seem to do without.

He deepened the kiss with a groan, nipping and biting lightly on the tip of her tongue and her lower hip, tugging and teasing until she had to wonder if lip-gasms were a real thing.

She had no idea her fingers were in his hair, yanking and pulling him exactly where she wanted. Not until she heard him growling. Crap, he was *growling*. A deep, rumbling sound that vibrated up through his chest and right into her soul.

No. Actually, those vibrations settled between her legs—right there where all good vibrations belonged.

Samantha was damn close to climbing into his lap right there, on a busy street in front of the ice cream shop, when Trey suddenly pulled back. He was breathing as hard as she was, his eyes reflecting the yellow glow of the nearby streetlamps. It only made him that much more mesmerizing.

"Tomorrow night…five o'clock?" he whispered, his warm

breath tantalizing against the sensitive skin of her lips. "I'll pick you up at your place again?"

It took a few moments for her rattled mind to figure out what he was even talking about, but when she did, all she could do was nod. He wanted to see her again tomorrow night. Yes, that was exactly what she wanted, too.

Grasping her hand, Trey stood, taking her with him, and they walked back to his Jeep. As he helped her into the passenger seat, then walked around to the driver's side, Samantha realized Crystal had been right. She was being absolutely stupid to risk the chance of being with Trey simply to learn a few secrets that probably didn't matter anyway.

CHAPTER 5

"YOU GOING TO FILL US IN ON HOW THE DATE WENT LAST night, or did you think we'd let you slide without telling us anything?" Connor asked from the far side of the tables they'd shoved together in the training room.

Trey looked up from the STAT file he'd been reading for the past few minutes to see Connor, Trevor, and Hale sitting in front of file folders of their own, scribble-filled notepads near at hand. Tuffie, the team's resident pit-bull-mix mascot, sat off to one side, while Kat perched on the table beside Connor, looking over his arm like she was actually reading the documents Alyssa had left them. Which, considering this particular cat, was a distinct possibility.

The four of them had come to the SWAT compound early that morning to go through Alyssa's files on the three dead victims, hoping to find some kind of connection between them. Trey didn't know about the others, but so far, nothing obvious was jumping out at him.

"The date was amazing," Trey said, unable to keep the smile off his face.

"What'd you guys do?" Trevor asked.

"We went out for burgers and then ice cream."

His buddies regarded him expectantly, clearly waiting for more details. But there was no way he was going to tell them about the kiss on the bench in front of the ice cream shop. No, that memory—of the most perfect kiss he'd ever had in his life—was for him alone. He still had a hard time believing it had been real, even if it had left him lying awake all night reliving it. Even now, all he could think about were Samantha's pillow-soft lips and the way her skin had smelled like cherry blossoms and spring air after a light rain.

Of course, he had no idea how to explain the fact that, in all the time he and Samantha had been around each other over the past two years, the moment on that metal bench had been the first time he'd picked up that scent. Considering the way everyone else in the Pack who'd found their soul mate had made such a big deal about picking up their unique scents right away, he didn't quite know what to make of his experience.

"Sounds like the perfect date," Hale observed.

"It was perfect," Trey said, what he knew was a dopey smile slipping across his face again. "Oh, who am I kidding? It was better than that. I haven't been able to think about much of anything but her since dropping her off at her place last night."

Connor exchanged looks with the other guys before leaning forward. "Do you think Samantha is *The One* for you?"

"Dude, they've been on a grand total of one date," Trevor pointed out. "How is he supposed to know if she's his soul mate yet?"

"Because he's been crushing on her since the first day he saw her," Connor said, as if that should explain everything. Then he looked over at Trey again. "So is she?"

Trey almost laughed at the eager expressions on his pack mates' faces. He should have known the question was coming. Over the past two years, more than half of the Pack had found their soul mates—aka that one person who could love a werewolf in spite of what they were. Every time he or any of the other single guys went out with someone, everyone automatically assumed they'd found *The One*. That was the way it seemed to work lately. He'd be lying if he said he hadn't been wondering the same thing when he'd knocked on Samantha's door last night.

There was just one problem.

"I wish I could tell you definitively that she is," he said, shocked at how true that statement really was. He hadn't realized until then exactly how much he wanted what most of the other members of his Pack had already found: a future of more than merely searching and hoping.

"But?" Hale prompted.

"But I think Samantha might be playing me."

Trey sighed, his gut twisting at the notion of thinking something like that, much less saying it out loud. He hadn't gone to bed with these doubts floating around in his head, but they'd relentlessly started popping up as the morning dragged on and he began to overanalyze every single minute of last night's date.

"I can't shake the horrible feeling that the only reason Samantha wanted to go out with me is because she's looking for dirt on the Pack," he continued. "You know she's been sniffing around our crime scenes for years. And after all the crap that got swept under the rug with that delirium case, I have no doubt she knows we're hiding something."

His pack mates looked at him dubiously.

"You think she knows we're werewolves?" Trevor asked.

Trey shrugged. "I don't know. I hope not, but you have to admit, the timing of all this is strange. The two of us have been flirting with each other forever, and then out of the blue she asks me out? You don't find that at least a little curious?"

"Not really, no," Hale said. "Is it so shocking that Samantha got tired of waiting for you to ask her and decided to take things into her own hands? This is the twenty-first century, you know. Women are completely comfortable going after what they want."

"Maybe," Trey admitted. "But you weren't the one sitting across from her as she asked me question after question."

Trevor laughed. "I may not be the greatest at the whole social thing, but isn't asking each other personal questions what people normally do on a date?"

"Yeah, personal questions I get," Trey answered. "But almost all

Samantha's questions were about how I got into SWAT, what kind of work we do, how tight I am with you guys, and how well I know all of you. And every time I tried to steer the conversation in her direction, she turned it right back around on me. After a while, it was like she was grilling me for information."

His friends were quiet for a while, considering that.

"So what are you going to do?" Connor asked.

"What can I do?" Trey ran his hand through his hair exasperated. "If I'm right, and the only reason Samantha is going out with me is to dig up dirt, then every minute I spend with her puts the Pack at risk. If I walk away now, and it turns out I was wrong about her, then I'd be giving up my chance at a soul mate."

"You can't do that," Hale said firmly. "Walking away from a shot at finding *The One* would be insane. Nobody in the Pack would expect you to do that."

"I know," Trey murmured. "That's why we're going out again tonight. It feels like I'm playing with fire, but the thought of walking away makes me sick to my stomach."

As they sat around, the files in front of them untouched, they talked about how much Samantha might already know, in between his buddies giving him suggestions on where he should take her on their second date. Connor was of the opinion that if things went well enough, maybe Samantha would give up her snooping and realize she was his soul mate. Trey thought that might be a little optimistic, but he couldn't stop himself from hoping his pack mate was right.

It was Trevor who finally pointed out they'd been talking about Trey's love life for the past hour, instead of finding clues on who was murdering men and leaving mummified remains at the city dumps.

"Never let it be said that I'm the adult in the room," he added. "But maybe we should actually get back to looking at these files, especially if STAT is right about the MO and there's a good chance the killer is going to strike again this weekend."

Trey couldn't argue with that logic. Pulling his pad full of notes a little closer, he flipped through the pages of scribbles he'd written. "I don't know about you guys, but I haven't found anything earth-shattering yet. Maybe we'll get lucky and find something STAT missed."

"STAT has an army of intelligence analysts on this, not to mention criminal profilers, data-mining and predictive analytic software tools, and loads of experts with experience dealing with supernatural killers," Hale pointed out. "You honestly think we're going to find something they missed?"

"We don't need a miracle here," Trey said. "Just something that will give us a place to start looking."

With that, Trey and his teammates spread out the papers from the three folders. Well, actually, two of the folders. Trevor was still sitting there holding one in his hand, his expression thoughtful.

"There's not much on the body found in the McCommas Bluff landfill. We know from his bone structure that the guy was approximately thirty years old. STAT says he was likely killed last Saturday or Sunday," Trevor said, holding up a piece of paper. "But they haven't ID'd the body yet."

"All right," Trey said. "With so little on that one, let's set him aside for the time being and focus on the other two."

Grabbing photos of the other two victims, Trey stood and walked over to the whiteboard at the front of the room. After hanging them up with some magnets, he picked up a marker and turned back to look at his pack mates.

"Let's start laying out everything we know about these two guys," he said, motioning at the "before" pictures. "Give me everything you got. No detail is too small."

"The first body, found in the truck at the Fair Oaks Transfer Station, was a man named Demario Harris," Connor said, skimming through the file. "He was twenty-seven years old and worked as a commercial plumber."

"Alden Cox was the one found at the DFW Landfill. He was a supervisor at a UPS distribution warehouse," Hale added. "Twenty-nine years old."

His teammates kept going like that, calling out information on first Demario and then Alden, helping Trey by focusing on equivalent data points. Trey didn't pay much attention to what he wrote, instead listing everything the files had on the two victims—home addresses, education, work history, bank accounts and credit cards balances, police records, nearby relatives and close friends, how often they went out at night, where they went when they did, sexual preferences, even the type of women they hung out with.

As they quickly filled the whiteboard, Trey decided it was more than a little creepy how much personal information STAT had been able to dig up about the two men, most of it probably coming straight from social media and other open sources.

After he finished writing, Trey stepped back to regard the whiteboard. While there were still no obvious slam-dunk connections, seeing everything laid out this way allowed him to realize the two men were surprisingly similar in many ways.

"We might only have these two victims, but I think we're already seeing a pattern," Hale said. "Both of these guys were physically fit, around the same age, attractive, and, if their social media accounts are any indication, extremely active in the club and party scene, which means our killer has a type."

Looking at what he'd written about Demario and Alden, Trey had to agree with Hale's assessment. According to the date and time stamps on their social media posts, both had gone out to a club almost every night in the weeks prior to their deaths, including the weekends when they'd been killed. But as he continued to compare the two men, he realized they had more in common than their social lives.

"These two were perfect victims," Trey said. "Neither seemed to be close with their families or have any good friends. Their interactions seem limited to casual acquaintances and a series of one-night stands."

"Yeah, and I'm willing to bet the killer picked them specifically because no one would notice them leaving a club or bar with a complete stranger," Trevor said.

"So we're all leaning toward the killer being a woman, right?" Connor asked.

"Or a man and a woman," Hale said. "The woman might be the bait. Her partner could be someone waiting for her to lure their victims outside."

"The guy we found yesterday did have his pants down around his knees," Trevor remarked. "That definitely supports the theory a woman enticed them to leave the clubs with the offer of sex, then whoever she's working with took them down while they were distracted. It's cold-blooded but effective."

Trey sighed. "While we're probably right about all of this, it doesn't help us much. STAT had their analysts go through both men's social media accounts. There were no women—or men—in common between them. There also weren't any bars, clubs, or restaurants in common, either. Whoever the killer or killers are, they're smart enough to stay away from any cameras. That's going to make it damn hard to find them."

"We could ask STAT to use their fancy computers to create a list of all the places the two victims spent time in the weeks before their deaths, then start hitting all of them with photos of Demario and Alden," Connor said. "Maybe we'll get lucky and someone will remember seeing something suspicious."

Trevor groaned at that idea.

Trey didn't blame him. "With only the four of us and the number of places those two guys frequented, that might take a while," he pointed out.

He left out the part about there being a good chance someone out there could get murdered this weekend, if they hadn't already.

Unfortunately, they had nothing really to go on when it came to stopping it from happening.

"You're right," Hale said. "We need a way to cut down the list of potential locations. If not, we could be canvassing clubs and bars for the next month and still never find anything."

They studied the board again, running through every detail they'd listed, wondering if there was something they'd missed. It wasn't until Trey went through the files again that he caught sight of a picture of the garbage truck where Demario's body had been found.

"Maybe we can use the fact that the killer appears to use dumpsters to dispose of the victims to our advantage." He dug through the photos until he found some from the DFW and McCommas Bluff sites. "I doubt the killer would have lugged those bodies very far after the murders. If we're right and the men were killed close to the bar, restaurant, or club where the killer picked them up, maybe it's as simple as looking for dumpsters positioned close to those kinds of places."

Trey could practically see the lightbulbs going on as his pack mates picked up on his reasoning.

"We could have STAT dig into the landfill records," Connor suggested. "See if they can figure out where the trash came from that the bodies had been found in. It should be easy for the truck that unloaded at Fair Oaks Transfer Station. Probably a little harder for the body at the DFW site. Once they have an ID on the body from yesterday, they could do the same for him. If they can figure out where the trash came from, they could compare that to the list of places the men went. That should give us a list of clubs, bars, and restaurants that have dumpsters nearby. It should cut way down on the number of places we have to check out."

"That theory depends on the killer being too lazy to haul the bodies anywhere before dumping them in the garbage," Trevor said. "That's one hell of an assumption, but at least it gives us a place to start. It might even lead us to the actual places the men were killed."

They spent a few more minutes talking before Trey called the number Alyssa had left for him.

"We'll have your requested info within twenty-four hours, if not before that," the woman on the other end of the line said. "I'll send the spreadsheets to each of your phones."

Trey frowned. "I'm not sure I can read spreadsheets on my phone."

The woman laughed. "You can now. I've updated your phones with the app. It's already been installed and authenticated. All you have to do is tap the document attachment when you get the email. Call if you need anything else."

As Trey hung up, he wondered if he should be worried that STAT could apparently get into his phone and do anything they wanted, whenever they wanted. Then he decided it wasn't worth his time to care. He had other stuff to worry about now that he and his pack mates had a plan to find the killer. Like figure out where he was going to take Samantha tonight.

Maybe he should have asked STAT if they could have helped with that.

CHAPTER 6

"I can't believe I've never been to this part of town." Samantha spun in a slow circle, taking in all the colorful shop fronts up and down either side of the street that ran through the middle of Bishop Arts District, surprised when she saw there was a live band playing on a stage set up at the end of the block. "I'd heard there were a few quaint shops and cafés here, but I never realized there were so many. Retail therapy is exactly what I need after spending the day dealing with those idiots on the Butcher task force."

Trey chuckled. "What happened?"

Samantha got that little twinge in her stomach as she worried once again that the only reason he wanted to spend time with her was to grill her for information on the Butcher case. She knew that was crazy and unfair, especially since a big part of the reason she'd manipulated him into asking her out in the first place was because she wanted to sniff out whatever secrets he and his teammates were hiding. But still, there was something about all this that made her feel more than a little crappy. Mostly because Trey was the kind of guy she could easily fall for if they both weren't so busy playing games with each other.

Trey took her hand as they walked into the brick-sided shop on the corner. It was filled from floor to ceiling and wall to wall, with vintage kitsch and knickknacks. From home decor, stationery, and candy, to collectible toys and original art pieces, the place was buried in stuff that was organized with no obvious rhyme or reason. There wasn't a thing in the store she needed and yet she wanted to buy it all.

"The detective in charge of the task force thought it would

be a good idea to spend the entire day having us go over every piece of evidence that we've collected so far, along with videos of the crime scenes and details from the autopsy reports on the off chance there's something buried in there we missed," she said in answer to Trey's question.

"How'd it go?" He picked up a lunch box covered in cartoon bunnies and frowned at it in confusion. "Did you find any new leads?"

Samantha pushed away the thought that Trey was only asking to gather information for his own purposes. "It was horrible. We spent six hours looking at the stuff and we're no better off than we were before. We still have no idea who the killer might be, who his victims are, or how he chooses them."

While they wandered around the shop, Trey commiserated with her about the lack of progress in the case, but mostly he simply let her vent. Samantha appreciated the hell out of that.

As they left the first shop and headed to another—an emporium apparently dedicated to all things weird and wonderful—she realized they were still holding hands. She wasn't the kind to normally do that. In fact, she'd never done it. But with Trey, it felt so right that the idea of not doing it seemed weird.

The contact suddenly made her think of the kisses the two of them shared last night, and the memory was enough to make her heart thump faster. Trey glanced at her from the corner of his eye. Could he hear the pounding of her heart? Or maybe he could feel her elevated pulse from his hand in hers.

Browsing at a shelf filled with ceramic vases and figurines, Samantha replayed the kiss through her mind for what had to be the thousandth time. Admittedly, she'd spent most of last night dreaming of those lips on hers instead of sleeping. Then again, she'd also whiled away a good portion of her wasted day with the task force thinking about them, too. She was pretty sure that kiss had been the stuff of fairy tales. Or romance books. Either way, she'd never experienced anything like it, and she was counting the minutes until they got a chance to do it again.

Being with Trey was almost enough to make her forget about all the weird stuff she was supposed to be digging into.

Almost.

"Aren't you going to buy anything?" Trey asked after she'd picked up the ugliest ceramic chicken in the existence of the earth and then put it right back down. "As part of your retail therapy, I mean. My treat. Movie, dinner, and a ceramic chicken of your choice."

Samantha laughed and shook her head. "You really don't understand the purpose of retail therapy, do you? It's searching for the thing that provides the therapy, not the buying. Besides, they're cute but I don't collect ceramic chickens."

He snorted. "I've seen what you collect in your office. I don't think we're going to find much in the way of antique medical equipment in the Bishop Arts District. Or old skulls. At least, I hope we don't."

Samantha laughed. Trey seemed to know her better than anyone she'd ever been with.

"Come on. Let's check out the rest of the shops," she said, tugging him toward the door. "They may not have anything for my office collection, but maybe I can find some Christmas presents for my family."

"Do they live in Dallas?" Trey asked as they hit the sidewalk, weaving through the crowd that was starting to get a little heavy now that the sun was edging toward the horizon and the searing late-day temperatures were finally easing off a bit.

"Just my sister, Loralei."

She subconsciously squeezed his hand tighter, so they wouldn't get separated in the press of people on the sidewalk. A part of her realized this was the first bit of personal information she'd revealed to Trey. It wasn't that she'd gone into the first date planning to withhold details about herself. It was simply that she'd been so eager to learn everything about Trey and his SWAT teammates that she'd sort of blown off all of his attempts to get to know her. Now, she felt kind of badly about that, especially since it'd probably seemed deceitful. Well, maybe not quite as deceitful as tricking him into revealing secrets he'd obviously rather keep hidden, but still.

"My parents and my two brothers live in Houston, but Loralei moved to Dallas after she graduated from college. She has a degree in biology, and since I know some people at a lab, I helped her get hired on there as a genetics tech. Now, they're paying for her master's program and she essentially owes me her firstborn child." She grinned. "Nothing down in writing, of course, because that would be weird. But trust me, that child is mine."

Trey chuckled, the sound deep and rich, and Samantha was stunned by how much she loved his laugh. It did things to her that, up until a few days ago, she would have taken as a sign of impending health issues. Now, having parts of her body fluttering, quivering, or growing warm at random times were being chalked up to attraction and arousal.

"So you're from Houston then?" he asked as they walked into a clothing store filled with denim jeans and other casual clothes that were exactly the kind of things her sister lived in. "I have to admit, even though your accent is so slight, I was sure you were from the Pacific Northwest. Washington State, maybe."

Samantha had never really thought about her accent one way or the other, but she found it adorable that Trey had taken the time and effort to figure out where she born and raised. At least that confirmed he didn't have a copy of her personnel records, like she had his.

"Actually, you're pretty close. I'm originally from a small town on the Kenai Peninsula called Homer in Alaska." She pulled out an artsy-looking T-shirt that Loralei would totally love. "We lived there until I was fourteen, when my dad got an offer to be the chief of cardiology at a hospital in Houston. My grandfather and grandmother still lived in Alaska, so I spent summer vacations with them and sometimes spring break when I was in college."

"It sounds like you're really close to them," he said, holding up a T-shirt and studying the graphic print on the front.

She wondered if she should point out that none of the shirts on the shelves in here had a snowball's chance of fitting him without being skintight. Not that there was anything wrong with skintight clothing. Not when a man had a body like Trey's. The image of a soft, cotton tee stretched across his broad chest made all kinds of body parts flutter, quiver, and/or go warm all over again.

"We were close," she finally said, turning to study a rack of sunglasses when she felt tears burn her eyes. "In some ways, I was closer to them than I am my parents. I know that probably sounds crazy. But they were just so…amazing."

"It's not crazy at all," he said softly. From the sudden warmth against her back, Samantha could tell he'd moved closer. "There's family we're born into and family we choose. They're both important, but some bonds are simply meant to be and there's no way to tell whom those bonds will develop with…or why. We simply have to accept and believe in them."

Samantha nodded. She'd never heard it phrased that way, but it sounded like Trey understood what she was talking about. Unfortunately, her mom and dad never really had. Sometimes, it seemed like they were upset that she'd been closer to her grandparents than she was to them.

"They passed away four years ago." Samantha picked up a pair of sunglasses and looked at them for a moment before putting them back on the rack. "They left their home, thousands of acres of wilderness property, and the wilderness tourism business they owned to me. I think they were hoping I'd move up there and settle down, but while Homer is breathtakingly beautiful, it's also small, which means there isn't much call for a full-time medical examiner there. I go up there a couple times a year to make sure the house and property are okay and check in on the business."

Taking a deep breath, she turned and gave Trey a small smile as she held up the T-shirt. "I think I'm going to get this."

When they got to the counter, Trey pulled out his wallet, and while she attempted to argue, he waved her off. "Your loss. You could have had a ceramic chicken."

They browsed around the other shops, laughing over the unusual and sometimes silly stuff they found. Trey picked up a few things, telling her it was never too early to buy Christmas gifts for his teammates. She swore for a second he almost tripped up and said *pack mates* but caught himself at the last second.

In between shopping and listening to the band, they stopped for food whenever something struck their fancy, from a French silk chocolate pie with pretzel crust at a bakery that smelled like absolute heaven, to half a pound of fudge at the fancy chocolatier shop at the far end of the district. Samantha thought they'd take the fudge with them, but it tasted so good, they ended up eating it all as they walked. She didn't even bother feeling guilty about it, either. The way she looked at it, all the walking would burn off the calories as soon as they ate them. That was her story, and she was sticking to it. Besides, Trey ate most of it.

"You mentioned that your dad's a cardiac surgeon and that your sister works in a lab, so making a career in medicine sounds like it's a family affair," Trey said as he held open the door to a rather eclectic-looking bookshop/café. "Did you always want to be a medical examiner?"

"Oh, yeah. I've wanted to work with dead people since I was a child," she said casually, perusing the mismatched books on the shelves across from the long wooden bar. Truly, she'd never been in a bookstore with a bar before. It was a match made in heaven as far as she was concerned. "So it was either an ME or a mortician."

She was disappointed when Trey didn't even bat an eye at her joke. "That must have been a tough choice. How did you decide?"

"Sorry for the gallows humor." She gave him a wry smile. "But you have no idea how many times I get asked that question. Dad still asks me at least once a year and he already knows the answer."

"I didn't mean to stick my nose somewhere it doesn't belong," Trey said. "If it's something you'd rather not talk about, I get it."

She shook her head. "It's not that. In my experience, doctors become medical examiners for one of two reasons. It's either because they lack the empathy and compassion to interact with patients, or they possess too much empathy and compassion and can't maintain the required emotional distance from their patients. It my case, it was the latter. I became close with an elderly patient in one of my practicums and when the woman died, it really did a number on me."

"Ah," he said with a nod. "Based on my experience as a combat medic and then as a paramedic, I'm thinking that probably happens a lot."

"Yeah, I know," Samantha admitted. "But there was no way I could ever put myself through that again. I talked to my advisers and at the end of that semester I transferred to a pathology program. It added another year onto my student loan debt, but I never looked back."

She turned, expecting to see some level of condemnation or pity on Trey's face. Her dad had certainly thrown enough of the first her way, while the friends she'd made during her pre-med program had provided the second. But Trey was regarding her with approval.

"This is going to sound selfish, but I'm personally glad you went the ME route." Settling his hands on her hips, he tugged her closer. "If you hadn't, we might never have met. And I think that would definitely have been my loss."

Samantha decided that had to be the cheesiest line she'd ever heard. But for some incredibly silly reason, she loved hearing it all the same.

"So," she said softy, leaning into him just enough to press her breasts against the hard planes of his chest. "What else is on the agenda for the evening? Beyond helping me reaffirm my career choice, I mean."

Trey tilted his head down, and for a moment, Samantha was sure he was going to kiss her right there in the middle of the bookstore. But instead, he inhaled deeply through his nose—like he was breathing in her scent—then flashed her one of those knee-weakening smiles.

"I figure there are at least a dozen more shops for us to check out as part of your retail-therapy session. Then we could go to the pizza place at the end of the block to grab a few slices before the movie, if you want. Maybe even stop by one more time to look at that ceramic chicken you had your eye on earlier before heading back to your place."

Samantha wasn't so sure about the ceramic chicken part of the plan, but the rest of it—especially the part about going back to her apartment—sounded excellent.

"You feel like some coffee?" Samantha asked as she opened the door to her apartment. "Or maybe something a little stronger."

"Coffee would be good."

Trey set down all the bags he'd been carrying for her on the floor near the couch. She might have said retail therapy was all about the looking and not the buying, but it was still nice to buy stuff, too. And yeah, she'd finally gotten that damn ceramic chicken even though she had no idea what she was going to do with it. Maybe give it to Louis for National Boss's Day.

But while they'd done their fair share of shopping, mostly

they'd spent the evening talking about her grandparents and the place in Homer; her sister, Loralei; and even a bit more about that brief moment in her life when she thought she was going to be a real doctor. Or at least the kind of doctor who helped living patients. She hadn't planned to be that open with Trey, but there was something about him that made him easy to talk to. She felt more connected to him than she ever had anyone else.

After she got coffee brewing, Samantha walked around the peninsula separating the kitchen from the living room, expecting to find Trey relaxing on the couch. Panic surged through her when she didn't. What if he'd found his way into her guest bedroom, where all her SWAT stalker stuff was set up? She practically hyperventilated at the thought of him seeing all the photos she had tacked up to her walls and various spreadsheets full of all the strange events that had occurred in Dallas over the past few years, as well as the colored yarn connecting those events to different members of his team.

But when she got to the hallway leading to the bedrooms, she found Trey gazing at the photographs hanging on the walls. His expression was intense as he took in every detail of the pictures that pretty much laid out her whole life in front of him.

"Are these your grandparents?" he asked, motioning to the largest framed photo in the center of the wall of an older couple sitting on the steps of a rustic stone-and-log home, smile lines crinkling the corners of their eyes as they held each other close. It was one of her most cherished memories of them, taken on her last visit before they passed away.

"Yes. In front of their place outside Homer." She smiled. "It doesn't get as cold there as it does other parts of Alaska, but they built their home to stand up to the fiercest winters just in case. They loved that place with all their hearts. That's why I'll never get rid of it."

She pointed out the other members of her family as well as her friends in the surrounding photos before leading Trey back to the living room. "When I'm not at work, I'm usually hanging out with either Loralei or Crystal, or both of them. No doubt, they'll call me later asking for details of our date."

He chuckled. "I hope you'll be able to tell them you had a good time."

She stepped closer until there were only a few inches between them, her pulse kicking up a notch at the proximity. "I think the odds are definitely in your favor," she murmured even as Trey's mouth came down to capture hers.

The kiss started slowly but didn't stay that way for long. First there was a slip of tongue, just enough to tease her with that masculine taste of his, then two strong arms wrapped around her and pulled her close. She let out a moan as Trey kissed her more passionately, his tongue delving deeper into her mouth, those sharp teeth nibbling on her lips in a way that had a knee-weakening throb already building up between her legs.

Samantha wasn't sure how they ended up on the couch, but the next thing she knew, Trey was leaning back against one arm of it, her knees on either side of his hips. She had his shirt half unbuttoned and was grinding down on his growing hard-on with enough force to make herself come if she kept it up. He must have somehow realized how close she was because he chose that moment to slide his hands down to her butt, rocking her against him even harder until she was practically riding him, her breath coming faster and faster.

Aroused beyond belief, Samantha didn't recognize how carried away she was getting until she found her mouth on Trey's neck, her teeth scraping harshly against his skin, the inviting throb of his pulse under her tongue. It was hard not thinking about how easy it would be to bite him right then.

Wait. What?!

"I'll be right back. I have to use the restroom!" she yelped, pushing up off Trey's chest and springing to her feet.

He immediately sat up, alarm on his face, mouth open to say something, but she waved him off, unsteady for a second before darting down the hallway to the bathroom. Slipping inside, she forced herself to stay calm and not slam the door.

Spinning around, she faced the mirror over the vanity, taking slow, cleansing breaths. "Get it together, girl," she whispered to her reflection. "You didn't actually bite him. That's the important thing."

Turning on the faucet, she splashed some cold water on her face, wondering when she'd actually gone so mental. Then again, maybe it was at the exact moment when she'd considered getting a new blood sample from Trey by biting him.

Admittedly, alcohol might have had something to do with that particular harebrained scheme. She'd come up with it after having a few glasses of wine with Crystal following that horrible episode with the contaminated blood sample she'd gotten from Trey's teammate. She'd been bemoaning the possibility of ever obtaining a clean sample from the SWAT guys when her friend had jokingly said something about getting it while sleeping with one of them. Samantha immediately envisioned her straddling Trey's powerful naked body, riding him like a hobbyhorse. Then, when she was right in the middle of driving him to orgasm, she'd lean forward to nip his neck hard enough to draw blood—blood she would use to finally gain a DNA profile of one of the SWAT cops. While she didn't know what she might find, the scientist in her insisted their blood was the key to figuring out what made him and his teammates different. Maybe it was something as simple as being on performance-enhancing drugs, but she wouldn't know for sure until she did an analysis.

Doing something as extreme as biting Trey to get a sample of his blood had been a stupid idea and she'd quickly dismissed it. There was no way she could bite Trey hard enough to make him bleed. He'd think she was a psycho. And he'd be right! But just now, as she'd been lying on top of Trey, kissing him like there was no tomorrow, the thought of biting him had popped into her head completely unbidden, like a bolt of stupid from the great beyond.

And now here she was, standing in her bathroom, doing her best not to freak out while the most amazing man she'd ever met was likely running out the door at that very moment. This obsession with finding out what made him different was not only taking over her life, but also jeopardizing any chance at a relationship with him. She needed to let this go before she completely ruined everything.

She took one more deep, calming breath before throwing another couple handfuls of water on her face, finally getting herself back under control. Then she turned and pulled a fresh towel out of the linen closet, ignoring the big first-aid kit sitting on the shelf mocking her. The kit held the sterile pads and resealable vials she would have used for those blood samples. If she'd actually been stupid enough to bite the man like a freaking vampire.

"Stupid first-aid kit," she muttered.

Samantha stood at the door for a moment with her hand on the knob, psyching herself up. Then she jerked it open and headed for the living room, sure Trey had left.

The sound of rattling and thumping from the kitchen caught her attention and she felt relief flood her. Apparently, she hadn't chased him off after all. Or maybe he was looking for a knife, so he could defend himself from the crazy woman who'd tried to attack him.

She walked into the kitchen to see him pulling two mugs out of the cabinet near the microwave, smiling over his shoulder at her as if she hadn't just tried to rip open his throat a few moments ago.

"Hope you don't mind me rifling through your cabinets, but I was really looking forward to that coffee."

Samantha had been so resigned to the fact that Trey had left that she hadn't thought of what she'd say if he hadn't. So she nodded, hoping she didn't come off as even more insane.

Silence filled the kitchen for a few moments as Trey moved over to the coffeepot, quietly pouring the rich, dark roast into the mugs. Samantha took coconut milk out of the fridge and held up the carton to him, giving it a questioning shake. Trey smiled but shook his head.

Samantha was adding sweetener and milk to her own coffee when Trey thankfully broke the silence.

"Sorry about that," he said softly, leaning a hip against the granite counter and looking over the edge of his mug as he took a small sip. "I didn't mean to scare you off by going too fast."

It was a good thing she had a mug in front of her face. At least that way, Trey couldn't see her jaw drop. It definitely wouldn't have been a good look for her.

"You don't have anything to apologize for," she murmured, sipping her coffee and enjoying the way the warmth of the beverage calmed her. "You weren't going too fast and you didn't scare me off."

"Okay." He regarded her in concern. "But if that's not it, then why did you run out? And don't say because you had to use the restroom."

She hesitated, not sure how to answer. "I'm not really sure I can explain it." She took a step closer, putting her coffee cup down on the counter. "I guess I got a little overwhelmed for a second."

Trey set his own mug aside on the edge of the counter. "Overwhelmed by what?"

She gave him a sheepish smile. "That's the part that's hard to explain."

She couldn't tell him the truth, but she didn't want to lie, either.

"When I'm with you, I get these crazy feelings," she started slowly. "Emotions I've never experienced before come bubbling up out of nowhere. They're so powerful, they take my breath away."

Even as Samantha recognized the complete truth of what she'd said, it was impossible to miss the effect her words had on Trey. He looked stunned.

"Crap," she muttered, wrapping her arms around herself protectively. "This isn't coming out the way I wanted. I must sound insane."

But instead of backing away like she expected, Trey took her into his arms, squeezing tight and making the most calming shushing sounds she'd ever heard.

"You don't sound insane," he said, tugging her close until her head was nestled comfortably under his chin. "I completely get everything you're saying. It's not crazy at all."

Samantha pulled away, opening her mouth to tell him she didn't appreciate being patronized. She was so focused on what she was about to say, she forgot about Trey's mug sitting on the edge of the counter. At least until her flailing hand slammed into it and sent it flying, spinning the thing into the tile backsplash hard enough to shatter it into a thousand pieces, dark coffee going everywhere.

She couldn't have explained what happened next if someone asked her to try. One moment, she was staring at the puddles of liquid and ceramic shards scattered over the counter, and the next, she was lunging for the mess as if she thought she could stop time and force the pieces back together if she only moved fast enough.

Samantha knew it was stupid even as she reached for the sharp fragments of the mug. Her mind screamed at her to stop, that she was a doctor who made a living with her hands. Slicing them to ribbons wouldn't end with her embarrassment. It would put her out of commission for a while.

But before she could grab any of the pieces, a blur of motion intercepted her hand. She stared, horrified as one of the bigger pieces sliced into Trey's palm. Bright red blood mixed with the coffee already on the counter and she gasped.

"Oh no! I'm so sorry!"

She quickly reached for his hand to see how bad it was. One glance confirmed it was as terrible as she'd feared. The gash slanted sideways across his palm, shallower near the thumb side and much deeper toward the outer part of his hand.

Samantha went straight into doctor mode, smacking Trey's free hand as he reached for the dishrag she had hanging on a hook by the fridge. "Don't use that…it's dirty," she said firmly as she pulled him closer to the sink so the blood would drip in there and not all over the floor. "I have a first-aid kit in the bathroom. I'll be right back. Keep pressure on it."

Her mind was a blur as she ran for the bathroom, bringing back the kit and snapping rubber gloves on her hands before seeing to Trey's wound. As she gently wiped the blood away, she realized the laceration wasn't nearly as bad as it seemed at first. The bleeding had already slowed to a trickle and the medial portion of the cut, which she'd been sure would need stitches, seemed to be sealing up quickly. But she cleaned the wound properly regardless, placing a swatch of gauze on it, then tightly wrapping a bandage around his hand.

"It's not bleeding as badly as it was a minute ago, but I still think we need to have a doctor look at this."

He chuckled, tilting her face upward for a soft kiss. "I did have a doctor look at it."

"I mean a real doctor." She frowned, not sure how he could laugh—or plant a kiss on her—at a time like this. "And I'm serious about your hand. You're SWAT, but that doesn't mean you're immune to infection."

"I'll get it checked out. Promise."

Samantha wasn't sure she could trust him. He had a look on his face that suggested he thought the slash across his hand was no big deal. She was about to tell him how serious she was when he stopped her with another soft kiss.

"But I'll do it later," he murmured against her lips, his warm breath tracing across her skin in a way that made her brain go all fuzzy. "Right now, I'd rather get back to what we were talking about before you murdered that poor, defenseless coffee mug. You know, those crazy feelings and emotions that take your breath away."

"I think I vaguely remember saying something about that." At times like this—when he was looking at her like he wanted to eat her up—it seemed his eyes almost glowed with an inner warmth. It was hypnotizing. "I hope I didn't scare you by admitting that."

He let out another soft laugh, then followed it up with an even softer kiss. "You definitely didn't scare me. In fact, I think I quite like the idea of being able to take your breath away."

Samantha realized then that she was in trouble. More trouble than she could ever have imagined. There genuinely *was* something about this man that took her breath away. It both scared and thrilled her at the same time.

"Then kiss me and see if it happens again," she whispered.

Trey's arms slid around her, pulling her in as his mouth covered hers, totally ravishing her...and yes, taking her breath away.

And yet, despite how transcendent the kiss was, Samantha found her gaze drifting toward the counter and the blood-soaked pieces of gauze lying there.

So much for letting her obsession with what made him different go.

CHAPTER 7

"ARE YOU REALLY SURE THIS IS A GOOD IDEA?" CRYSTAL ASKED from the passenger seat of Samantha's car. "I mean, it's not too late to turn around and go home. Act like this was never a thought in your clever but overactive imagination."

Samantha glanced at her best friend, who was nervously holding a plastic bag filled with the vials holding Trey's blood and a file folder filled with DNA profiles Samantha had collected over the past couple years from some of the more bizarre cases SWAT had been involved in. The folder wasn't much, but those vials of Trey's blood caught and held her attention. From how much blood there'd been, she once again wondered how the wound had stopped bleeding so quickly. Considering the number of sopping wet gauze pads she'd bottled up, anyone would assume there'd been some serious damage involved. But obviously, there hadn't been, or she and Trey wouldn't have spent fifteen minutes making out in the kitchen. They would have been in an emergency room getting stitches.

Tracking her gaze up from the plastic bag to her friend's face, Samantha realized Crystal seemed genuinely nervous. She'd like to think Crystal was simply worried about driving across town with this many bloody bandages sitting in her lap, but she knew that wasn't it. No, it was far more likely Crystal was regretting her decision to join Samantha on this late-night expedition. Saying that Crystal strongly disapproved was putting it mildly. Samantha couldn't honestly blame her. She'd been the one who'd come up with this scheme in the first place and she still wasn't so sure it was the right thing to do.

Crystal had shown up at Samantha's apartment right after Trey left, eager to hear all about the date. Samantha doubted Crystal expected to find her wearing rubber gloves and stuffing bloody pieces of gauze into glass vials. The situation had gone from confused to tense when Samantha admitted the blood was Trey's and that she planned to take the samples to Loralei, so her sister could run a full-DNA analysis on it. The idea of having Loralei compare the results with some of the previous crime scenes involving torn-up bodies had been a spur-of-the-moment kind of thing.

"Good idea or not, this is what we're doing," Samantha said, pulling into one of the visitor spaces at Loralei's apartment complex.

"Unless you have one of those proverbial mice in your pocket, don't use the word *we*," Crystal muttered. "This stupid scheme is totally on you, and when it blows up in your face, I'll be right there saying I told you so."

Samantha turned off the SUV with a heavy sigh. "You know I'm the kind of person who can't let a mystery go unsolved."

Her friend reached over the console to take her hand, giving it a gentle squeeze. "And that's what makes you such a great medical examiner. But at the moment, it's making you a crappy girlfriend."

Samantha didn't say anything as the import of the word *girlfriend* hit her. Crystal was right. She and Trey might not have defined their relationship yet, but they were headed in that direction. Analyzing his blood like he was a suspect in a crime was all kinds of wrong for a girlfriend to do. But if this thing between them was ever going to work, she had to know what he was hiding.

She looked at Crystal. "I have to do this."

"And if there is something weird in his blood, what are you going to do then?"

"I haven't thought that far," Samantha admitted quietly.

It was her friend's turn to sigh. "If Trey finds out what you did, you could lose him. You know that, right?"

The idea of losing Trey made Samantha feel physically ill. "He isn't going to find out."

Crystal opened her door. "I think you're making a huge mistake."

Samantha couldn't say her friend was wrong. But it wasn't like she hadn't made a ton of other stupid decisions in her life. This would simply be one more on the list. She ignored the voice in the back of her head telling her this idea was raising stupid to a whole new level as they climbed the steps to the second floor.

Loralei opened the door on the first knock, a worried expression on her face. Samantha's younger sister was wearing a pair of SpongeBob SquarePants pajama pants and matching tank top, her shoulder-length blond hair tousled from sleep. Loralei eyed the plastic bag with the samples Crystal was holding as she closed the door behind them.

"You wake me up at midnight, tell me you're coming over and that it's an emergency, then you just hang up," Loralei said. "I've been sitting here worried sick. What. The. Hell?"

Samantha winced. "I'm sorry. I didn't mean to worry you. Something came up with this case I've been working on and it couldn't wait."

Her sister perked up at that. "You mean the Butcher case?"

Like everyone else in town, Loralei had gotten caught up in the grisly murders and had helped out any way she could, even if it was as a sounding board for Samantha to bounce ideas off.

"No," Samantha said. "It's related to something else." Grabbing the plastic bag and file folder from Crystal, she held them out to her sister. "I need you to run a full DNA profile, compare the results to the other profiles in the folder, and generally look for anything strange."

Loralei held up the bag, studying its contents. "Strange, how?"

"Just look for anything that shouldn't be there. And I need you to keep this top secret. No one can know anything about these samples. Don't tell anyone, no matter what you find."

Loralei eyed the bag again, then looked at her. "Okay, but why you aren't you doing this DNA profile at your own labs? Your equipment is as good as the stuff we use at mine."

"The chances of me getting anything this complex done on the down low at the institute is almost nil." That wasn't a lie. Each medical examiner had access to their fellow ME's computer files. She'd never be able to analyze Trey's blood without someone knowing. "Besides, you're used to dealing with proprietary customers who don't want anyone knowing they've given you a sample."

Loralei seemed to consider that for a moment before nodding. "Okay. I'll toss these in the fridge, then start on them first thing Monday morning and get the info to you as soon as I can. But you know, you could have brought this stuff over tomorrow at a decent hour, instead of waking me up."

She gave her sister a sheepish look. "Yeah, I know."

But then she might have come to her senses and bailed on the whole thing.

Thanking her sister for the help, Samantha apologized for waking her up, then gave her a hug before she and Crystal left.

"You are definitely going to regret this," her friend said as they walked out of the apartment building.

Based on how guilty she felt right then, Samantha agreed. But it was too late to turn back now. There was a possibility that these samples would come back completely normal. If so, she had no idea what the hell she was going to do. At the end of the day, she knew there was something going on with Trey and his teammates. If the answer didn't show up in his blood, she'd like to think she'd be able to simply let this all go and focus on this relationship she was developing with Trey, but part of her worried she'd never be able to do that. It was an obsession at this point, and all she could do was pray she could stop before it was too late.

CHAPTER 8

"YOU SURE YOU'VE NEVER SEEN THIS GUY IN HERE BEFORE?" Trey asked the bartender, leaning over so the woman behind the wide granite counter could get a better look at the photo of Alden Cox. "It would have been last weekend. His social media accounts suggested he was in here and we're hoping you might have seen him. Maybe with someone?"

There were a boatload of bars and clubs along this stretch of Pacific Avenue, but this particular place seemed even more crowded than the others, especially for a Sunday night. But the dark-haired woman mixing the drinks at least paused long enough to look at the photo. "Yeah, I recognize him," she said after squinting in the bar's dim light before looking back up at Trey and Connor. "He's in here pretty regularly. I don't know his name though, and I don't think I've seen him this weekend. But he's a player. What he'd do, assault some woman who wouldn't pay attention to him?"

The bartender had pegged him and Connor as police officers the moment they'd walked in, even though they were both dressed in civilian clothes. She'd eyed them up and down and informed them that no one had called the cops, then visibly relaxed when she heard they were there looking for someone.

"No, nothing like that," Connor said. "But he might have left with a woman—or a couple."

The bartender shook her head. "I think I saw him last Friday, though it might have been Saturday. Didn't see him with anyone that I can remember. Sorry."

Trey thanked the woman, then he and Connor walked around and asked a few of the servers to see if maybe they'd seen anything the bartender had missed. They hadn't.

"That's another one off the list," Trey said, pulling the afore-mentioned list out of his back pocket and drawing a line through the name of the bar with a pen.

Connor groaned as they walked out of the place and started down the sidewalk lining Pacific Avenue. "So that only leaves what, twenty more places or so?"

"About that," Trey replied.

It had taken them over two hours to work through the first four clubs Alden Cox had been to. At this rate, it would take them days to get through the rest. Unfortunately, by then there'd almost certainly be another dead body showing up in one of the local landfills. If it wasn't there already.

Following Trey's suggestion, STAT had built a list of clubs, bars, and restaurants that Alden Cox and Demario Harris had visited in the days right around their supposed times of death. Then they'd compared those locations with the routes taken by the garbage trucks that could have picked up the bodies. Since they'd known exactly which truck had picked up Demario Harris's body, that list—which Hale and Trevor had—was much shorter than the one Trey and Connor had been stuck with. But both were longer than they'd hoped. Demario and Alden had covered a lot of ground on the weekends of their deaths. As if they'd both been looking for one last shot at life before it was all over.

Trey and Connor didn't talk about how hopeless this exercise probably was as they walked. Instead, they moved from bar to club to restaurant, flashing Alden's picture to anyone they thought might remember him. Lots of people did. He was a regular at almost every place in the Pacific Avenue district. On the downside, no one could remember seeing him with anyone specific.

"How'd your date with Sam go last night?" Connor asked as they left a large nightclub that had taken them over an hour to work their way through. "Do you still think she's going out with you simply to get information about us?"

That was a loaded question if there ever was one. Unfortunately, he wasn't sure how to answer it.

So, instead, he checked his list, then his watch, before motioning down the block toward the bar on the corner. "It's getting close to last call for most of the places in this part of town. We'll probably have time for one more, then we'll have to call it a night."

Connor fell into step beside him. The sidewalk was still crowded. "So, what about Samantha? Since you don't want to talk about the date, does that mean you were right about her?"

Trey's mouth edged up. "The date was fantastic. Even better than the first one, if that's possible. We went out to the art district and walked around the shops, then grabbed pizza. We didn't even talk about SWAT or you guys or anything."

"But?" Connor prompted.

"I still don't know if she's playing me." Trey sighed. "Even though I'm sure she's definitely *The One*."

The crazy emotions she admitted feeling were more than enough to convince him that she was the woman he was meant to be with. Not to mention make his inner wolf sigh in contentment. And yet, his human side still urged him to be cautious.

"I don't want to be the one to say I told you so, but I told you so." Connor grinned.

Trey slanted him a glance. "Did you miss the part where I said I'm not sure if I can trust her?"

Even now, the gauze Samantha had used to clean the cut on his hand nagged at the back of his mind. Why hadn't he cleaned up the mess and tossed everything in the trash before he left? Did his inner wolf somehow instinctively already know she wasn't a threat to the Pack?

Dammit, why couldn't things be simple? But finding *The One* hadn't been easy for any of his teammates, so why should it be different for him?

"I still think you should tell her that she's your soul mate," Connor insisted.

"Yeah right." Trey snorted. "We've been on two whole dates and you think it would be a good idea to throw her in the deep end of the pool. I can see it now. *Hey, Samantha, you know those weird feelings you've been experiencing? Well, you're getting them because I'm a werewolf and you're my soul mate. But don't worry, I promise not to bite.*"

Connor scowled. "Okay, I guess I see your point. But you know you'll have to tell her at some point, so maybe you should come up with a plan now on how you're going to do that. Unless you want it to all blow up in your face."

Maybe Connor was right. Maybe if he sat Samantha down and explained everything in a very straightforward, scientific way, she'd realize what they had was too important for her to ever expose that he and his pack mates were werewolves. He needed to stop overcomplicating things and put his faith in the bond developing between them.

When he and Connor came to a rather unassuming bar illuminated by a series of soft orange and red neon signs in the windows, Trey had to admit it didn't look like the kind of place Alden would have hung out. It seemed a little too low-key for the guy's taste.

"We're on last call," an older man behind the bar announced as he and Connor stepped inside. "I'll pour you two some drinks, but you'll have to down 'em fast."

"Thanks for the offer, but we're not here for a drink," Trey said, flashing his badge. "We're looking for information on someone." Taking the photo out, he placed it on the wooden bar. "Have you ever seen this guy around?"

The man behind the bar barely looked at the photo for more than a second before nodding. "Yeah, I know Alden. All the regulars do." He motioned to several other people sitting at the bar. "Comes in every weekend like clockwork. Sometimes during the week, too. I haven't seen him in a while, though."

"That's because he was murdered two weeks ago," Trey said.

"Murdered?" The older man looked devastated at the news. "Damn."

"We're trying to pin down the last place he was seen that weekend. Do you remember if he came in here?"

The bartender nodded sadly. "Yeah, he was in here both Saturday and Sunday night. He came in around this time both nights."

"Did you see if he left with anyone?" Connor asked.

"I saw him with a woman Sunday night," a man at the end of the bar said. "She was tall with shoulder-length dark hair. I remember thinking she was definitely Alden's type."

Trey opened his mouth to ask the guy if he'd be able to describe her to a sketch artist when a woman's voice interrupted him. "I know the person you're talking about."

Trey turned to see a petite redhead standing there holding a drink tray full of empty glasses and beer bottles. "She was in here earlier tonight. She left a little while ago with some guy."

Trey exchanged looks with Connor.

"Do you remember what she was wearing?" his pack mate asked.

The waitress nodded. "A short skirt and red silk blouse."

"When did they leave?" Trey asked.

She shrugged. "Fifteen minutes ago, maybe."

Thirty seconds later, Trey was running south on Saint Paul Street, his nose going at a hundred miles an hour as he tried to pick up a scent that might lead him to the woman and the man she'd left the bar with. Unfortunately, the waitress hadn't seen which direction the couple had gone. He and Connor concluded she wouldn't have taken her prey toward the crowds of people still hanging around outside the other clubs in the area, so they'd headed farther down Pacific, praying for a little luck.

A hundred yards later, they split up, Connor continuing along

Pacific, while Trey turned down Saint Paul. It was a desperate gamble. There were a hundred different places the woman could have taken her victim if she were planning to kill him—or lure him into someone else's trap. Trey only hoped their theory was right and that she'd try to murder the guy somewhere close to the bar where she'd picked him up. If the guy had gotten into a car with her, there'd be no chance of ever finding them. At least not while the man was still alive.

When Trey reached the green spaces of Main Street Garden Park, his instincts had him slowing down and turning that way. He had no idea why, but it felt right.

The park filled a whole block between Main and Commerce, most of that being wide-open grassy areas with a few walking paths here and there and a big fountain in the front. The trees and light shrubs growing along the north side—along with the large construction dumpster near the far northeast corner—caught his attention.

He'd barely taken more than a step in that direction when he heard a sound halfway between a groan of agonizing pain and a gasp of pleasure that made the hair on the back of his neck stand up. Pulling his off-duty SIG, he sprinted in that direction.

Trey picked up an overly sweet odor mixed with a hint of something old and dried out underneath it. The smell made his nose tingle, like dust in the air. He was still trying to imagine what kind of creature could possibly possess such a scent when he rounded the corner of the dumpster.

Despite the glow coming from the streetlamps and nearby buildings, it was still dark behind the dumpster thanks to the shadows cast by the trees. Trey's night vision was near perfect even without having to partially shift. But when he saw the tall, slender woman in a red silk blouse and miniskirt holding the large, struggling man against the side of the dumpster with one hand, he couldn't comprehend how someone her size was able to manage it.

The man's shirt had been ripped open and his pants were undone and hanging loose. That strange groan of pleasure and pain came again, and Trey realized the woman had her lips planted firmly against the guy's chest.

Thinking he was on the verge of stepping into the middle of a kinky sex scene, Trey started to back out of the situation as fast as he'd arrived, but then he saw the man's face twist in torment, his skin shriveling right before his eyes. Like every ounce of youth and vitality was being sucked out of him.

Nope, so not a kinky sex scene.

"Drop him!" Trey shouted.

As Trey moved toward them, the woman immediately released her victim, the man's body falling limply to the ground. She spun around, taking a half dozen steps toward Trey in a blur.

Shit, she is fast.

Her strides put her directly in a halo of light coming from a nearby streetlamp, giving Trey his first clear look at the woman.

Who…maybe…probably…wasn't a woman at all.

Lidless eyes the size of baseballs, solid black and glossy as glass, dominated a pale face framed in dark hair that seemed to flutter in a nonexistent breeze with an energy of its own. The creature's nose was little more than two slits above a pair of colorless lips, and when it opened its mouth to hiss at him, Trey saw dozens of short, ragged teeth.

But even with the huge eyes and manic hair, possibly the most disconcerting part of the creature's appearance was the fact that it was wearing clothes. There was something unsettling about a creature this scary-looking wearing a miniskirt, silk blouse, and high heels. It was just wrong.

Another groan from the guy on the ground distracted Trey for a fraction of a second. That's when the creature attacked. One second, she was hissing at him, the next she was on him, both hands slamming into his chest hard enough to crack ribs and send him flying fifteen feet through the air. He vaguely felt his SIG tumbling into the darkness and decided he might be in a little bit of trouble.

Something in his back broke on impact, a spike of pain ripping down both legs to leave them throbbing and partially numb. But Trey didn't have much time to worry about how bad the damage might be as the creature came at him again. Apparently, the thing didn't like Trey interrupting whatever it had been doing to the guy on the ground.

Trey scrambled painfully to his feet, claws and fangs extending with a low growl, ready to face the thing this time. Unfortunately, he still wasn't ready for how fast the creature was. He barely got his hands up before she was hitting him with a combination of punches and shoves that had him stumbling back step by step.

Pissed, Trey let out a snarl and slashed at the creature's face, hoping to at least back her off. Amazingly, his claws connected somehow, ripping four deep gouges across the left side of the thing's face and down its neck. The thing shrieked and stumbled back, falling to the ground, clear, watery liquid that Trey assumed was blood gushing out. The wound was gruesome, and Trey wondered if he'd somehow managed to kill the creature.

He wasn't that lucky.

The creature slowly got to its feet, a bizarre sound coming from its throat. Crap, was the thing laughing? Freaky beyond description, the sound made his skin want to crawl away and hide in the nearby dumpster.

The slashes on the creature's face healed within seconds, disappearing without a trace. Even the clear liquid that had been running down its neck was reabsorbed until there was no sign he'd injured the thing at all. Werewolves healed fast, but not that fast.

Damn, he might very well be fucked.

Trey tried to slash the creature's face again when it charged at him a second later, but it blocked the blow, both hands clamping down on his arm and yanking hard. He panicked, thinking she was going to rip the damn thing off, but then he was flying through the air again. He had about half a second to contemplate how much this was going to hurt, then he was slamming into the side of the big construction dumpster. The metal gave under the impact. Unfortunately, he felt parts of him give, too.

He hit the ground a few feet from the woman's victim. The guy looked like shit, eyes closed, his face haggard and exhausted. Trey could hear the man's heartbeat, so he knew he was alive, but it was a lot slower and weaker than it should have been. Whatever the creature had been doing to the man, it had nearly killed him.

A blur of movement out of the corner of his eye made Trey realize he should have been a little more concerned about the creature killing *him*. Then the thing was on him, long, narrow fingers wrapping around his throat to crush the life out of him at the same time she picked him up and slammed him against the side of the dented dumpster.

Trey punched, slashed, and shoved at the creature, air running out as he was once more stunned she could be so strong. The creature ripped open his shirt, its cold lips pressing against the bare skin of his chest right where his wolf head tattoo was. Pain ripped through him, as if the creature was pulling his soul out right through his chest.

The pain shoved Trey's shift further than it already was, fangs and claws fully extending, muscles across his back and shoulders twisting and contracting, bones beginning to crack and lengthen as his body fought to assume a shape more conducive to this fight. The pain in his chest lessened and Trey threw every ounce of his strength into breaking free, slashing and ripping at the creature's throat and chest in rapid succession.

He knew he was hurting the creature because it was shrieking and hissing like mad, but he was weakening at the same time. It was a toss-up as to which one of them would collapse first.

In the distance, he heard the rapid thud of approaching boots, too fast to be a regular human. Connor's scent reached him just as Trey finally succeeded in shoving the creature away. It stared at him for a moment before its head snapped around in the direction of those footsteps. With one more quick hiss at Trey, the creature was off, running as fast as hell across the park toward Main Street. A second later Connor was hauling ass after it, his handgun out—along with his fangs and claws.

Trey stayed on his feet for all of five more seconds before he slowly slid down the side of the dumpster and onto the ground, more exhausted than he'd ever been in his life. He knew he should get up and help his pack mate chase the thing, but he was too damn tired.

A glance at his chest showed no real wound beyond some redness, as if the creature had been trying to give him a hickey. That thought was actually more repulsive than the idea of the thing biting him.

Giving up on the idea of going after Connor, Trey instead crawled over to the guy on the ground, getting him flipped over and hopefully in a position that would make breathing easier. The guy's heart rate wasn't any better than it had been before, but at least it wasn't any worse. Looking closer at the man's skin, Trey realized it looked severely dehydrated. Not nearly as bad as the body they'd found at the landfill, but obviously well on the way to that condition. Trey wondered how much longer the guy could have survived whatever the creature had been doing to him.

The sound of heavy footsteps in the grass drew his attention away from the man and he turned his head to see Connor racing across the park toward him. A few seconds later, his friend was at his side, asking if he was okay. Trey couldn't do much except nod.

"What the hell was that thing?" Connor whispered, moving over to check the other guy on the ground. "I heard you yelling from a couple blocks away and came running, but she was already on the move by the time I got here. I tried to chase her…it…whatever the hell we're supposed to call the thing, but it was too damn fast. I almost caught up to it until it ducked into an alley and ran right up the side of a frigging wall."

"I'm not sure what that thing was, but it's definitely the same thing that's responsible for the bodies in the landfills," Trey said weakly. "She was well on the way to draining this poor guy when I arrived."

"Draining?" Connor prompted, curious.

Trey questioned why he'd used that particular word but decided it actually fit. He described what he'd seen upon first getting on the scene and what it had felt like when the creature latched onto his chest.

"I think it was feeding on me," he added. "It felt like she was sucking the life out of me. Hurt like a son of a bitch, too. I'm exhausted and she was only on me a couple seconds. I have no idea how long she'd been going at this guy."

Connor looked over at the man on the ground. "What are we going to do with him? If we call an ambulance, the hospital won't have a clue what to do with him."

Trey agreed. "I say we call STAT and get them out here to help, then send a sketch artist back to that bar we just left and have them work on a drawing of our suspect. We need to tell Gage and the deputy chief that we definitely have a supernatural creature hunting people in our city. One that's stronger and faster than we are and damn near immune to injuries."

Connor reached for his phone, shaking his head. "When the hell is the weird crap in this town going to end? If it's not serial killers that steal body parts, it's supernatural soul suckers with big, freaky eyes."

Trey sighed and leaned back against the dumpster. As his mom always liked saying, when it rained, it poured.

CHAPTER 9

Samantha was staring at her computer screen lost in thought when Crystal walked into her office a few minutes after eight Monday morning.

"Having second thoughts about asking your sister to analyze Trey's blood?"

Samantha sat back with a sigh as Crystal slipped into one of the chairs in front of her desk. "Second, third, and fourth. I know that sounds crazy, especially since I've been obsessing over this forever, but what I'm doing—going behind Trey's back like this—I feel like I'm betraying him."

"Wow. Betraying." Crystal did a double take. "That's a heavy word."

"I know, right?" Samantha gave her a small smile. "Want to hear something even crazier? We've only been on a few dates, and I already feel a connection with him that I've never felt with anyone else."

Her friend leaned forward. "Then talk to him and ask him to explain all the weird stuff you saw at those crime scenes the past two years. You're a medical examiner. It's not a bizarre question coming from you."

Looking at it that way, what Crystal said made a lot of sense. If she asked Trey a straightforward question, he would probably be honest with her. More importantly, she wouldn't have to feel so crappy about deceiving him. Then again, what if being up front with him backfired on her and he broke up with her?

Crystal opened her mouth to say something, but before she could, the thud of heavy boots in the hallway interrupted her. A few moments later, Trey appeared in the doorway, the delicious scent of bacon and eggs wafted from a fast-food bag in one hand, a cardboard tray with two cups of coffee balancing in the other.

"Hope I'm not interrupting anything," he said, flashing both of them a charming grin before looking at Samantha. "I was in the area and thought you might want breakfast. I only brought two cups of coffee, Crystal, but you're welcome to take mine."

Crystal shook her head as she got to her feet. "I wouldn't dream of it," she said with a smile. "I already ate and have a freshly brewed pot of coffee in my office waiting for me, but you two go for it." She caught Samantha's eye. "I'll see you later. And what I was saying earlier? Think about it, okay?"

Giving Trey another smile, Crystal walked out, leaving Samantha alone with Trey.

He set the bag on her desk, then took one of the cups out of the tray and offered it to her as he sat down in the chair Crystal had just vacated.

"Milk, two packs of sweetener, right?"

If Samantha wasn't already feeling so crappy about how she was treating Trey, this would have pushed her over the edge for sure. Not only had he thoughtfully brought her breakfast because she happened to mention the other night that she ends up skipping it because she's usually running late, but he remembered how she liked her coffee, too. Could he be any more perfect?

"Right." She reached for the cup with a smile. "Anytime you feel like stopping by with breakfast, feel free."

Breakfast turned out to be a breakfast burrito the size of her forearm stuffed with eggs, sausage, and hash browns, all smothered in a thick ranchero sauce. There was no way Samantha could eat the whole thing herself.

As Trey settled back into his chair and pulled his own burrito out of the bag, Samantha realized he wasn't wearing a bandage around his hand any longer. She opened her mouth to tear him a new one for not protecting the wound when she saw the faded bruising around his neck. More light bruises colored both forearms, some extending all the way up to where those droolworthy biceps disappeared into the sleeves of his uniform shirt. Forensic mind kicking into high gear, she immediately recognized the marks on his arms as defensive bruising, and the yellowish-green smudges around his neck looked like someone had tried to choke the life out of him—with a pair of Vise-Grips.

"What happened?" she asked, not sure why her heart was suddenly thumping way too fast. "It looks like someone tried to choke you to death."

Unbelievably, Trey chuckled. "It was nothing," he said, not even looking up from the burrito he was busy unwrapping. "Connor and I were down on Pacific Avenue flashing a photo of a guy around a few clubs and bars. He was murdered two weeks ago, and we were trying to ascertain if anyone had seen him. We ended up running into someone we think was involved in the guy's death and they weren't exactly friendly."

Samantha didn't think Trey was lying, but something told her he was leaving a lot unsaid. She knew the Dallas SWAT team was involved in a lot more stuff than a normal SWAT team might be, but she still couldn't understand why they'd be downtown wandering around the bars with a dead guy's picture. That's not what SWAT cops did for a living.

Unless there was something weird going on that he wasn't ready to share yet.

Doubting he'd tell her anything, she opened her mouth to ask anyway when she got a good look at the palm of his injured hand. Except it wasn't injured now. For a moment, she thought she was looking at the wrong hand. But that wasn't it at all. In fact, there was a line of pink scar tissue across his right palm exactly where it should be, completely sealed and well on its way to disappearing. She might work with dead people who didn't heal from wounds, but she still recognized one that looked at least ten days old.

Her first thought was: *What the hell?* But then she remembered how many times she'd heard outlandish stories about members of the SWAT team being injured in the line of duty without ever going to the hospital. She'd always thought those stories were urban legends, the law enforcement equivalent of the fish that got away.

Looking at Trey's hand, maybe not.

Samantha was still trying to figure out a way to get a closer look at the scar—short of grabbing his hand and telling him she was going to read his palm—when a slight cough from the doorway interrupted her thoughts. She looked up to see Louis and Hugh standing there. While Louis smiled at them with a fatherly expression, Hugh's sour grimace made her think he'd rather throw something at her.

"Morning, Officer Duncan. Sorry to interrupt," Louis said, stepping into the office with Hugh on his heels. "I just got a call from DPD dispatch. It seems they've found another possible body dump near that homeless camp south of the George Bush Turnpike off West Renner, and the task force lead wants you there ASAP, Samantha."

"I'd be happy to tag along if you need some help," Hugh added quickly.

She just bet he would. He stopped by her office at least twice a day to check on the progress in the investigation.

"I can drive Samantha to the site and make sure she gets back here whenever she needs to," Trey said with a smile that didn't quite reach his eyes.

While she could have driven herself, Samantha wasn't going to turn down Trey's offer, especially if it gave her a chance to get a closer look at his hand. She thought Hugh might insist on going, too, but to her relief, he turned and walked off in a huff.

As they drove to the crime scene that likely involved one or more dismembered bodies, Samantha tried to get a peek at Trey's right hand. Unfortunately, he kept it on the wheel the entire time, so she didn't get a chance to check out the well-healed scar again.

Samantha ate slowly as Trey turned onto the George Bush Turnpike and headed north. The burrito was the best thing she'd eaten for breakfast in a long time, but it was kind of heavy for the situation she was heading into. As they slipped through morning traffic, most of it heading south at this time of day, they chatted about the shops they'd seen in the Bishop Art District and where they should go on their next date. Samantha loved seeing Trey again, even as her stomach twisted at the way she was going behind his back with the whole blood-sample thing.

She felt a lot better when the conversation got around to Trey trying to get her to talk about the Butcher case while Samantha pumped him for more details on what happened to him and Connor at the bar last night. Neither one of them ended up getting what they were looking for, both of them dancing around each other's questions, talking but saying little.

The moment Trey turned onto West Renner, Samantha caught sight of the crime scene. In addition to all the emergency vehicles lined up along the road, there was also a large collection of tents set up in the nearby tree line.

"Wow," Trey murmured, looking out at the dozens of tents nestled in the shade provided by the scraggly pines. "This camp gets bigger every time I see it. There must be close to a hundred people living out here."

Samantha didn't doubt his estimate. The homeless camp was one of many that had sprung up throughout the city over the years.

As she gazed at the crowded camp, Samantha wondered if the cops had made a mistake and that the body found out here had nothing to do with the Butcher case. All the previous dumps had been in the middle of nowhere. Why the sudden change in MO?

Then she realized that most of the cops and gawkers were standing on the other size of the road from the homeless camp, staring at a section of high grass near the side of a rundown building. She couldn't see what they were looking at, but it wasn't hard to guess that's where the body was located.

Trey must have thought the same thing because he turned into the building's overgrown parking lot, stopping a short distance away from the grassy area where a handful of young cops were busy setting up crime scene tape. She glanced out the passenger window at the tents spread out among the trees across the road. Based on the heavy puddles scattered around the area, it must have rained late last night or early this morning. Assuming the body had been dumped in the dark during that time, it was possible the Butcher hadn't known there was anyone out here.

Chief Leclair was there to greet Samantha as soon as she stepped out of Trey's vehicle. The chief looked back and forth between her and Trey curiously before raising a questioning brow at Samantha, clearly expecting an explanation as to why the ME assigned to the Butcher task force had decided to show up at a crime scene in the company of one of her SWAT officers. But there was no way in hell Samantha was getting anywhere near that conversation, so she just nodded toward the grassy area and the young cops busy with their rolls of yellow tape.

"So, what do we have, Chief?" she asked, taking her kit out of the back seat of the SWAT SUV, noticing Trey had moved away to talk to some of the other officers farther across the parking lot. He probably didn't want to get cross-examined by the chief, either. "Another mutilated body, I'm assuming?"

"Not quite." The chief grimaced and motioned toward the crime scene with a hand. "Maybe you should take a look yourself rather than have me try to describe it."

Curiosity definitely stoked now, Samantha fell into step beside the chief, pausing for a moment when they got closer to the grassy area and one of the younger cops suddenly turned and stumbled before bending over to throw up. Okay, that probably wasn't good.

As they reached the edge of the parking lot, Samantha slowed for a few seconds to watch one of the techs from the ME's office masking off some tire tracks there in the mud between the pieces of asphalt. She was guessing, but based on the width and tread pattern, the tracks were from a large truck or SUV. Almost certainly the one that had dumped off the body. The tread pattern looked generic, but maybe they'd get lucky.

"I'll leave you to it," the chief said as they reached the entrance to the crime scene and the young officer standing there writing down the names of everyone who entered the taped-off area. "But as soon as you can, I need to know if this is connected to the Butcher case. It would help if the mayor hears it from me before he gets it from the press."

Just inside the tape, right before the grass started getting thicker, Samantha found a boot print in the mud. She leaned down to get a closer look before calling back to the tech still working the tire tracks, telling him to get on this print next. It looked identical to the ones she'd seen at the other Butcher body dumps and seemed like the connection the chief had been looking for. She'd be happy—or unhappy, depending on her point of view. The high grass and brush had been completely crushed down by the killer as he'd moved through the area, and once again, Samantha wondered how big the Butcher was. At least as large as Trey, maybe bigger.

Another few feet in, Samantha finally saw the reason the young cop had run off to throw up earlier and the meaning of the chief's equivocation when Samantha asked about this being another body dump. It wasn't a body. It was part of a body.

First, there was a portion of a man's arm, neatly and cleanly amputated at the wrist and elbow. Directly beyond the arm was a fully intact left leg, amputated a few inches above midthigh. There was also another lower arm and a hand missing the fingers. It only took a quick glance at the slightly different skin tones among the parts for Samantha to realize the three pieces hadn't come from a single victim.

She took another step forward but stopped cold when she caught sight of the pile of what could only be called scraps left strewn across the grass just short of the building's wall. In addition to bits of skin, there were bigger chunks of internal organs and long lengths of mangled muscles and ligaments. She saw pieces of bones buried deeper in the grass. She wasn't quite sure what part of the body they'd come from. Maybe broken rib pieces. There was an ear to one side of the bones and, nearby, a handful of knotted and twisted hair.

There was blood slopped on the wall, where the earlier rain hadn't reached it to wash off. The way it was spattered made her think the killer had slung a bucket full of the stuff in their desire to get rid of it quickly.

Samantha swallowed hard. Even with her extensive exposure to upsetting scenes like this, she regretted her decision to eat that breakfast burrito. She'd seen a lot of vile stuff in this job, but this was hard even for her. She pushed the thoughts aside and pulled her camera from her bag, starting with wide-angle shots before moving in for close-ups.

"Is it the Butcher?" the chief asked from behind her. "I know you can't say for sure until you do an autopsy, but I'll take your best guess."

Samantha turned to see Chief Leclair standing just beyond the crime tape, Trey at her side. "The boot imprint in the mud over there is a visual match for the ones at the previous crime scenes. And from a cursory look at the ends of the three amputated limbs, I can tell you they were cut with a high-speed oscillating bone saw. Unless we have two nearly identical killers using identical cutting tools, we can assume that this is another Butcher scene."

Mouth tight, the chief gave her a nod, then left, heading over to talk to several detectives Samantha recognized from the task force. She knew the exact moment when the chief told them that they were almost certainly dealing with another Butcher killing. None of them seemed surprised; instead they all looked pissed. This psychopath was making a laughingstock out of all off them.

"Some of the people who live in the camp saw a large truck pull into this parking lot early this morning, a little after four a.m.," Trey said, looking down at some notes he'd scribbled on a small pad. "They described the guy who got out of the vehicle as frigging huge. Well over six feet, easy. He was wearing some kind of long coat with a hood, so even if it hadn't been dark and raining, no one would be able to describe him."

She sighed. "Well, that all matches the details of the crime scene, from the tire tracks at the edge of the lot to the boot print and the crushed grass. It's not much to go on, but this is the first time anyone has caught sight of the killer. Even if it only confirms the gender and build of the suspect, that's still more than we had before."

"If that was all there was, I'd definitely take it," Trey replied as she leaned in and took detailed shots of the thigh end of the leg. "But in this case, one of the witnesses over in the camp gave us something else. Something big."

Samantha stopped what she was doing to raise a brow questioningly. "How big?"

"The big guy got out the passenger side of the truck," Trey said, nodding when her eyes widened. "Yeah, there was someone else driving. The person didn't get out to help, and between the darkness and the rain, the witnesses couldn't see much, but they said the silhouette they could make out was definitely a man."

Samantha considered the implications of that. As far as she knew, serial killers were a solitary lot, regardless of what some of the people on the task force thought. The fact that this one had a partner must be significant. It also called into question another previous assumption. Namely, the idea that the big man who'd been leaving the deep boot prints behind was the killer might be wrong. Maybe he was simply the muscle of the operation. Maybe the man who stayed in the vehicle was the killer. Considering the combination of precise and inexact cuts she'd found on the bodies, it looked like the people who'd been pushing the theory about two killers might be right.

"I don't suppose anyone got a look at the vehicle's license plate?" she asked.

While it was interesting to know there were now two suspects in the Butcher case, it didn't necessarily help them very much.

Trey shook his head. "The truck was here for less than five minutes and no one in the camp even considered coming out of their tents to take a closer look. Not that I blame them. Hell, none of them even bothered to look at what they dumped until this morning."

From the corner of her eye, Samantha saw Trey move a little further along the crime scene tape, staying outside it, but obviously trying to get a better view of remains. She even saw him lean in a little and take a sniff, though she had no idea what the hell that was about.

"Do you think these parts are from the previous bodies we already recovered?" Trey asked curiously. "Or does this mean there are even more victims out there that we don't know about?"

She grimaced. "I won't know until I get a closer look at everything, start blood typing, cross matching, and running DNA profiles. But man, I hope these aren't completely new victims. If they are, this killer is even more bloodthirsty than we thought."

Trey watched while she finished the last of the photos, then mapped out where all the parts were positioned, taking pages of notes on each. He let her work without interruption, even though he probably had hundreds of questions. Samantha discovered she liked his company. It was the most pleasant time she'd ever had at a crime scene.

There is something wrong with you, a little voice whispered in the back of her head. *Very, very wrong with you.*

She was at a crime scene, standing over a gruesome collection of amputated body parts, thinking about how much fun she was having. Like she was on a date.

Samantha was halfway through bagging up the partial arm, noting the circular-shaped scar on the center of the inner part of the forearm, when Trey spoke.

"I know this is probably a weird time to ask," he said softly, obviously concerned about being overheard by the other cops nearby, "but I thought you might want to get together tonight."

She smiled. "Sure. I'll text you later and let you know when I'm wrapping up at the institute."

He returned her smile. "Sounds good."

Trey went back to watching as she continued picking up the various remains. Samantha tried to focus on what she was doing, but saying she was a little distracted would be an understatement. Especially when she was so keenly aware of his gaze on her.

"Are those burn scars on the leg?" he suddenly asked, almost making her jump.

Samantha looked over to see him leaning across the tape, pointing toward the leg she'd been in the process of picking up. She'd noticed the built-up scar tissue along the top and inside of the thigh area earlier, but looking at it again, she realized it was even worse than she'd first thought, the burns wrapping all the way around to the back of the leg and down past the knee. She could see the crosshatch markings indicative of extensive skin graft work and pressure dressings. Whoever this poor guy had been, he'd lived a life filled with pain.

"Yeah," she finally answered. "Pretty bad burn scars, too."

Trey looked thoughtful at that but didn't comment, and Samantha found herself wondering what kind of experience he had with burns. Had he seen them often during his time as a medic in the army?

She was putting the remains of the leg into an evidence bag when she caught sight of Trey leaning forward, his nostrils flaring as if he was trying to catch a stray scent. She wasn't sure why it struck her that way, but she couldn't help thinking the movement was almost predatory.

"What's that smell?" he asked, sniffing the air. "It smells like a cleanser or disinfectant, but it's kind of flowery, too. Like perfume. There's a bit of a burnt electrical odor to it as well, but it's really light."

Samantha didn't have a clue what Trey was talking about, but she leaned closer to the leg and took a good sniff anyway, surprised when she actually picked up a scent that seemed out of place on a chunk of human remains. And while she couldn't say she smelled anything that even hinted at burnt electricity, she was sure she smelled flowers...and something sharper. But it was really faint. She could barely smell it even with her nose almost touching the skin. She had no idea how Trey had been able to pick up the odor from ten feet away.

"I think it's some kind of antiseptic body wash," she said slowly.

"Antiseptic body wash?" Trey repeated, looking as baffled as she felt. "You mean like the stuff they give patients to use before they go in for surgery?"

She nodded, kind of surprised he knew that, even with his medic background. "It's definitely used for that. But I've known doctors, nurses, and other people in the medical field who use it to wash up after work."

Trey frowned as he considered that. "But why would something like that be on the remains of a serial killer's victim?"

All Samantha could do was shrug as she finished bagging up the leg for transport. Because she'd been wondering the exact same thing and didn't have a clue.

CHAPTER 10

"THANKS FOR COMING WITH ME," TREY SAID, AMAZED AT HOW nervous he felt as he pulled into the parking lot of the low-budget motel off Interstate 20 near Lawson. "I have to warn you in advance that Kyson can be a little intimidating. He's a big guy and sort of intense."

Trey smiled as he thought of his old army buddy Kyson Daughtry. Well over six feet tall and super muscular, his blond, blue-eyed friend was a monster of a man, so calling him "big" was putting it mildly. He cursed under his breath when he heard Samantha's heart begin to beat a little faster. Realizing he was making her nervous, he did his best to backtrack.

"But don't worry," he added quickly, parking in a space around the backside of the building. The rooms there were the cheapest the motel had, and the only ones his friend could afford with his veteran's benefits. "I think you and Kyson will hit it off. He might be kind of gruff, but he's a teddy bear at heart. He'll be thrilled to meet you."

For Trey, introducing Samantha to Kyson was like bringing her meet his family. He and Kyson might not be related by blood, but after everything they'd gone through in Afghanistan together, they were as close as brothers. Maybe closer.

"That's cool you and Kyson stayed in touch after you guys got out of the army," she said, hopping out of his Jeep before he could come around and open the door for her.

Trey nodded as they walked toward his old friend's room. It was even cooler that she hadn't minded stopping to see Kyson on the way to dinner. Being around the homeless camp today had reminded him that he hadn't checked in on his buddy in a while and that he was way overdue for a visit.

"Kyson is actually the reason I ended up in Dallas after getting out of the army," he admitted. "Remember that firefight in Afghanistan I told you about that happened right before I was supposed to reenlist? Kyson was that best friend who ended up in worse shape than I did."

"What happened to him?"

"A rocket-propelled grenade slammed into the truck we took cover behind. It hit the gas tank and sent me flying, but Kyson wasn't so lucky. When the truck blew, flames engulfed him, covering the lower half of his body." Trey winced at the memory. "It was so bad that he got transferred to the military hospital in San Antonio for long-term care. I moved to Dallas to be close to him and would drive down there a few times a month to see him. He stayed in the army a lot longer than I did, but spent all of that time rehabbing his injuries. They finally medically discharged him about three years ago."

"That's terrible." Samantha looked around, taking in the run-down motel and its dirty surroundings, the empty beer cans and other trash lying in the corner of the stairwell. "No one should have to live in a place like this, but it seems even more of a shame for a veteran who's served his country."

"Unfortunately, his VA benefits aren't enough for him to afford anything else," Trey said. "Kyson hasn't handled the transition back to civilian life very well and there's still some stuff he's working through that makes it hard for him to hold down a job. I do what I can to help, but he won't take any money from me, so I have to settle for stopping by to see him every week or so."

Damn, now he was babbling, not to mention telling her way more than she probably wanted to know. But the connection he had with Samantha made it easy to confide in her about things. Maybe that came with the territory when a werewolf found *The One*, making it easier to tell your mate what you were.

"I'd do so much more for him if he'd let me," Trey added. "I told him he could move in with me until he saved up some money for a nicer place, but he's proud as hell, and if I do too much, he gets pissed and thinks I'm trying to take care of him. He thinks it makes him a charity case and he hates that."

"Does he have anyone in his life besides you?" Samantha asked, empathy clear in her eyes. "Any family?"

Trey shook his head. "Not really. He doesn't have any family, and after what happened in Afghanistan, he does a good job of pushing people away. God knows he tries hard enough to get me to walk away. I've seen him with a homeless woman named Shaylee at the food bank a few times, though. She frigging adores Kyson, but he refuses to see it. He doesn't think he's good enough for her."

He smiled a little when they got to Kyson's room. Unlike the rest of the place, the exterior walkway was clear of all trash and dirt. Kyson liked his surroundings neat and orderly, always had. He might be down on his luck right now, but that didn't mean he wanted to look like it.

"I can't wait for you to meet him. I promise you're going to like him," Trey told Samantha again as he knocked on the door.

When Kyson didn't make an appearance, Trey knocked again, a little harder this time, leaning in closer to the door to try to pick up any sounds from within the room. His friend was always home by this time of the day, since all of the manual labor temporary jobs usually finished up by six o'clock. And while Kyson would occasionally buy some beer and drink a little bit too much when he did, then go to sleep early, that was normally on the weekends when he didn't have to get up with the sun in order to find work.

"He's gone," a rough voice said from their left. "Manager already cleared out the room and everything. Gave away all his stuff... what there was of it."

Trey turned to see a skinny guy with a scraggly gray beard standing there.

"What do you mean *gone*?" Trey asked.

He got a sinking feeling in his stomach while he waited for the man to answer. It hit him then that the familiar scent he associated with his friend was so faint it was almost nonexistent.

"He killed himself three weeks ago," the guy said bluntly. "I found him hanging in his shower. I heard some noise in his room and thought he might be in trouble, so I came over to check, but I was too late."

Trey stopped listening, his whole world coming to a screeching halt. There was no way in hell that Kyson could be dead. He wouldn't kill himself. He would have called Trey if he even thought of doing something like that.

That was a lie. Kyson had never called him when he'd needed help or anything else. How many times had his friend told him that he didn't want to be a burden? And how many times had Trey told him that he wasn't?

Trey vaguely heard Samantha talking to the man, heard the guy say something about Kyson being fired from a job for getting mad and punching someone. From what the man said, Trey got the feeling his friend had been fired from quite a few jobs lately. He and Kyson had shared a couple boxes of pizza and breadsticks a little over three weeks ago, and his friend had never breathed a word of any of this to him.

Dammit, why hadn't he realized his friend was hurting?

Trey didn't pay much attention to the rest of the conversation as Samantha continued to talk with the man, getting a small cardboard box from him before asking who had come to pick up the body. Trey knew all of that was important, but right then, he simply couldn't process any more. Kyson was gone. Nothing seemed to make sense at the moment.

A little while later, they ended up at Samantha's office at the institute, though Trey could barely remember even getting back in the Jeep, much less her driving them there. He was somewhat baffled about why they'd gone there until he heard Louis explain to Samantha that Kyson's death had been ruled a suicide and that there was no need for a full autopsy. He even showed them paperwork to prove it.

"UT Southwestern handles burial assistance for Dallas County in cases like this," Louis added softly, his eyes kind behind his glasses, seeming to know that Kyson had been important to him. "We were able to confirm his military background, so the VA paid for most of the cremation. The county covered the rest. With no next of kin, there was no one to send the ashes to. I'm sorry, but he's gone."

Trey mumbled his thanks, then let Samantha guide him out to the Jeep again. Fifteen minutes later, he was sitting in a chair at the small table in her kitchen, sipping on the whiskey she'd pulled out of the back of a cabinet, numbly watching as she made soup and sandwiches for dinner.

"You don't have to make anything." He took a large swallow of his drink even though it was nearly impossible for a werewolf to get drunk on anything less than a case of whiskey. "I asked you to dinner, so we should go somewhere."

Samantha gave him a small smile as she continued to stir the soup. "I thought maybe it would be better if we hung out here and talked for a while."

And in that moment, Trey realized he was so completely done for. Even if he attempted to ignore the whole damn soul-mate thing, he was going to have to accept that Samantha had slipped in and taken up residence in his chest—right where his heart was. After spending little more than a long weekend with him, she was smart enough to know he was in no shape to be going anywhere, so she'd taken him to her place and made them soup and sandwiches. If she pulled out a bag of Fritos, he was going to have to do something serious, like wash her windows or something.

"Talking would be good," he answered, enjoying this little domestic moment, even if it came in the middle of the shittiest night he'd had in a long time.

When Samantha brought over the soup and sandwiches, she was carrying a bag of corn chips, too. Which, yeah, put a smile on his face. Sitting down across from him, she pulled the small cardboard box he'd seen her get from the neighbor at Kyson's apartment closer. Trey stared down at the bowl of tomato soup in front of him as she opened the box and reached inside.

"What's this?" she asked, holding up a piece of framework covered in rectangles of colorful cloth and tiny bits of metal.

Trey's breath caught as he stared at the thing in Samantha's delicate hand. He hadn't realized his friend had even kept anything from his days in the military.

"It's Kyson's ribbon rack." Spoon in one hand, he reached out the other to run a finger over the stiff pieces of fabric. "They're his award and campaign ribbons from when he was in the army. They're worn on a soldier's dress uniform on the left side, over his heart. I didn't know he kept his."

Samantha was silent for a while as she ate spoonfuls of soup. "Do you have one?" When Trey nodded, she pointed at the rack of ribbons. "I assume the different colors mean something special, right? And these little pieces of metal in the middle of these ribbons mean something, too?"

Trey knew exactly what Samantha was doing. She was dragging him out of the darkness in his head and he loved her for it.

"Yeah. Every ribbon has a meaning, especially to the soldier who receives them." He tapped the rack. "And these little pieces of metal as you call them are oak leaf clusters and knots that signify multiple awards. One cluster means the second award and two clusters means the third award. The rules with the knots are a little different simply because the army refuses to make anything easy, but you get the basic idea."

Samantha laughed as she took a bite of her turkey and cheese sandwich. "Tell me about the ribbons and what they all mean. And if you know why Kyson got them, I'd love to hear the stories."

Just when Trey thought she couldn't possibly get any better, she did.

So they sat there at her small kitchen table, eating their soup and sandwiches, while Trey walked her through every single ribbon on the rack, from the simplest Army Service Ribbon, through all the campaign ribbons for Afghanistan, Iraq, and the Global War on Terrorism, and finally finishing with Kyson's Purple Heart and Bronze Star for the battle the two of them had been in together in Kabul. In between, there were a lot of other awards for achievement and commendation. And Trey had been around for all of them. He told Samantha every one of those stories, even the one about the last battle they'd fought in together. Talking about everything he'd been through with Kyson brought tears to his eyes and made it feel like his heart was being ripped out of his chest, but he told her everything and felt better afterward.

When every bit of food was gone, every ribbon explained, and every story told, they pulled the cardboard box closer and began to go through its contents together. There were copies of Kyson's awards and discharge paperwork, patches off his old uniforms, trinkets and keepsakes from years spent traveling the world. Underneath all the knickknacks was a picture of an enormous Kyson standing with an arm around a petite, shy-looking blond who barely came up to the middle of his chest.

"That's Shaylee," Trey whispered, tears blurring his vision again. "I knew he liked her, too, even if he refused to admit it to me."

He wondered if anyone had told Shaylee that Kyson was dead. The poor woman was going to be devastated.

If Trey was surprised by the photo of Kyson and Shaylee, he was even more stunned when he saw the picture at the very bottom of the box, this one of Trey and Kyson rigged out in full battle rattle taken only days before that miserable mission in Afghanistan that had nearly killed both of them.

Samantha grabbed the picture away from him excitedly. "You look so young in this! I swear you somehow look smaller than you are now."

Trey shrugged as he let out a chuckle. How could he tell her that going through his werewolf transition had slapped forty pounds of muscle on him and about five inches in height? "That's what I get for standing beside Kyson. I told you the guy was frigging huge. He looked even bigger in all his gear. Made me seem like a small guy in comparison."

Samantha studied the photo again and then him, as if trying to work through the size differences and the scale of the picture. Fortunately, there wasn't much there for her to work with to prove him wrong.

"You two look like the very best of friends," she said with a smile as she handed the picture back to him. "I'm sorry I never got a chance to meet him."

"Me, too."

Trey gazed at the photo for a long time, replaying the moment when it had been taken, and all the moments that had happened since, culminating in some stranger telling him that his best friend had killed himself.

"I should have done something," he whispered brokenly. "I knew he was having problems transitioning back to civilian life and getting past what happened in Afghanistan. I should have dragged him to more VA meetings, forced him to get counseling for his depression. He was my best friend and I failed him."

"Stop," Samantha said firmly, her hand coming out to cover his own, which was still holding the picture. "You didn't fail him. I'm not going to act like I knew the details of the situation, but it's obvious you were there for your friend. Sometimes, even that's not enough. Kyson wouldn't want you blaming yourself for his death."

Trey knew she was right, but he still felt like shit anyway. He replayed every conversation he'd had with his friend over the past few months, trying to understand why he didn't see this coming and berating himself because he hadn't.

He and Samantha talked for hours about Kyson, their friend-ship, and all the things he wished he could have done for his friend. She was amazing at letting him get it all out without letting him wallow in it. By the time midnight rolled around, Trey felt like he might be okay. Yeah, Kyson's death was going to hurt for a long time, but with Samantha's help, he knew he'd get through it.

"As much as I hate to leave, we both have to be up early tomor-row," he said, brushing her hair back as they sat cuddling on the couch.

She straightened up to look at him in concern. "Are you okay to drive home?"

He pressed a soft kiss to her lips. "Yeah. Thanks to you."

Trey slipped off to use the restroom before he headed home. He was gazing at a photo of Samantha and her sister, Loralei, standing in the snow somewhere in the Alaskan wilderness, a smile tugging at the corners of his mouth, when he noticed the door to the guest bedroom was slightly ajar. Trey found himself moving toward it without realizing what he was even doing, his inner wolf guiding him.

What he saw in the room knocked the air out of his lungs. The space wasn't a guest room at all, but a home office, with a desk and a series of filing cabinets. Three of the walls were covered floor to ceiling with photos of Trey, his pack mates, and dozens of crime scenes. He recognized many of the pictures from those situations when the Pack had come damn close to revealing itself. She even had pictures and articles from New Orleans and Los Angeles, including a blurry picture of a large wolf running down a dimly lit street in the rain. Lengths of different colored yarn connected the various crime scenes to different members of the Pack, with a scary number of them connecting back to him.

Two fast strides brought him over to the desk and the file

folder left open on top of it. It was filled with stuff about him, from his performance evaluations at work to his friends and family to medical history, even details from his time in the military. It was his whole damn life.

Worried Samantha would come looking for him, Trey quickly slipped out of the bedroom, careful to leave the door ajar like it was before, then headed out to the living room, all the while fighting to calm his breathing even as his insides churned like water in a washing machine.

He'd known Samantha was suspicious all along, so what he saw shouldn't have bothered him, but it did. She wasn't merely suspicious about him and his pack mates. She was frigging *stalking* them. Even as she stood and wrapped him in another hug, asking him again if he was going to be okay, all Trey could think about was that every word she'd spoken to him this evening had been nothing more than a ruse to get him to trust her. To get him to spill everything to her. And it had been working.

"Text me when you get home," she murmured, lifting up on her toes to kiss him. "I want to make sure you get there okay."

Trey nodded and kissed her back, telling her he'd definitely text even though his head was spinning so fast he was practically dizzy as he walked to his truck.

CHAPTER 11

"WHY DIDN'T YOU GUYS TELL ME YOU WERE OUT LOOKING FOR the killer tonight?" Trey asked as he slipped into the booth in the nearly empty bar where Connor, Trevor, and Hale were sitting. "I would have come with you."

Trey had been planning to drive over to Connor's place to talk to him after leaving Samantha's apartment, but when he'd texted to see if his friend was still awake, Connor had messaged him back, telling him to meet them at a bar.

"We didn't want to interrupt your date," Connor said, motioning toward one of the waitresses, then at Trey and the beers on the table. "What happened? You look like crap."

Sighing, Trey slipped into the booth beside Hale, ready to tell them about what he'd seen in Samantha's spare bedroom, but then he noticed the police sketch on the table in front of Trevor that completely distracted him. Reaching over, he grabbed it, realizing it must have been the woman who'd attacked him at the Main Street Garden Park. Well, at least what she looked like before turning into a big eyed, pasty-faced, soul sucker.

Earlier in the day, he and Connor had taken one of the department artists to the bar on Pacific Avenue, asking the bartender and the server to help work up a sketch of the woman they'd seen leaving with that guy last night. Unfortunately, Trey had been pulled away on a domestic violence call before the drawing was anything more than a couple of circles and a few lines on a pad. The picture he was looking at now was a finished product with enough detail to hopefully make her easy to identify. Even if she didn't look a thing like the creature who'd almost killed him. Attractive, in her midthirties, the woman in the picture was heavily made up with lots of eyeliner, bright red lipstick, and dark wavy hair that skimmed her shoulders.

But as good as the sketch might be, it was still only a two-dimensional drawing of a real person. He knew from experience how difficult it could be identifying a suspect from a sketch. It was hard enough with men, but with their makeup and hairstyles so easy to change, it was even harder to do with a woman.

"Have you found anyone who recognizes her?" Trey asked as the waitress brought over his beer.

He was glad his teammates had stayed together tonight. Trey didn't want to think about how dangerous it would be for one of them to confront that thing on their own again.

"Yeah, a couple people," Hale said. "Especially when we showed them the photos of Demario and Alden at the same time. But while they definitely know her face, nobody has a clue what her name is. And since she always lets the guys buy her drinks, we can't pull credit card receipts and get a name that way. Worse, it seems she has an almost preternatural ability to avoid surveillance cameras. We haven't caught a glimpse of her face on video yet."

"We're planning to hit a few more bars before we call it a night, but she's going to be hard to identity, even with this drawing," Trevor said. "She's a trained predator and people are her prey. She's not going to slip up and make herself easy to find."

Trey took a sip of his beer. "Speaking of prey, any word on that guy we rescued in the park last night? Has he woken up yet?"

"I talked to STAT a couple hours ago and as of then, the guy was still in a coma," Trevor said. "They're giving him fluids and trying to replace all the crap the creature sucked out of him, but they have no idea when—or if—he'll wake up."

Connor leaned forward to regard him thoughtfully. "Back to your date for a minute. Why are you here instead of rolling around in bed with a certain attractive medical examiner?"

Trey frowned, rubbing his thumb over the fancy label on the

beer bottle. When he didn't respond right away, his pack mates looked back and forth at each other like they were playing a silent game of rock paper scissors to see who would have to dig the issue out of him.

"What happened?" Trevor finally asked.

Trey opened his mouth to tell them what he'd found at Samantha's place, but at the last second, his tongue made a wide right turn and decided to go in a different direction. "You remember that buddy of mine I served in the army with, Kyson? Samantha and I went to visit him tonight and found out that he killed himself a couple weeks ago."

No one said anything, then they were all talking at once, asking why Kyson had committed suicide. Trey told them about the issues Kyson had been dealing with since being medically discharged from the army but had to admit he had no idea what had ultimately pushed his friend to take his own life.

"I'll probably never know why he did it," he finally said. "I'm just sorry that when it really mattered, he didn't reach out to me. After everything we went through together, he decided to go it alone."

"You doing okay?" Connor asked. "I know you guys were close."

Trey nodded. "I'm okay, thanks to Samantha. After I found out about Kyson, I kind of shut down and she was there for me. I don't know what I would have done without her."

"Dude, if that isn't proof that she's *The One* for you, I don't know what is," Connor said.

Trey felt the corner of his mouth edge up. "I'm not even going to try to fight you on that anymore. Samantha is definitely *The One*. That only makes it even harder to accept the fact that she's planning to betray us."

His pack mates exchanged looks, clearly confused.

"What do you mean?" Connor asked.

Trey blew out a breath. "I got a look in her guest bedroom, and it's one big stalker haven. Three walls were covered with pictures of the Pack, and she's got all these pieces of yarn connecting each pic to other shots of various crime scenes where we used our werewolf abilities. I don't know how, but she even has stuff from when we were in New Orleans and LA. Worse, she has a file on me with my whole life in it—military records, work evaluations, even medical stuff. And I'm willing to bet she has similar files on all of you guys, too."

"Damn," Trevor breathed. "How much do you think she's figured out? Does she know we're werewolves?"

Trey shook his head. "I don't think so. But considering what happened Saturday night, I'm guessing it's only a matter of time before she has proof."

"What happened Saturday night?" Hale murmured. "And why are we just hearing about it now?"

"We were in her kitchen making out when Samantha broke a coffee mug. She started to reach for the pieces and I instinctively put my hand out so she wouldn't get cut." Trey held up his right palm. "I sliced myself pretty good, too. Blood went everywhere."

"Shit," Connor groaned.

"Yeah, exactly," Trey muttered. "I didn't tell you because I didn't even think about it at first. I assumed it was an accident. But in light of all the stuff I found in her apartment, now I'm wondering if she orchestrated the whole event to get a blood sample."

That announcement was met with complete and total silence. Trey didn't blame them. This was huge.

"What do you think she's going to do with it?" Trevor asked. "I mean, what can she do with it? I'm not exactly up on the science of werewolf blood. Can she find something to prove you're a werewolf?"

Trey shrugged. "Samantha is a doctor and a medical examiner with access to a multimillion-dollar DNA lab. If anyone could rip my blood apart and pull out the werewolf bits, it would be her."

"What are you going to do?" Hale asked.

Trey would have laughed if there were a single thing about this effed-up situation that was funny. "I don't know. I mean, seriously, she could be in the process of outing the entire pack as we speak. So if any of you guys have a suggestion, I'm all ears."

He didn't honestly expect an answer, especially since they seemed as blindsided by the whole thing as he was, so he wasn't surprised when the first piece of advice was less than brilliant.

"I say we grab her," Trevor suggested. "You know, to protect the Pack."

Trey gave him a wry look. "And what do we do with her then? Keep her locked up in the arms room at the compound?"

Trevor winced. "Okay. Maybe that wasn't the best idea. But we have to do something."

"Agreed," Trey said firmly. "But not that."

"This might sound crazy, but maybe you should simply talk to her," Hale advised. "Put your cards on the table and see what she has to say."

"Put my cards on the table?" Trey snorted. "And what do you expect me to tell her, that yes, the entire Dallas SWAT team is a pack of werewolves, but that she shouldn't hold that against us because we're really nice people? Or maybe I should tell her she's my soul mate? Because I'm sure that would go over really well."

"Maybe it would," Connor said. "If Samantha is *The One* for you, then she's going to feel the connection, too. Do you think she'd honestly out the Pack once she knows the two of you are soul mates?"

Trey did a double take. "You're willing to risk the Pack's safety on the chance that Samantha would be willing to drop everything she's spent the last two years collecting simply because she's my soul mate? That's damn risky, don't you think?"

"Maybe," Connor replied. "But it's not like we have a lot of choices here. If you won't talk to her, the only other option would be for the whole Pack to go on the run."

A weight dropped into the pit of Trey's stomach and settled

there. The thought of the whole SWAT team and their mates leaving the homes they'd built in Dallas was gut-wrenching. But that was why their pack alpha and team commander had a plan in place to do exactly that if and when this very situation came up.

"Connor's right," Hale said. "Either you talk to Gage and prepare for the likelihood that we'll all have to leave the country. Or trust in the soul-mate connection and talk to Samantha."

———

Samantha was so preoccupied with thoughts of Trey that she didn't realize her electric toothbrush had turned off and she was standing in front of the bathroom mirror slowly pushing the bristles back and forth across her teeth like a robot. Considering how much foam was in her mouth, she could have been brushing for the last ten minutes for all she knew.

She spit, then rinsed, her mind still spinning with everything Trey had been through that evening. The anguish in his voice as he'd talked about Kyson, the agony in his eyes when he'd looked at the photo of the two of them together when they'd been younger, the desolation that had seemed to consume him as he'd talked about failing his friend. Seeing him like that had hurt her like nothing she'd ever experienced. She swore it was like she was grieving over a loss of her own.

When Trey told her that he was going to head home, the urge to stop him and make him stay there so she could take care of him was so overwhelming it was almost scary. To make matters worse, the worry she'd felt for him all night had actually gotten more magnified when he left. She was terrified he was sitting in his apartment right now, alone with his grief. The thought of Trey being in pain was enough to make her want to cry. The idea of going to bed and trying to sleep was ridiculous. There was no way she'd be able to do anything but stare at the ceiling all night.

When she heard the soft knock on her door a moment later, Samantha didn't even pause to think. She was certain Trey had come back. Pulse racing, she hurried to the door and jerked it open without looking through the peephole.

"Trey, thank God!"

Only it wasn't the big sexy cop she was very quickly falling for.

"No, sorry." Loralei looked at her in concern as she stepped inside. "Did you guys have a fight or something?"

Samantha closed the door and turned to follow her sister. "No. He just learned that a friend of his passed away and he took it pretty hard."

Loralei nodded and sat down on the couch. "Sorry to come over so late, but I got the initial DNA results on those blood samples you gave me and thought you might want to hear what I found. Even if none of it makes sense."

Samantha's heart beat a little faster. "What do you mean it doesn't make sense?"

Her sister frowned. "The blood you gave me matched two of the other profiles you provided—the ones labeled Airport Sample Six and Loft Sample Three—but that isn't the freaky part."

"Freaky?" Sam repeated softly, still trying to come to grips with the confirmation that Trey's DNA was on two of the bodies that coyotes had supposedly nibbled on. Airport Sample Six was from the throat wound of a body recovered from the scene where the SWAT team had gone toe-to-toe with a band of criminals working for an organized crime family. Loft Sample Three was from the throat of an Albanian criminal SWAT had tangled with a few months later. Cause of death in both cases had been rapid exsanguination—common when a person gets their throat ripped out. Of course, the final reports out of the ME's office had implied the initial wounds could have been from a gunshot with the majority of the damage coming postmortem courtesy of the apparently invisible coyotes. But while Samantha had never believed that part, nothing in her wildest dreams had made her think she'd find Trey's DNA in the wounds.

"Yeah, freaky," Loralei said. "What else would you call human and wolf DNA blended together? Are you sure the samples didn't get mixed together somehow?"

Samantha was sure she'd heard her sister wrong. "Definitely not. I watched the blood pour out of the guy's hand after he cut it open, so I know for a fact they weren't contaminated."

"Not contaminated," Loralei said. "Blended. As in there are pieces of wolf DNA attached perfectly to the human genetic material. It's not corrupted in any way, but it's—"

"Impossible," Samantha finished.

Her head was really spinning now. What her sister was describing didn't make sense. But then the little voice in her head reminded her that the other sample she'd sent to an outside lab had come back *contaminated* with wolf DNA as well.

Samantha took a deep breath. "I know you're really good at what you do, but is there any way you might have contaminated the sample?"

Her sister shook her ahead. "I thought the same thing when I first came up with the anomaly. So I started with a fresh sample and ran it again and got the same results. I thought maybe you'd been messing around with some gene-splicing techniques and were trying to see if I would catch it, but I'm guessing from the look on your face that isn't the case?"

Samantha sank down on the couch beside her sister. "I wish I could tell you that was the answer."

Loralei pulled up a knee, turning to face Samantha. "Well, as long as we're complicating the situation, I might as well tell you what else I discovered."

"There's more?" Samantha asked, not sure she wanted to know.

"Afraid so. I'm not sure how to explain it, but it looks like the wolf DNA I found is slightly…unusual, I guess is the best way to describe it. I have to run some other comparisons to be sure, but I think the material is prehistoric."

"Huh?" Samantha croaked, not even trying to come across as intelligent at this point. This whole thing was getting too strange for words.

"Yeah, my thoughts exactly." Her sister smiled. "And before you say it, yes, I know how crazy this sounds. But there's no other explanation for the fact that the genetic material is definitely in the Canis genus, with wolflike traits, and yet it doesn't quite match anything in our current database."

Samantha didn't say anything, too busy trying to figure out what all of it meant. How could Trey have prehistoric wolf DNA blended with his own? Even if it were possible, what did it mean?

"This feels like something out of a Marvel movie." Her sister leaned forward and grabbed one of Samantha's hands. "What the hell did you get yourself involved in?"

"I wish I could tell you, but I can't," she said softly. "At least not right now. I'm going to need you to trust me, okay?"

Loralei gazed at her for a long time before squeezing her hand again. "Okay, I won't push for now. But you will tell me at some point, right?"

Samantha nodded, and that seemed to be enough to satisfy her sister.

"There's more I can do with the blood if you want me to," Loralei said. "I have a contact in the paleontology department at Baylor who can get me DNA samples from extinct wolves for comparison with no questions asked. I can also isolate exactly which parts of the human genes have been affected by the wolf DNA."

Samantha thought a moment. "How hard will it be to hide what you're doing?"

She didn't want her sister getting in too deep. Getting fired might be the least of Loralei's problems if someone found out.

Loralei shrugged. "I won't lie, I'll have to come up with some pretty fancy BS to cover up why I'm doing this. Maybe you could help me come up with a false request from DPD animal control? Make it look like the city is looking for details on an animal attack or something. I need to have something to justify the time and money I'll have to put into this. This testing is expensive."

Samantha nodded, promising to send over some ME paper-work that would probably pass a cursory inspection. "Be careful, okay? Absolutely no one can know what's really going on here, especially not anyone in the DPD."

Loralei assured her that she would, then headed home a little while later, leaving Samantha sitting on the couch wracked with guilt over the fact that she was betraying Trey more and more the further she took this. But she couldn't stop now, especially after learning there was wolf DNA mixed with his. There was some-thing strange going on, and no matter what her heart might be feeling when it came to Trey, she needed to know what it was.

The conversation she'd had with Crystal that morning came back to her. The one where her friend suggested coming out and just asking Trey what was going on. But how could she ask him about something so bizarre?

CHAPTER 12

TREY PULLED HIS JEEP INTO A PARKING SPACE AT THE institute but didn't turn off the engine right away. Instead, he sat there with the AC on, wondering if coming here had been a good idea. Connor *had* suggested it, so probably not.

Trey and Connor had spent a good portion of the morning cleaning weapons at the SWAT compound and talking about his conundrum with Samantha. Connor kept pushing the *trust your instincts* and *believe in your soul mate* angles, while that little voice in the back of Trey's mind continued to warn him that Samantha was likely playing him for a sucker.

But Samantha *was* his soul mate, even if she didn't know it, which meant he needed to come up with a way to talk to her. While that might sound easy, it was going to be the toughest thing he'd ever done. If he messed this up—or waited too long—there was a good chance she might expose all the pack's secrets.

He'd been stuck in an endless loop of second-guessing himself when Trevor had come into the armory and told them that the Butcher had struck again. Taking that as a sign he needed to go talk to Samantha, he had headed to the institute, hoping to come up with what to say to her on the drive over. Twenty minutes later and here he was, sitting in his pickup outside her office still wondering what the hell he was supposed to do.

Cursing under his breath, Trey hopped out of his truck and headed for the entrance. He was so busy thinking about how to broach the subject of soul mates with Samantha that he almost missed the sound of raised voices coming from her office. Trey recognized Hugh's voice at the same time he picked up the man's scent and that of the other ME he'd met before, Nadia. It was obvious from his tone of voice that Hugh was angry.

"If Louis had given me this damn case, the Butcher would have already been caught and people would be commending this institute for its performance instead of laughing at it. You weren't ready for a case this big, Samantha, and you never will be. If you were better at your job, you could have pegged that scene this morning as a copycat faster and saved everyone a lot of time and energy."

Hearing someone bad-mouth Samantha filled Trey with a rage he couldn't remember ever experiencing. It hit him so hard he felt his claws extend, could taste his own blood on his tongue as his fangs tore through his gums. Knowing there was no way he could show up in Samantha's office like this, he stopped a few feet from her door, fighting to get his inner wolf back under control. He'd had full control over his werewolf side for years, so this shouldn't even be happening, but the mere thought of his soul mate in danger was enough to unleash the beast in him.

"Hugh, you're an idiot. If Louis put you on the Butcher case, you would have been fired already," Nadia said sharply. "Being a good brown-noser doesn't make you a good medical examiner."

Trey was surprised Nadia had come to Samantha's defense. Finally getting his claws and fangs back where they belonged, he walked into Samantha's office. She was standing in front of her desk, arms crossed and a perturbed look on her face. Catching sight of Trey in the doorway, she smiled, relief in her eyes.

Hugh turned to look his way, heart suddenly beating nervously at the expression on Trey's face. Maybe the ME had picked up on the fact that Trey would like to rip Hugh's face off right now.

Mouth tight, Hugh threw a glare at Samantha, then stormed out.

"Don't let him get to you," Nadia said, reaching out to rest her hand gently on Samantha's arm, giving it a gentle squeeze. "He's a jealous asshole who knows you're better at your job than he is every day of the week. If you need help on the Butcher case, let me know. I'm more than willing to slip in and do a little work off the books. Unlike Hugh, I can live without the recognition. I just want this bastard caught."

Nadia gave Trey a smile as she left, saying it was nice to see him again. The woman's expression seemed legit, but he couldn't be sure. When he gave Samantha a questioning look, she shrugged.

"Hugh was being his usual self, trying to shoehorn himself onto the Butcher task force again, and I guess Nadia decided to take the honey instead of vinegar route to get on my good side. While I appreciate what she said to Hugh, I'm still not sure I trust her motives."

Trey was about to agree with that assessment, but before he could say anything, Samantha stepped forward, her arms coming up to loop around his neck as she pressed her body to his, her face buried against his chest. He heard her breathing deeply as she squeezed him tight, and he found himself wondering what she thought of his scent.

"How are you doing?" she asked. "I've been worrying about you ever since you left last night."

He wrapped his arms around her waist, holding her close and burying his face in her silky hair, breathing in the scent of cherry blossoms and spring rain. It brought a sense of calm he hadn't even known he was lacking.

"I'm okay," he said, "Better than I probably have any right to be, honestly. I have you to thank for that. You kept me sane last night and I'll never be able to thank you enough."

"You don't have to thank me at all." She smiled up at him in a way that lit up his whole world. "You here to get the latest on the Butcher?"

He grinned. "Actually, I really just wanted to see you. But the rumors that you'd been called out on another body dump gave me a good excuse to come over here. Did I hear Hugh say something about it being a copycat?"

Samantha sighed as she walked around her desk and sat down. Trey followed suit, dropping into the chair in front of her desk, feeling inexplicably cold without her arms around him. It occurred to him then that she looked more tired than she had when he walked in, and he chided himself for keeping her up so late last night.

"I got a call early this morning about body parts scattered around a section of the Hinton Regional Landfill off Elm Grove Road," she said. "It didn't take long for me to figure out they all belonged to the same victim, and since the hands still had fingers, the detectives on the task force ID'd the woman and connected her to a guy who got released from Coffield Unit less than a month ago. They picked him up immediately, sure they had the Butcher."

Trey didn't have to ask to know where this was going. The Butcher task force was under pressure to find a suspect, so he didn't blame them for jumping on the first one that offered themselves up on a silver platter. "I'm guessing you had to burst their bubble?"

"Yeah." She sat back and lazily swiveled her chair back and forth. "I took my time because I didn't want to get this wrong, but in the end, it was obvious whoever killed that woman wasn't our guy…either of our guys. Not only was the gender of the victim wrong, but so were the cut marks and defensive wounds. The detectives on the task force aren't happy with me, but at least they were able to catch the guy who really killed her."

"Was he trying to look like a copycat to throw them of his trail?" Trey asked.

"Not in a premeditated way, if that's what you mean. He got into a drunken argument with his girlfriend and accidentally killed her, then decided to cut her up and dump the pieces at a landfill barely a mile away from where they lived. He was still trying to clean up all the blood in his garage when they kicked in the door."

Trey winced at that image. "Well, like you said, at least they caught him."

"Unfortunately, the case this morning only highlights the way the cops on the task force expect the Butcher case to go. Find a lead, follow it to a bad guy, arrest the bad guy. The fact that the clues I'm finding are only making this case more and more confusing isn't helping anything."

Trey hated seeing Samantha down on herself like this. She was frigging amazing. Didn't she see that?

"Did you find anything new?" he asked.

She stopped swiveling in her chair and flipped open one of the folders on her desk. Turning it around so it was facing him, she spread out several photos displaying extreme close-up views of bones, muscles, and ligaments. Seeing all of it in such detail was the definition of unsettling, even if he had far more experience with the subject than he wanted to think about.

"What am I looking at?" he asked.

"These are magnified views of two of the pieces we recovered the other day," she explained. "This one is the hand and lower arm. This one is the forearm section from wrist to elbow." She tapped one photo, then the other. "I found evidence that the parts had been amputated and then reattached. There are pin, bracket, and screw holes along several areas on the bones. There are also suture marks along the ends of the muscles, ligaments, and tendons. If that's not strange enough, I also found evidence of new growth and advanced healing in both the tissues *and* the bone. This might be a leap, but I think the parts had been reattached and were starting to heal for some period of time until something went wrong and had to be removed. The healing's less advanced in some areas, more advanced in others, making me think the killer may have chopped off some parts multiple times and started over."

Trey frowned, not sure what all of that meant. Then it hit him. "Wait a minute. There's something off here. These bodies have been showing up for about two weeks, which means this killer has been doing his thing for three weeks at the most. Even if these parts you found were attached at the very start of that time frame, they still wouldn't have shown that healing. I don't know much about this kind of thing, but doesn't it take a lot longer than that for bones to regrow?"

Samantha nodded. "Normally, I'd agree with you, but I found some unknown chemical substances in the tissue of the two parts in question. It's too soon to know for sure—and I haven't mentioned it to anyone yet—but it's my theory that the killer has come up with a medical protocol that speeds up the regrowth process drastically."

Trey ignored the fact that Samantha had described a *medical protocol* that didn't—couldn't—exist and focused on the implications. "So what you're saying is that the serial killer is grabbing random people off the street, cutting parts off of them, and attaching those parts to someone else using a drug that no one has ever heard of, only to start the process over when the parts start to rot?"

She gave him a shrug. "Like I said, I haven't mentioned my theory to anyone yet, but yes, that's where we seem to be right now. You can see why the cops on the task force are starting to grumble. Hugh was here because he overheard the task force lead ask Louis about assigning another ME to the team."

Shit.

There was no way in hell he could bring up the subject of soul mates now, not after the absolutely crappy day Samantha was having. She needed to be clearheaded for a conversation like that.

"That sucks," he said. "What are you going to do?"

"Louis wants me to go over every single body we've recovered as part of the Butcher case and see if I can find any more evidence of reattachment, bone, or tissue regrowth. He also asked me to prepare tissue samples so our analysis lab can start trying to identify what chemical the killer has been using during these surgeries. I'll be lucky to get out of here before the sun sets."

"I'd better let you get started then." He got to his feet. "If you're not too tired afterward, do you want to get together for dinner tonight?"

Samantha stood and came back around the desk and kissed him. Despite everything going on with the investigation—not to mention the secrets they were both hiding from each other—Trey found himself kissing her back with a passion that was definitely not safe for work.

He wasn't sure who pulled away first, since both of them groaned in disappointment. He chuckled when he saw Samantha blush. Another minute and they'd have been making out on her desk. Trey got the feeling she would have been just fine with that.

"Why don't you come over to my place?" she suggested softly.

Trey grinned. "Sounds good to me."

It would definitely be easier to have the conversation about soul mates in her apartment than at a restaurant, that was for sure. And by then, maybe he'd actually figure out what to say.

CHAPTER 13

Eyes closed and body completely relaxed, Samantha let the shower gently sluice the foamy body wash off her skin. She knew she should hurry up so she'd be ready before Trey arrived with the takeout he'd said he was picking up, but she was more tired than usual after the day she'd had. Besides, the water felt *so* damn good.

After hours spent examining amputated body parts and a second run-in with Hugh and Nadia, Sam had been pulled into yet another task force meeting. The lead detective had once again insisted on slogging through every piece of evidence they'd collected in the Butcher case. But other than the fact that there were now two suspects and a pretty good idea of what kind of vehicle they were using, they'd discussed very little of interest. Nobody on the task force had a clue how to deal with Samantha's theory that the killer was attempting to reattach the parts he'd cut off, so they all ignored it. The only worthwhile outcome of the meeting was a task force decision to put surveillance teams on every landfill in the county and a good number of the parks in the hopes of catching the killers if they tried to dump another body. The city was going to freak out over the cost, but there was very little else they could do.

Just when Samantha thought she might get out of the institute at a half-decent time, Louis had pulled her into an office staff call, where the assistant MEs were expected to lay out the cases they'd been working on over the past few weeks. This was something they did once a month, under the theory that the MEs could learn from each other's efforts, but mostly it was simply a chance for Hugh and Nadia to try to one up each other when it came to clearing cases. After the day Samantha'd had, looking at endless photos of suicides, overdoses, and murder victims was hard to deal with.

To pound the final nail in the coffin of exhaustion, the staff meeting had been followed by a private one with Louis, where he'd asked her to rehash everything the task force had talked about earlier. Samantha appreciated her boss's willingness to help her find things she might have missed, but by that point she'd been done for the day.

When falling asleep standing up under the spray of water started to become a real concern, Samantha finally forced herself to step out of the shower, toweling her hair dry and finger comb-ing it to save time. Fortunately, her hair was straight enough that she could get away with that because she definitely didn't feel like getting out the iron and spending the next fifteen minutes in front of the mirror.

Padding over to the walk-in closet off her bedroom, Samantha slipped into one of her fancier bras and panties before turning her attention to what she was going to wear for her date with Trey. She gave the issue about five seconds of thought before grabbing a pair of sleep shorts and an Alaskan tourism T-shirt she'd picked up the last time she was in Homer. Tonight was about being relaxed and hanging out. A pair of shorts and a soft tee were the definition of relaxed and casual as far as she was concerned.

Still barefoot, Samantha moved around the apartment, clean-ing up a little and forcing herself to think about anything other than body parts, task force politics, and coworkers. Of course, the first thing that popped into her head was Trey and what the hell she was going to do about everything her sister had told her. She'd had no choice but to push those issues aside while at the office because there was no way she could do her job and think about the impossibilities the DNA had revealed at the same time. But now that Trey was on his way over, it was hard to think about anything else.

The man she was falling for like a ton of bricks had wolf DNA blended in with his human genetic material. And not just any wolf—an extinct, prehistoric wolf. Because if you're gonna go wolf, go hard.

How the hell was she supposed to handle this? Seriously, there was no way to act like this wasn't a big deal. Even if she could somehow overlook the whole wolf-DNA thing and convince herself it was as inconsequential as being born with a cleft chin or dimples, there was still the fact that Trey's DNA had been found in the wounds of two men who'd had their throats ripped out.

It wasn't like those traces of DNA could be explained away with a hangnail or a paper cut. No, his DNA had ended up on those men because he was the one who'd done the damage with something sharp and savage enough to cause those kinds of wounds. And when you put *wolf*, *sharp*, and *savage* together in a single sentence, it was surprisingly easy to come up with a very disturbing visual of Trey with really big fangs.

That entire train of thought should have had her laughing her butt off, but she wasn't laughing at all. She'd known for a while that the SWAT team was hiding some kind of enormously big secret. Could this be it?

If Samantha had two functioning brain cells in her head, she would have dumped all of this on Louis's desk right this very minute and let someone above her pay grade deal with it. But the mere thought of doing something like that twisted her stomach so violently, she thought she might pass out. Betraying Trey like that felt beyond wrong. But what else was she supposed to do?

Maybe she should simply talk to him.

As logical as that idea sounded, Samantha wasn't sure if she could do it. There were so many different ways that conversation could go wrong.

Samantha was still lost in thought when the doorbell rang fifteen minutes later. Putting on her game face, she headed that way, her heart starting to beat faster. It was funny how merely thinking about Trey being close to her could do that. Nothing compared to what it was like when he kissed her, of course. Today at the institute, she'd been damn close to jumping him right there in her office.

"Hope you like Indian food," Trey said, holding up two over-sized takeout bags in his hand. "There was a place on the way I've been wanting to try out, but if you aren't a fan, we can call for something else."

Samantha held the door open wider, noting the way his gaze caressed her legs as he walked in. She had no doubt it was a trick of the lights, but damn, it seemed like his eyes lit up from within when he saw all that skin. Yup, definitely a leg man.

"I *love* Indian food," she said, taking in the jeans that showed off those muscular thighs and the T-shirt stretched tight across his broad chest. She patted herself on the back for her decision to go casual. It had been the right call. "I haven't had any in forever, but I definitely love it."

"Good." He motioned toward the kitchen with the bags. "Want me to set everything out on the table?"

"Let's hang out on the couch instead." She smiled. "Just between you and me, that's where I eat most of the time anyway."

Trey chucked, admitting he did the same thing, and Samantha felt something loosen in her chest. Yes, there was a truckload of baggage to deal with when it came to being with him, but when he smiled at her like that, none of it seemed that important. What was a little wolf DNA if it came with dimples like that?

While Trey unpacked the bags of takeout, Samantha grabbed a bottle of beer for him and poured herself a glass of wine. By the time she walked back into the living room, her big, hunky cop had all the cardboard boxes out of the bags and spread around the coffee table. As she'd expected, there was way more food than necessary. That made her smile.

"I wasn't sure what you liked to eat, so I got a little bit of everything," he said.

Trey's idea of a little bit of everything included four different entrées—chicken tikka masala, pork vindaloo, lamb rogan josh, and a vegetarian saag paneer—plus a family-size box of naan bread.

"I'm pretty sure your definition of a *little bit* is somewhat different than mine," she said with a laugh. "There's enough food here for five or six people with leftovers."

She thought it possible that Trey actually blushed a little at that, and Samantha wondered if he could hear the thud when her heart hit the floor all over again. A guy as big and tough as Trey getting embarrassed over buying too much takeout? Could there be a better man on the planet? That prehistoric wolf DNA was looking less and less important by the minute.

They sat there together on the couch, her bare feet tucked under her as they passed the takeout containers back and forth, oohing and aahing over the food as they talked about their respective days. Samantha definitely liked the masala, but the vindaloo, while delicious, was way too spicy for her taste. The soul-warming rogan josh was so tender it fell apart on her fork, so she used the naan flatbread to scoop it up. Since she didn't want to eat too much, she only ate the cheese out of the saag paneer, figuring she'd be nice and leave the spinach for Trey. That was her story and she was sticking to it.

He didn't complain, letting her have first pick of everything. But even with ridiculous amount of food Trey inhaled, Samantha knew she was going to have leftovers for days. Then again, maybe she'd invite him over tomorrow night to eat the rest. The idea of that made her damn near giddy. And she definitely wasn't normally the giddy type.

In addition to talking about work, they also talked about family, friends, and things they enjoyed doing. When Trey asked her about the property her grandparents had left her up in Homer,

Samantha ended up spending the next hour describing everything about the place.

"Being up there must make you feel close to your grandparents," he said softly.

With those few words, she realized Trey got her better than the entire rest of her family. Most of them assumed the property was nothing more than a long-term investment. Samantha almost started tearing up when she told him about the old chair in the living room she would spend hours sitting in every time she went up there. It was a silly thing to talk about, but with Trey, it didn't seem to matter. It was easy to talk about anything with him.

Then why was it so difficult to bring up the topic of his wolf DNA?

They ate in comfortable silence for a little while before Trey got a pensive look on his face. Suddenly worried she'd gotten too mushy too fast, Samantha quickly stood and began to collect the scattered food containers.

"Sit and finish your beer," she said when Trey started to stand to help. "It'll only take me a second to get this stuff put away in the fridge."

He ignored her of course, grabbing the rest of the takeout boxes and following her into the kitchen, chuckling as Sam stood on her tiptoes to try to reach into the back of one of her upper cabinets for the plastic containers.

"Good thing I came in here to help," Trey said, moving closer to reach over her head, his warm, firm body pressing against hers in the most delicious way. "How would you have ever gotten these out?"

"I'm sure I would have figured it out," Samantha murmured, nudging her butt back playfully against his crotch, smiling to herself when she felt the bulge in his jeans. "How hard could it be?"

Trey snorted as he took down a few of the plastic containers and spread them out on the counter. "Seems pretty hard from where I'm standing. But I'm sure you already knew that."

Samantha bit her lip to keep from laughing, enjoying how easy it was for them to flirt with each other. As they stood side by side putting away the leftovers, their arms and hips touching occasionally, she could almost forget all the secrets they were keeping from each other.

"You up for dessert?" She turned to face him after finding a place in her crowded fridge for the containers. "I always keep some cookies around in case of emergency."

Grinning, Trey reached out to snag the waist of her shorts and tug her closer. "If we're talking about dessert, I can think of something I'd like even more than cookies."

Samantha opened her mouth to tell him that had to be the cheesiest line she'd ever heard, but then Trey was pulling her into his arms and kissing her, and suddenly she had a difficult time thinking about anything other than his lips on hers.

One moment, Trey's big hands were resting casually on her hips, his fingers sliding under her T-shirt to tease the sensitive skin above the top of her shorts; the next second, he was picking her up and setting her butt down on the counter. She automatically spread her knees to make room for him to slip between them, then wrapped her legs around his waist like it was the most natural thing in the world.

He slid one hand into her hair, tugging just the way she liked, while his other slipped down to her bare thigh, fingers tracing up and down her skin, electric tingles chasing his touch.

"Maybe we should do this somewhere else?" he murmured against her mouth. "The last time we tried to make out in here, you attacked me with a coffee mug."

Samantha laughed, refusing to think about the fact that she couldn't even see the scar on his hand now. "I promise to stay away from coffee mugs from now on, but if you want to take this somewhere else, like my bedroom, let's say, I'm not going to complain."

Trey pulled back and stared down into her eyes, his gaze

intense. "I wasn't implying we have to rush anything if you aren't ready for that."

Samantha caught her breath, pretty sure her heart had never beaten this hard in her life. "And if I am ready?"

Gaze never leaving hers, Trey slipped his hands under her butt, picking her up easily. She instinctively locked her ankles together behind his back, wrapping her arms tightly around his broad shoulders and holding on like a koala bear even though she knew in her heart that he'd never let her fall.

Samantha expected Trey to make a beeline straight down the hallway to her bedroom, but it turned out he was in no hurry, slowing when he was halfway across the living room to gently set her butt on the back of the couch. She kept her legs wrapped around him as he kissed her again, his tongue teasing hers, the taste of him enough to nearly drive her crazy. When she felt his jean-covered hard-on pressing against the sensitive area between her thighs, her hips started rolling as if they had a mind of their own.

She slid her hands under Trey's T-shirt, letting her fingers trace their way up his muscular abs as she pushed the soft material up his chest. She did her very best not to gasp out loud, but as he moved back so she could get the garment over his head, she found herself hypnotized by the tattoo of a wolf head on the left side of his chest.

She'd seen it before, when he flashed it briefly at the restaurant on their first date, but now it took on a whole new meaning. She was surprised he'd so blatantly put his wolf secret out there for the whole world to see. Then again, maybe it was his way of dealing with something so overwhelming—tattooing the truth of it right on his chest was the only possible way for him to deal with it.

Reaching out, she glided her fingertips across his heavily muscled chest, up from the deep divide between his pecs, slowly tracing the outline of the wolf. The work was exquisite, the exposed fangs making the creature appear both savage and protective at the same time. She could easily spend hours staring at the tattoo, memorizing every single line and curve of it.

"Do you like tattoos?" he asked softly, the deep rumble of his voice seeming to vibrate up from deep in his chest. The lights from the lamp beside the couch reflected off his eyes in that crazy way it seemed to do with him, making his irises almost glow with a yellow-gold glimmer. It had to be the most amazing, arousing thing she'd ever seen.

"I like *this* tattoo."

She scraped her nails down the figure like she was running her fingers through the creature's fur. The wolf gazed at her, the intensity in those eyes making it seem like the animal could see into her soul, and she caught her breath. She couldn't wait any longer. She had to tell Trey the truth. Right now.

She lifted her head to look at him. "I have to tell you something."

"Later," he said, the words almost sounding like a growl as he said them. "Much later."

Trey moved so fast Samantha barely had time to do more than yelp before he was slipping one arm under her knees and the other behind her back, scooping her off the couch and heading for the bedroom. She'd never realized she was the type of woman interested in being swept off her feet, but she had to admit, when Trey was the one doing it, she could get used to it.

She hit the light switch on the wall as they stepped through the door and into her bedroom, laughing as he tossed her casually on the bed, kicking off his shoes before reaching forward to grab the hem of her T-shirt, pulling it slowly over her head, leaving her lying there in her shorts and bra. The way Trey's eyes roamed over her partially nude body at that moment felt like a caress.

"Well?" she prompted softly as he continued to gaze down at her like she was something he desperately wanted to devour. "Were you planning on joining me?"

A smile tugged up the corners of his sensuous lips as he took a slow step forward. "Maybe I want to stand here and worship you with my eyes until I memorize every line and curve of that perfect body of yours."

She couldn't help returning his smile, if for no other reason than because it helped hide the blush she felt rushing to her cheeks. "Wow. I need to keep you around all the time. You're seriously great for my ego."

"I agree," he murmured in that rumbling growl that went right through her as he reached down to unbuckle his belt and pop the buttons of his jeans. "You should keep me around all the time. But I think I can help with more than your ego."

She opened her mouth to say something witty in response, but as Trey shoved down his jeans and briefs at the same time, revealing the rest of his positively stunning body, she found herself suddenly unable to speak. Because now that she was able to see everything, it was impossible to dismiss the reality that he was beyond perfection.

She'd been mesmerized by his muscular upper body, and the arms, chest, and shoulders that made her wonder precisely how many hours a day he worked out. But now she realized that his legs were equally as powerful as the rest of him. And the hard erection nestled between them was long, thick, and already pulsing with need.

Taken altogether, it was nearly enough to make a grown woman weep. And perhaps question what the hell she'd done to attract the attention of such a man. Hell, at this moment, all her worries about Trey's wolf DNA and the weird crap he'd been involved in seemed kind of irrelevant. The only thing that was important was right here in front of her.

Completely naked.

Samantha was off the bed and on her knees before she even thought about what she going to do. Then again, what she had in mind didn't required much thought. All it took was reaching out a hand to wrap around that hard shaft and a quick dip of her head, and she had her mouth right where she wanted it to be.

Trey tasted exactly the way she imagined he would—musky and masculine—and the flavor drew a moan from deep inside her as her tongue flicked around the head of his cock. Based on the groan of pleasure he let out, he obviously liked what she was doing.

It was so easy to fall into a rhythm as she knelt there in front of him, one hand caressing up and down while her mouth moved in counterpoint, swirling and licking, then swallowing deeply every once in a while just to keep him guessing. Feeling him throb in her hand, hearing those growly sounds he made every time she took him to the back of her throat, the way his essence became more and more intoxicating with every swipe of her tongue, Samantha decided she might have found heaven.

There hadn't been a plan when she'd dropped to her knees in front of him, but the general idea had been that she would get him excited, then hop on top for the next part of this evening's entertainment. But now that she was in the moment, the thought of stopping seemed like the most insane idea in the world. She wanted to finish him—needed to do it—simply so she could hear him growl her name and taste him when he exploded in her mouth.

With that sexy image motivating her, Samantha began to work her hand and mouth faster, eager now that she'd made her decision. But just when she felt his cock start to pulse in a clear sign of an impending orgasm, Trey reached down and pulled her to her feet, his mouth coming down to kiss the breath out of her when she started to complain.

"I'm not saying I wasn't enjoying that," he murmured as he broke the kiss and nudged her back toward the bed. "But in the interest of making sure this evening lasts, I think it's time for me to return the favor."

Samantha supposed she could have put up a fuss, tried to convince him that she wanted to get back to pleasing him. But seriously, Trey had just volunteered to go down on her. What woman on the planet would complain about that? And the part about making sure this evening lasts? That was definitely a yes vote on her part as well.

Trey stopped her as the back of her legs hit the edge of the mattress, slipping a hand around her back to hold her up while undoing her bra at the same time. She let the lacy material slide from her shoulders, shivering as it fell away and his big, warm hands came up to cup her breasts. Her shivers turned to gasps when he started gently squeezing her nipples between his fingertips, the pressure sending little sparks of pleasure straight to her core. Trey leaned down to trail hot kisses along her jawline and down her neck, drawing little moans of pleasure from her throat. But when those warm kisses turned to bites and sharp teeth sliding across hypersensitive skin, she thought her knees might give out.

She was shoving her shorts and panties over her hips and to the floor even as she scrambled back onto the bed, Trey chasing after her to run his warm lips and tongue slowly down her naked body. He took his time, licking and nibbling his way around the curve of her breasts and her nipples before heading lower, settling between her legs.

"I never knew I liked the nibbling thing," she breathed as he gently worked his way down her stomach and around her belly button, alternating between little kisses and gentle bites that had her body writhing all over the place. "But I think I'm addicted."

He stopped his teasing, glancing up at her with a heat in his gaze that absolutely consumed her. Like she was the only thing in the world that existed for him. Having him look at her that way was intoxicating.

"There are worse things in the world to be addicted to," he murmured, his lips pulling back in a sexy smile before he dipped his head back down, heading farther south. And right before that brilliant grin was fully hidden from view, Samantha was sure she caught site of something that shouldn't have been there.

Fangs.

She instinctively tensed, but before she could even question what she might have seen, Trey's talented tongue was on her clit and all rational thought became impossible. It didn't matter what she might have seen. All that mattered was the way he made her feel.

Samantha had been aroused since Trey walked in the door. When they'd moved from the living room to the kitchen to clean up—and make out—the low embers of heat that had been kindled low in her belly had roared to blazing life. By the time they'd made it to the bedroom, she'd been burning up. So when she felt those familiar tingles building up within seconds of his mouth on her, she wasn't surprised. The truth was, this moment was the culmination of about two years of foreplay, and she was ready to explode.

Her first orgasm hit her when Trey closed his mouth over her clit and began to lightly suck. Her back arched and her thighs clamped down tightly on his strong shoulders, pleasure rolling through her in waves that made her eyes blur. It was as she was coming down from that plateau, tremors still rippling through her body, that he slipped two big fingers inside her and began to firmly caress that secret spot that turned her insides to mush. Then she came unglued.

Samantha cried out as she climaxed that time, her body convulsing as it tore through her with a savage intensity she felt all the way down to her toes. Where the first orgasm had been a vision of white static behind her eyelids, this one was all darkness as she teetered on the edge of passing out.

By the time the last wave and tremor faded away, Samantha was so wrung out that all she could do was lay there on the bed gasping for air. That had been beyond amazing.

She came back to herself when she felt a familiar nibbling, this time to the inside of her right thigh. It was difficult to believe, but the feel of those sharp teeth on her flesh had her warming up all over again. After two big orgasms, she'd thought she might be done for the night.

Apparently not.

Trey was still between her legs when Samantha finally opened her eyes. She lifted her head to look at him. That smoldering smile was back on his lips, revealing enough of his teeth to confirm there were no fangs to be seen, leaving her to wonder if it had merely been some kind of hallucination.

"You okay?" he whispered, looking half-amused, half-concerned. "Thought I lost you for a little bit there."

"I think maybe you did." Laughing, she rolled over to the edge of the bed and the nightstand on that side. A few seconds of digging around in the top drawer and she came out with a handful of foil-wrapped condoms. "That doesn't mean we're done yet, though. In fact, I tend to remember you saying something about making this evening last."

Eyes glinting, Trey took one of the foil packets from her and quickly tore it open. She pushed herself up and moved across the bed until she was in front of him. Reaching out, she helped roll the condom down his shaft, which was as rock hard as it had been while she was licking him. She couldn't stop herself from giving it a few light caresses, loving the way his stomach muscles flexed and jumped at her touch.

"Do you want me like this?" she whispered playfully as she rolled over on her hands and knees, looking over her shoulder at him. "Or on my back?"

The question earned her another one of those sexy growls and firm hands on her hips dragging her closer to the edge of the bed. She laughed. Something told her Trey would be into doing it doggy style, though she refused to allow herself to think about why that might be.

The anticipation as she knelt in front of him, waiting for him to touch her, was unworldly. Fortunately, Trey didn't make her wait for long, one hand coming down to hold her hips steady as the other one positioned the head of his cock at her very wet opening.

She was more than ready for him—man, was she ready—but the feel as he slid in all the way was enough to drag a moan from deep in her throat. Trey ran the fingertips of his free hand down her back before settling on her other hip. She took a deep breath as his grip tightened, spreading her arms a little wider to steady herself for that first thrust.

They were slow and shallow at first, but within seconds, he was moving faster, her entire body bouncing from the force of his thrusts. The sound of his hips smacking her butt was deliciously delightful and she cried out a little louder each time. It was so exquisite, she actually started to see stars. Resting her face on the bed, she reached one hand between her legs to softly rub her clit.

When Trey slid out a half second later, Samantha rolled over without any prompting, scooting back a little on the bed and spreading her legs for him, then wrapping them around him, pulling him in even deeper. She didn't know how it was possible, but he felt even better in this position. Draping her hands around his neck, she gazed into his eyes to see them glowing with that inner light she'd seen so many times. She tried to make sense of it but couldn't understand where the reflected glow was coming from. Then Trey was burying his face in her neck, chanting her name as he kissed and nibble the skin there, pounding into her hard once again.

The angle was perfect, the head of his cock nudging that spot that no other man had ever been this successful at finding. She clawed her nails up and down his back, squeezing her legs around his waist so tightly it was a wonder he could move, but neither seemed to bother him in the least. He had stamina she'd never experienced before, and all she could think about was whether the thing that made him so different was to thank for that.

"Don't stop," she demanded when the tingling sensation grew into a lightning storm inside her body. "Please don't ever stop!"

He growled, his teeth lightly clamping onto the skin at the junction of her neck and shoulder, and she swore those teeth were sharper than any teeth had the right to be. But then the pleasure/pain pushed her over the edge, and she was coming so hard she didn't care if he bit her.

Samantha screamed his name so loudly she had no doubt Crystal could hear it across the hall and would be bringing up the subject tomorrow. But right then, she didn't care. And yeah, this time, she might have passed out...just a little.

Trey slipped into the master bathroom to clean up and was back in bed with her by the time she pulled herself back. Dragging the blue paisley comforter over them, he lay on his side, head propped up on the palm of his hand while his other hand casually traced circles through the moisture still glossing the skin of her stomach.

Samantha gazed at his mouth, then his eyes, looking for a glimpse of fangs or glowing eyes, but there was nothing unusual to see now. She absently lifted her hand to run her fingers over the skin where her neck and shoulder met. The area was a little tender and slightly raised up...like a welt. She glanced at Trey out the corner of her eye to see that, while he didn't exactly appear to be panicking, there was definitely something in his eyes. Guilt, maybe?

If anyone should feel guilty here, it was her. She took a deep breath. It was time to come out and put her cards on the table, then give him a chance to do the same.

Samantha opened her mouth to start, but Trey started talking first. He stopped when he realized he was interrupting, and they ended up stopping and starting twice before he held up his hand.

"You first," he murmured with a soft chuckle.

She laughed nervously as she gathered her courage, trying desperately to think of what she could say that wouldn't make her sound like the worse stalker on the planet.

Then Trey's phone rang.

Samantha seriously didn't think he would answer it, especially since she was about to say something so important, but before she knew it, his perfect, naked ass was leaping out of bed and digging through the jeans on the floor to come out with his cell phone.

"Conner, this had better be important," he muttered the moment he thumbed the green button on the screen. "I was in the middle of something."

Whatever Connor said must have been serious because Trey's whole body stiffened.

"That's not even five minutes from here," he said, reaching for boxer briefs. "I'll meet you there."

Trey dropped his phone on the bed, then hurriedly pulled on his underwear and jeans before snatching up his shirt. "Someone thinks they saw the Butcher carrying a body through the woods not far from here. Connor and the other guys are on the way, but I'm closer and can get there first. I have to go. I'm sorry."

Before Samantha could say anything one way or the other, Trey kissed her hard on the lips, then turned and ran for the door, leaving her to figure out what the hell she was supposed to do now.

CHAPTER 14

"I WANT YOUR WORD THAT YOU WON'T EVEN THINK ABOUT getting out of this truck," Trey said as he pulled off Mountain Creek Parkway onto the narrow road leading deeper into the Cedar Ridge Preserve.

Samantha remained silent in the seat beside him for so long Trey was sure bringing her with him had been the dumbest idea of the century. Right up there with how they'd decided to end the TV show *Game of Thrones*.

"You don't have to worry about me staying in the truck," she finally said. "I'm an ME, not a cop. I have no interest in dealing with any suspect until he or she stops moving."

Trey could tell from Samantha's elevated heart rate that she was nervous. Of course, those nerves had started building long before she'd demanded he take her with him to the heavily wooded area only a short trip from her apartment complex.

He'd first picked up on the tension filling her beautiful body shortly after coming back from the bathroom. It was obvious she'd been trying to tell him something important before Connor called. It was possible she was having one of those *defining the relationship* moments, but part of him had hoped she would broach the subject of her stalking him and the Pack. Maybe admit she knew they were werewolves or at least confess to stealing his blood. When she'd gotten stuck, Trey had tried to talk first, finally deciding to tell her what he was. Then the phone had rung, and a minute later, both of them had been dressed and running for his pickup. Bringing her with him was stupid, no doubt. But it wasn't like he could have stopped her from following if he'd left her back at her place. At least this way, he knew where the hell she was.

"There's no one else here yet," Samantha announced unnecessarily as he turned into the gravel parking lot surrounded by acres of thick pine forests and one poorly lit building that held the park's education center. "You're going to wait for backup, right?"

Trey shook his head as he reached for the door handle. "There's no time for that. It's been at least ten minutes since the witness who called Connor saw the man carrying a body into the preserve from the direction of the Mountain Creek subdivision. Even if the suspect was moving slowly, he's probably already on the way back out of the woods. I have to try to cut him off before he reaches the perimeter of the preserve."

"What kind of witness would be out here this late at night?" she asked desperately as Trey stepped out of the vehicle. "And if they saw the Butcher, why would they call Connor instead of 911?"

Trey sighed. He really didn't have time for this. But that didn't keep him from turning around to lean back in to look at her.

"The witness who called Connor was out here in the woods looking to score some drugs. Nearly every street cop in the DPD knows him, but Connor has helped the guy out a few times, so he called him first. Connor called dispatch the second he got off the phone with me. The cavalry will be here soon, but it won't matter if the Butcher is already gone."

"But what if it's not the Butcher?" she pressed.

He bent down a little lower, catching her eyes. "Whoever this person is, if they were actually carrying a body, I have to stop them because there's no scenario where a man in the woods in the middle of the night with a body is a good thing. I have to go, Samantha. This is my job. Connor and my other teammates will be here soon."

Samantha looked like she was close to crying but nodded and sat back a little in her seat. "Promise me you'll be careful."

"I will," he assured her. "I left the keys in the ignition, so lock the doors after I get out. There's a flashlight under the seat, but if you feel the slightest bit nervous about being in this parking lot alone in the dark, I want you to start the vehicle and get the hell out of here, okay?"

He closed the door before Samantha could start asking questions about whether she had a good reason to be apprehensive. As he headed south past the education center, he fingered his badge, hanging by the chain around his neck, then slipped a hand down to make sure his off-duty weapon was secure in its ankle holster.

Trey was running at full speed by the time he got to the start of the Cattail Pond Trail and headed due south. Out of the corner of his eye, he caught sight of the warning sign for the place being a poisonous snake habitat, declaring the existence of all kinds of slithery killers out here. He almost laughed. Maybe they'd get lucky and a rattlesnake or moccasin would take out the Butcher for them.

A little farther in, Trey slowed enough to send out a quick text to Connor, letting him know where he was. Connor replied immediately, saying that he, Hale, and Trevor had just pulled off Belt Line Road and would come in from the west in an attempt to herd the killer Trey's direction. More of their pack mates were on the way, and dispatch was trying to get enough patrol units together to establish a perimeter around the preserve. A helicopter was en route, too. But the Cedar Ridge Preserve was huge. There was no way to get enough cops out here to cover that much real estate. Not quickly enough to matter at least.

There was a stillness to the overgrown pine forest as he ran through it, like the other creatures who normally prowled these woods sensed the tension that came with having an unnatural killer in their midst. He swore he could feel every living thing out here stop what they were doing to watch the drama unfolded.

He was at least a half mile into the woods, leaving Cattail Pond Trail far behind as he continued working his way south, when he picked up that familiar burnt electrical odor. He slid to a dead stop, lifting his nose to test the wind direction before shooting a quick text to Connor and the others: Caught his scent south of Cedar Break Trail. Heading east toward Straus Road. Trying to cut him off.

Trey left the trail then, running hard in a southeasterly direction. The scent he'd come to associate with the Butcher was definitely stronger in this direction, but getting through the undergrowth was much tougher now that he was going cross-country. Thickets and vines tore at his arms and legs as he moved, actively resisting him and drawing blood here and there. The only bright spot in the situation was that the killer was also having to deal with the same terrain. Hopefully, it would slow him down even more than it did Trey.

As he ran, his inner wolf tried to make sense of the burnt-electrical scent. It was one of the killers, that much was obvious, but he'd never encountered a human who smelled even remotely like this odor. Sure, there was a slight undertone of humanity there, but for the most part, whoever it was smelled like a science experiment gone wrong.

A vibration from his back pocket distracted him for a second, and he yanked out the phone to see a text from Connor: It's another body dump. A leg, an arm, and organs.

Trey grimaced at the image, then pushed it away as he replied back: A quarter mile from Straus Road. I'm close.

He'd barely put his phone away when a blur of movement from off to the right caught his eye. Someone big, but surprisingly fast and quiet, was running through the woods, crossing the track he'd been taking and heading straight for Straus Road. The burnt-electrical scent with the hint of something almost human underneath it grew stronger by the second. It was definitely the Butcher.

Trey moved to the left, feeling the muscles of his legs and back begin to shift as he put on more speed, a growl rumbling up through his chest as he set a course that would intercept the killer.

As he got closer, he could tell from the man's silhouette that he was close to seven feet tall and broad in the shoulders and chest. Then again, it was difficult to be sure, given the heavy robes the guy was wearing. There was even a hood that covered his head and made it impossible to see his face.

Shit. He was chasing a damn monk.

Even in a frigging robe, the big man ran fast. Way faster than someone his size should have been capable of in these woods, especially in the dark on a moonless night.

Unless he is a supernatural.

Trey kept having to adjust his intercept angle until he was running parallel to the killer, twenty or thirty yards separating them. Every once in a while, the heavy cowl would shift, and Trey was able to catch a quick glimpse of the guy's nose or jawline. Never enough to describe him to anyone, but even with the parts he could make out, there was something damn familiar about him. Trey sprinted faster, needing to see that face.

A subtle movement a few hundred yards south of the big man snagged Trey's attention and he glanced that way to make out the shadow of someone else running through the woods with them. This guy was average height and slower but heading in the same direction. Trey got the feeling the big man in the robe was running interference to make sure he couldn't reach the other man.

The wind wasn't quite right to let Trey get a whiff of the second guy's scent, but from what he could make out through the trees, he was definitely a normal human, even if he was one who ran with a killer.

The sound of a twig snapping underfoot from somewhere way too close snapped Trey's attention back to the monk he'd been trying to catch up to only to realize the man was nowhere to be seen. The burnt-electrical scent hung in the night air, so he knew the guy was somewhere nearby, but he didn't have a visual on him. Trey couldn't even pick up a heartbeat. All he saw were trees and shadows and the unsettling reality that a man who weighed close to three-hundred-pounds and ran faster than an Olympic sprinter could also apparently turn invisible.

He heard the loud thump of a single heartbeat at the same time as a veritable mountain stepped out from behind a pile of thickets and hit him with a tree trunk.

A rational part of Trey's mind told him it hadn't actually been a mountain. Or a tree trunk. It had simply been a very large man with an equally large tree limb. But as he felt the ribs on the right side of his chest crack and cave in, the less-than-rational part insisted that it really had been a mountain. And a tree trunk.

He seemed to fly through the air for a very long time. Long enough to hear another one of those incredibly slow heartbeats. Then gravity reasserted itself in the form of the ground coming up to meet him and any air left in his lungs was immediately lost when the impact cracked a few more important-sounding bones. It was only when he felt something big and bulky under him that Trey realized the guy had thrown him through one tree and that he'd landed on another.

Trey would have preferred to stay right where he was for a second to get his lungs working again, but the thudding of extremely heavy boots coming his way convinced him he didn't have that option. With a groan, he forced himself to roll to the side, ignoring the grating of bone on bone as things in his chest shifted painfully. Scrambling to his feet, Trey considered going for the gun holstered at his ankle but knew he didn't have time. The huge man was only a few strides away, closing on him fast.

Trey extended his claws, cut loose a savage howl of anger, and launched himself at the man. His claws slashed through the thick material of the cloak and the flesh underneath. With the insanely slow heart rate, he didn't draw nearly as much blood as he should have. Not that the big man seemed to care one way or the other. He lunged forward and slammed a shoulder into Trey, sending him tumbling backward through the pine needles and other debris covering the forest floor.

Trey somehow ended up back on his feet even as his ribs exploded in pain all over again. Stepping forward with a growl, he stood toe-to-toe with the giant, the two of them punching and slashing at each other over and over. The damage Trey inflicted on the man was horrendous, deep, slicing gashes across the arms, chest, and shoulders that went all the way down to bone. The wounds didn't heal like they had on that female soul-sucker thing downtown, but the man never flinched. Hell, he never even made a sound. He simply kept swinging and punching, each blow more powerful than the last, as though all the trauma Trey was causing didn't even faze him. It shouldn't have been possible for any creature—even if it was supernatural—to sustain this much damage and not feel it.

A stray punch caught Trey in the chest, sending him flying yet again, bouncing him off a tree hard enough crack a few more bones in his back. When he hit the ground, there were a few moments as his vision started to fade and he had to waste precious seconds fighting off the approaching wave of darkness. If he passed out, he was dead.

Going on pure instinct, he scrambled for the weapon holstered at his ankle, even as the voice in the back of his mind pointed out that if his claws hadn't slowed the behemoth down, a little 9mm round probably wouldn't even tickle him.

Not that it mattered. By the time he got his weapon out and pointed in the right direction, he realized the big man in the robe was nowhere to be seen. After shoving himself upright and staggering forward a few steps, he came to the conclusion that the guy was already gone. The revving of a vehicle engine from the direction of Straus Road a few seconds later told him there was absolutely no chance of catching the man.

He stood there in the darkness, wondering why the monstrously huge man hadn't finished him when he had the chance. The only answer he could come up with was that the guy had attacked him simply to give his slower partner time to get away. Of course, if that was the case, he couldn't help but wonder how much more dangerous the guy would be if he had really wanted to murder Trey. He had to admit it was rather disturbing that the guy may not have been trying to kill him and had still been doing a bang-up job of it.

Trey turned and started walking slowly in a northerly direction, taking shallow breaths to ease his aching ribs as he pulled out his cell to let Connor know that the bad guys had gotten away. Connor passed the information on to dispatch, hoping for the best.

He just made it back onto Cedar Break Trail when he caught wind of Connor, Trevor, and Hale approaching, along with a scent he definitely hadn't expected. A few minutes later, he saw a flashlight bobbing up and down in the darkness, coming his way.

"We found her at the intersection of Cattail and Cedar Break trails trying to figure out which way to go," Connor said as they all reached him a minute later. "We thought it was better to keep her with us than to try to send her back to the parking lot."

Trey was about to thank his pack mates, but the moment he stepped into the beam from Samantha's flashlight, she let out a shriek and came running toward him. He held up his hands to stop her, but it was too late. She slammed right into the busted-up ribs on the right side of his body. He tried to hide his grunt of pain. And failed.

Expression bordering on panic, Samantha's heart rate—which had already been way too fast—shot through the roof. Yanking up his T-shirt, she aimed the beam of her flashlight at the exposed skin and the bruising already forming across his torso. He tried to push the shirt back down as quickly as he could, praying she wouldn't notice the places where his broken ribs stuck out at strange angles.

"Crap," she said. "You look terrible. We have to get you to a hospital. On second thought, maybe you should lay down here and wait for the paramedics to arrive."

Trey grabbed the hand swinging the flashlight wildly around and pulled her closer before she hit him—or herself. "Samantha, I'm okay," he said softly, getting an arm around her and rubbing little circles on her back with his hand, trying to soothe her. "I'm a little roughed up, but nothing I can't handle. I promise."

Samantha looked like she wanted to argue, but then took a deep breath and let it out with a shuddering sigh, her eyes coming up to meet his in the darkness. "Sorry. I was sitting in your truck completely losing my mind worrying about you, so I got out to come help. When I saw the bruises, I kind of lost it. Like I told you, I'm not really good with living patients."

He wanted to be mad at her for getting out of his pickup, but seeing her so freaked out, he simply couldn't do it. He promised himself they'd talk about it later. Because the thought of Samantha being in the same woods as that huge psychotic monk scared the hell out of him.

"We'd better get back to the parking lot before too many people show up," Trevor said. "Or we're going to have cops wandering around these woods all night trying to find us."

After they got moving, Hale deftly fell into step on the other side of Samantha and distracted her with a vivid description of the body parts they'd found about a half mile to the west of their location. Trey didn't have to wait long before Trevor and Connor tugged him back a few yards to talk.

"Samantha wasn't exaggerating," Connor murmured quietly. "You do look terrible. What the hell did you run into out there?"

"Truthfully? I don't know have a clue," Trey admitted, keeping an eye on Samantha to make sure she couldn't hear them talking. "The guy was big, fast, strong as hell, and I'm pretty sure he could control his heartbeat. At one point he was hiding behind a tree only a few feet away and I know for a fact that I didn't hear a beat for at least twenty seconds."

"Are you saying the Butcher is a supernatural?" Trevor asked.

"Any chance he's working with the one you went up against the other night?"

"It sure seems like he's a supernatural to me," Trey said. "As for whether he's involved with the creature who's going around turning people into mummies, that's anyone's guess."

As they walked, Trey described the fight in detail, emphasizing how much damage he'd inflicted, to little effect. He also told them about the second guy he saw.

"I'm not sure what it means, but I think the guy in the robe could have killed me if he'd wanted to," Trey added as they reached the parking lot area already filled with cop cars. "Or at least screw me up a lot more than he did. But as soon as I was temporarily out of action and the second guy had gotten away, the big man disappeared."

Hale, who'd clearly been eavesdropping on the conversation from several yards ahead, looked over his shoulder at Trey, surprise on his face.

"Why would a supernatural serial killer decide to let you live after he just dumped body parts of his latest victim?" Trevor asked.

Trey shook his head grimly. "I wish I knew."

CHAPTER 15

At the light knock on her open office door, Samantha looked up from the autopsy records she was reading to see Trey standing there holding a paper bag from the deli down the street. Her pulse skipped a beat. She didn't know why, but everything seemed a little bit lighter and brighter when he was around.

"Hey," she said, pushing back her chair and walking around the desk to meet him. "You brought dinner? You didn't have to do that."

He flashed her a grin. "I wanted to. You didn't eat already, did you?"

"No, and I'm starving," she admitted.

She'd spent what was left of last night and much of the morning working the Cedar Ridge scene, then come straight to the institute to go over everything they'd collected. To say she was exhausted was an understatement, especially considering she hadn't gotten a bit of sleep last night. Not that she was complaining. She'd gladly give up endless nights of sleep for sex that good.

"I ate a pack of cheese crackers and a Snickers from the vending machine around noon," she added as they sat down on the couch along the wall. "Do I get any credit for that?"

Trey snorted as he pulled out a bottle of water and a small plastic clamshell filled with pickle spears, then two sandwiches wrapped in paper. "Absolutely none. I had no idea what kind of sandwich you liked, so I went with ham and swiss on rye. Hope that's okay?"

"It's perfect."

Unwrapping the sandwich, she took a bite, then helped herself to a crunchy dill pickle spear. She resisted the urge to shove it in her mouth along with the ham and swiss. Dang, she really *was* hungry.

While they ate, Trey told her about the browbeating he'd gotten from Chief Leclair, admitting he wasn't sure if she was more upset he'd gone into the woods after the Butcher by himself or that the killer had ended up getting away. Samantha glanced at him as she nibbled on the pickle, looking for any sign of the damage she knew he'd sustained last night in the fight with the bad guy.

After a few minutes of looking him over, she decided that if she hadn't seen the bruises with her own eyes, she would never know that anything had happened at all. Which was absolutely insane. Yes, it had been dark when she'd pulled up his T-shirt and looked him over, and he'd done his best to keep her from getting a clear view, but she'd seen the unnatural dips and ridges along his chest. There was no doubt in her mind that he'd sustained at least three broken ribs and what she was guessing had been some pretty serious cartilage tears.

Trey should be in the hospital right now, with surgery as a distinct possibility, serious painkillers an absolute must, and breathing a chore to accomplish. The one thing he shouldn't have been doing was sitting in her office, chatting and gesturing like it was just another beautiful day in the neighborhood.

She wanted to ask him about it, demand answers, but she refrained, choosing to focus on her sandwich and pickles instead. Her office wasn't the place for that conversation. They needed privacy, and it was too easy here for someone to overhear. Besides, what did she expect him to say anyway? That yes, he had broken several ribs, but not to worry about it because he was fine now.

The scary part was that Trey truly was fine. He'd had his chest nearly caved in last night, and now, barely more than twelve hours, he was fully healed. It shouldn't have been possible, but obviously it was. A part of her knew that somehow, it was the wolf DNA that had allowed him to heal so quickly, but for the life of her, she couldn't explain how something like that could be possible.

The puzzle nagged at her, but in the end, she was simply glad he was whole and healthy. That was more important to her than having answers.

"Have you gotten anything from the blood samples I showed you at the crime scene?" Trey asked as she finished eating. "I know it's too soon to have anything conclusive as far as DNA, but I was wondering if maybe you'd noticed anything strange about the blood?"

With all the bizarre stuff she'd seen the past two years, she should be immune to one more sudden left turn into the *Twilight Zone*. Apparently not. His odd question, and the fact that he was obviously hiding some important details concerning last night's attack, still caught her off guard.

When Trey had led her to the stretch of forest where he and the larger member of the Butcher serial-killing duo had fought, she expected to see a few disturbed piles of pine needles, some broken tree branches, and maybe a drop or two of blood. What she'd gotten was a war zone of gouged earth, broken tree trunks, and what looked like two or three pints of blood spattered absolutely everywhere. It had helped some when Trey had assured her the blood wasn't his, though he'd been seriously short on the details when it came to how that much blood had ended up spattered so far and wide.

If she had to guess—and she had to because his answers were vague BS—she'd say Trey had gone at the killer with a knife or even a machete. But Trey hadn't been carrying a weapon like that when they'd left her place. Having essentially frisked him while getting naked with him, she knew that for a fact. And he definitely hadn't taken anything from his truck because she would have seen him doing it.

Which meant that there was yet another secret Trey was keeping from her.

"The blood?" he prompted when she didn't say anything.

Crap. How long had she been sitting there in a daze?

"Oh, sorry. I was lost in thought," she said. "To answer the first part of your question, no, nothing on the DNA yet. Even with a priority rush, it will be a couple days before we can check to see if the samples match anyone already in the system. As far as the other part of your question, yes, there was something strange with the blood."

Trey waited patiently, one brow lifted.

"This is going to sound insane," she admitted. "But the blood I collected at the Cedar Ridge Preserve can't be typed and doesn't have a definitive rhesus factor."

Trey considered that for a moment before nodding. "Okay, you're right. That does sound insane. What exactly do you mean?"

"I mean I've tested multiple samples. The results either come back inconclusive or as a random mix of blood types. Same with the rhesus factor. It either comes back as positive, negative, or both. It's like the samples were taken from a combination of a different people's blood. You're sure you saw the blood come straight from the big guy you fought, right?"

Trey nodded. "It was his blood for sure. Is it possible for a person to have mixed blood like that? Maybe if they'd gotten a transfusion?"

Samantha shook her head. "No way. For one thing, no doctor worth a crap would ever do a transfusion without typing and cross matching the blood for compatibility. And if something like that happened anyway, the person would have one hell of a nasty incompatibility reaction. He wouldn't be running around the woods fighting. He'd be laid up in a hospital waiting for his kidneys to fail."

"Then how do you explain what you've discovered with the samples?"

"I can't." She sighed. "Which is why I've hidden the results from Louis and everyone else. I only hope it doesn't affect the

DNA profiling. If we can match these blood samples to someone already in the system, we'll have the killer."

They talked for a while longer about the evidence collected at the preserve, Samantha admitting she'd been getting ready to examine the body parts Connor and the others had found before Trey had shown up with dinner. Trey seemed to take that as a sign she needed to get back to work. He wasn't wrong, but Samantha still hated to see him leave.

"Hey, before you go," she said as they got to their feet. "We didn't get a chance to talk, but I wanted to tell you how much I enjoyed last night."

Mouth quirking, Trey casually rested his hands on her hips, sending her heart rate soaring with that simple touch. "Last night? Oh, you mean running around the woods collecting blood samples? Yeah, that was fun, wasn't it?"

She slapped him in the chest, only remembering his broken ribs after the fact. Not that he seemed to care. "No, I don't mean running around the woods collecting blood samples, you eejit. I was talking about earlier at my apartment. In my bed."

He chuckled. "I know what you meant." He stepped closer until all Samantha could see was his broad chest and those powerful arms, his low, rumbling voice making her shiver a little. "And yes, I enjoyed last night, too. More than I could ever say. It was special beyond words."

Feeling exactly the same way, Samantha went up on her toes, dragging his mouth down at the same time for a kiss she simply couldn't go another minute without. She moaned at the electric tingles running all over her body from that simply contact, suddenly wishing they were anywhere but in her office.

It hit her then that this had moved well past the *falling* stage at some point when she wasn't looking and was now hovering dangerously close to the L-word, leaving her to wonder when the hell that transition had happened. Was it the sex? It seemed likely, since she'd never had orgasms that good in her life. But even as that thought popped into her head, she knew it wasn't just about sex. The moment things between them had changed so drastically was well after the bedroom gymnastics. It had been when she'd been sitting in Trey's truck all alone, terrified out of her mind for him.

"I didn't realize how scared I was until I heard that howl coming out of the woods," Samantha murmured, not realizing she'd said the words out loud until she looked up and discovered Trey was gazing down at her, his face full of concern. "It was so loud that I could hear it right through the windows. I started freaking out then, knowing you were out there on your own. I had the door open and was running through the woods before I even knew what I was doing. It was insane, and I can't even begin to explain what the hell made me think I could find you in that pitch-black forest, but I couldn't leave you out there on your own. Something inside wouldn't let me sit there and do nothing."

Trey's arms wrapped around her, pulling her to his chest and hugging her tightly. He made gentle shushing sounds and little relaxing circular motions on her back with his hand. "You don't have to explain it. I completely understand. When you showed up with the guys, I nearly lost my mind. I can't believe you did something as crazy as come into the woods after me. But then I realized I couldn't expect you to leave me behind any more than I would have left you behind."

If his admission of how worried he'd been hadn't melted her into a gooey puddle, the kiss he gave her would have. Gazing up at him afterward, thoroughly kissed and thrilled at the knowledge that this thing between them wasn't one-sided, Samantha decided then and there that it was time to tell him everything. Yes, it had the potential to blow everything up in their faces, but she needed to tell him now. Before it was too late.

Then Louis walked in the door.

"Officer Duncan," he said warmly, ignoring the fact that she and Trey had been in each other's arms a moment ago, clearly in the middle of making out. But her boss was cool that way. "I heard someone up front say you were here and thought I'd check to see how you're doing."

Trey exchanged looks with her before giving Louis a frown. "How I'm doing?"

"Yes." Louis reached up to adjust his glasses, eyeing Trey up and down like he was a corpse on his exam table. "I heard someone say you got into a physical altercation with the Butcher. One of the techs who was at the crime scene last night said you were so beat up, you could barely stand up straight."

Trey chuckled. "I think that might be an exaggeration. It wasn't anything more than a few bumps and bruises. Nothing a couple of ibuprofen couldn't fix."

Louis nodded. "Well, that's good to hear." He looked to Samantha. "Don't stay too late. After last night, you must be exhausted. The Butcher will wait until tomorrow."

Giving Trey a nod, Louis walked out, leaving them alone.

"You want to get together tonight?" Trey asked, giving her a smile. "I promise to have you in bed at a decent hour."

She laughed. "I like the way you think. But let's go to your place instead. I haven't even seen it yet. Unless you live in a van by the river, of course."

He chuckled and kissed her again, promising that he did, in fact, have a place nicer than a van by the river. "I'll text you my address."

Another kiss and he was out the door. Promising herself she'd tell him everything that night, Samantha grabbed her lab coat from the coat rack and slipped into it. If she wanted to get out of there at a decent hour, she needed to get to work.

The institute was nearly empty as she walked toward the lab. Not all of the assistant MEs had their own labs, but the senior ones like her, Hugh, and Nadia did. It was nice having a room set up exactly the way she liked it—with equipment and supplies arranged so she could find everything quickly—and knowing she didn't have to worry about anyone messing with stuff.

She spent the next hour on the dismembered leg, taking pictures, weighing, and measuring it, recording all the details in the institute's digital forensic database. Photos were uploaded automatically, but everything else had to be manually entered into descriptive forms that went along with every photo. It took forever, but once it was in, the computer system made it easy to bring up anything she wanted.

Samantha found very familiar burn scars on the leg, making her almost certain it had belonged to the same victim as the leg she collected Monday morning out by the homeless camp. That would make this the first time a second part had been found from the same person. She wasn't sure why yet, but she knew it was significant.

It wasn't until she started working on the arm that she found something that might finally help them find the Butcher—a tattoo of a winged horse, with five stars arranged above it and a six digit number below. This thing wasn't some generic *I love Mom* ink. No, this was super original and specific. For the first time since the investigation started, she had a distinctive mark that should make ID'ing the person the arm came from a slam dunk.

She was in the middle of taking multiple photos of the artwork, trying to capture it from every angle, when she stopped mid-click.

Crap.

She'd seen this tattoo before.

Setting down the camera, she hurried over to the computer and logged out of the forensic database, then placed the remains back in cold storage and hauled butt back to her office. One glance at the darkness outside told her she'd already worked way too long, and that Trey was probably wondering where she was, but she had one thing she needed to check before leaving.

Back at her desk, she jumped on her computer, pulling up the files from yesterday's staff meeting. She had to flip through nearly a hundred crime scene and autopsy photos, but when she found the picture she'd remembered, it stopped her cold.

Aidan Bridges, thirty-two-year-old male, found dead in his Preston Hollow home. Cause of death was an opiate overdose. The photo of the man's body on the exam table showed the winged-horse tattoo on the right arm clear as day. Hugh, the ME who'd performed the autopsy, confirmed that because Bridges had no family or next of kin, the body had been cremated by the county two weeks ago.

That obviously wasn't true because Aidan Bridges's arm was sitting in cold storage in her lab.

Her head spinning at the implications, Samantha went through all of Hugh's autopsy records from the staff briefing, stunned at how many cases the man cleared in a month. She wasn't exactly sure what she was looking for until she found a John Doe with a circular-shaped scar on the inner part of his left forearm—the same scar she'd seen Monday morning on the arm from the body dump near the homeless camp. The John Doe had been picked up in the woods west of Cockrell Hill, with Hugh declaring the man's death a suicide. Like Aiden Bridges, this body had been cremated about two weeks ago.

Samantha wasn't sure how long she sat there staring at the photos of Aiden Bridges and the John Doe, wondering how many more of the Butcher's victims had first been on Hugh's autopsy table. She finally closed the file and logged out even as she tried to understand what exactly was going on. Had Hugh murdered those two people himself, then used his position in the ME's office to cover up the crime so he could give them to the Butcher? Or had those men actually committed suicide, then Hugh gave the bodies to the Butcher so he could dissect them? Or was Hugh the Butcher, doing some kind of insane experiments on people using the parts from these two corpses? Considering his medical and surgical training, that made sense on some sick level. No wonder she'd been having such a hard time coming up with any viable clues in the case. Who better than an ME to know how to hide stuff like that?

Samantha stood and ran for the door. She needed to tell somebody about all of this, and fast.

CHAPTER 16

"Trey, it's Samantha," she said into her cell, knowing how stupid it was to drive with one hand and operate a phone with the other. But she needed to talk to him about what she'd found. Unfortunately, she got his voicemail. "I stumbled onto something really big with the case I need to talk to you about it. Call me as soon as you get this."

Samantha almost said *I love you* before hanging up, but then chickened out at the last second. Yeah, maybe it was too soon for that. She should probably wait to see if they made it past the part where she confessed to stealing his blood and sending it out to a private lab for testing.

As she drove through the well-maintained streets and fancy homes in Westover Hills, Samantha began thinking she had the wrong address. When she reached the house taking up the entire end of the cul-de-sac, she was even more sure she'd taken a wrong turn. With its stacked stone walls and turreted roof, the three-story structure looked more like a castle where a king would live than a house belonging to a chief medical examiner.

She pulled her car into the broad driveway and stopped, staring up at her Louis's home in disbelief. Even with the light streaming through the leaded-glass windows on the lower floor, "dark and foreboding" was the best way to describe the house. Not that it wasn't beautiful. It simply wasn't the kind of place she'd ever want to live.

Getting out of the car, she headed for the front door, taking in the manicured lawn and impeccable flower beds. She knew Louis came from money—or at least that's what the rumors around the institute were—but if the man could afford a place like this, why the hell did he keep working? Especially as county medical examiner.

She rang the doorbell and waited, praying he was home. If he wasn't, she'd have to go with her backup plan—going to see the task force lead detective or Chief Leclair. Truthfully, she wasn't comfortable with either one. She didn't know the lead detective well enough to refer to him by anything other than his title. She didn't know his first name and couldn't remember his last name. And while she'd at least talked to the chief a time or two outside of the Butcher case, the woman had always struck her as overwhelmingly busy and not very interested in the thoughts of anyone not wearing DPD blue.

It didn't help that Samantha had no idea how well her theory would be received. The idea that Hugh was either the Butcher or working directly with him was a little out there. Especially when the only evidence she had at the moment was that two of the body parts she'd recovered had come from corpses that had been on his examiner's table. It's why she wanted to talk to Louis first and see if she was completely off base. If he found her ideas sane and reasonable, the task force would be more likely to take them seriously.

She lifted her hand to ring the doorbell again when the front door opened. Louis stood there in the entryway wearing a Mr. Rogers cardigan, clearly surprised to see her.

"Samantha! What are you doing here so late?"

"I discovered something disturbing about the Butcher case and wanted to talk to you first before I told anyone else."

Louis's expression quickly became all business, and he opened the door wider, motioning her forward. "Of course. Come in and we can talk."

Samantha stopped inside the large foyer, completely awed. The circular space was breathtaking, open all the way up to the third floor, with lots of marble and gilt edges, beautiful curving stairs leading to the floors above. But the most unexpected find were the gleaming suits of armor positioned on pedestals all around the perimeter of the room, each holding a weapon that looked real as hell to her.

"Forgive my taste in home decor," Louis said with a laugh, motioning toward the suits of armor. "My family name has historical roots in sixteenth-century Italy, hence an obsession with antique armor and weapons from that time. Feel free to look around if you wish, or if you prefer, my study is ahead and to the left. I have to take care of something I was in the middle of when you knocked."

Samantha spent a few moments looking at all the armor and weapons but was too distracted to pay them any attention, so she instead headed for the arched doorway Louis had pointed out.

The study was as nice as the entryway, with antique furniture and shelves loaded with leather bound books. While she waited for her boss to take care of that thing he'd been in the middle of, Samantha looked around. Taking in the books, paintings, and the glass case filled with more edged weapons and a handful of extremely modern handguns and rifles, she was pretty sure this one room was worth more than her whole apartment.

One particular painting on the back wall behind the desk caught her attention. It was extremely well done, depicting Louis with a teenage boy and a pretty, dark-haired woman. The boy was obviously the son she'd heard about that had died years ago. The woman in the painting must have been his wife, but Samantha had heard rumors they'd gotten divorced a little while after that.

"Jamison was killed in a car accident several years ago," Louis said from behind her and Samantha turned to see him standing in the arched doorway, gazing up at the painting she'd been studying. "I'm sure you knew that already, though. But the fact that my wife divorced me less than a year later is probably something not as widely known. Not that I blame her for leaving. I was an inconsolable prick after my son's death and gave her no reason to stay."

Samantha couldn't help but feel badly for Louis. He'd gone through a lot of tragedy. "I know saying this doesn't mean much, but I'm sorry for your loss."

Louis nodded, continuing to gaze up at the painting for some time. Then he seemed to come back to himself, walking across the room to move behind the desk and take a seat there. "Thank you for that. And thank you for waiting so patiently while I took care of that other issue. But I'm sure that you didn't drive all the way out here at this time to night to talk about my family. You mentioned discovering something about the Butcher case?"

Samantha took a seat in one of the two fancy armchairs in front of the desk. "I have good reason to believe that Hugh is the Butcher. Or at the very minimum, is working directly with the killer."

Louis lifted a brow. "I think you'd better tell me everything— and I do mean everything."

Taking a deep breath, Samantha laid it all out for him—the body parts she'd identified from Hugh's staff briefing, the paperwork trail the assistant ME had left showing that Aiden Bridges and the John Doe had been cremated, her theory that Hugh was helping to make sure the Butcher case was never solved and that he was conducting some kind of macabre experiments using cadaver parts, trying to reattach them to other bodies. She told Louis everything she knew or suspected, no matter how insignificant she thought it might be.

Louis sat there speechless for what felt like five minutes after she finished, and Samantha wondered if she'd screwed up and thrown in too much conjecture when all her boss wanted was the facts.

"To say this is bad is the understatement of the century," he finally said, and Samantha could almost see the wheels in his mind turning as he considered the various ways this could play out. "But I think you've found the Butcher."

Before she could say anything, Louis reached for the fancy

French phone on the corner of his desk. "Have you told anyone else about this yet? You might have put them at risk if Hugh figures out you've told them. At this point, I doubt there's anything left the man wouldn't do to cover up his crimes."

That was probably true. She shook her head as Louis asked to be connected to the lead detective for the task force. How bad was it that her boss knew the full name of the task force lead when she didn't?

"I called Trey...Officer Duncan, but got his voicemail, so I left a message for him to call me back," she said. "I didn't think this was the kind of thing you leave on someone's voicemail."

Louis nodded, waving his hand when Samantha was about to ask if she should call Trey back. "The head of the task force just picked up."

Samantha leaned back in the chair, listening as her boss explained everything she'd discovered. He covered it in detail, answering what seemed like an endless list of questions. She couldn't help but notice he kept using her name over and over, making sure the detective knew she was the one to get credit for this discovery. It was difficult to put into words how much she appreciated this.

After another minute or so of conversation, Louis hung up, a smile on his face.

"The police are heading to Hugh's place to pick him up." Louis leaned back in his leather office chair. "They're also sending someone over to take your statement."

She nodded. She would rather have headed over to Trey's place, but it made sense the cops would want to take her statement. She was a little surprised they hadn't asked him to go to the station to do it, though.

Getting to his feet, Louis moved around the desk to sit on the edge, gazing down at her with kind eyes.

"I'm glad you came here and told me all of that," he said quietly.

"It completely destroys my established timeline, but it could have been so much worse."

Samantha frowned, trying to understand what Louis was talking about. Apparently seeing the confusion on her face, her boss picked up the rest of his thought.

"Unfortunately, it's going to force me to do some things earlier than I would have preferred, but it would have been much worse if you'd told anyone what you'd discovered. That would have ruined everything."

Samantha straightened in her chair, alarm bells going off.

Hugh wasn't the Butcher.

Louis was.

Crap.

Suddenly, a hand came around in front of her face and slapped a wet cloth across her nose and mouth. She struggled immediately, trying to stand up, then clawing at the hand over her face when that didn't work.

But whoever was behind her was incredibly strong and held her down like she was a little kid. Louis stepped in then, grabbing her flailing hands and shoving them down to the arms of the chair. Her heart felt like it was about to explode in her chest even as her mind recognized the ether-like odor of chloroform.

Everything started to get fuzzy then, her last thoughts of Trey and wishing she'd told him she loved him on that phone message she'd left.

———————

"Are we seriously about to Skype with someone from STAT on the top level of an uptown parking garage?" Trey asked as he watched Connor boot up his laptop. "Isn't this some kind of security violation? Couldn't our conversation be hacked and show up on TMZ or something?"

"STAT loaded an encryption program on my laptop," Connor said with a snort, not bothering to look up from the screen of his computer. "Yours, too, by the way. Something tells me even the NSA would have a hard time eavesdropping on this call."

Before Trey could say anything, the echoing squawk of tires on concrete caught Trey's attention, and he turned to see Trevor's blue Ford Thunderbird coming up the ramp to the top level of the parking garage. Hale was sitting in the passenger seat of the beautifully restored classic, looking as confused about the last-minute meeting as Trey was.

"What the hell is going on?" Hale demanded as he stepped out of the convertible and strode toward them. "Trevor and I were at a club in the middle of talking to a cocktail waitress who's sure she saw Ramiro Cordova Sunday before last, then we got your text telling us to meet you here ASAP."

"Sorry about that," Connor said, still focused on the laptop sitting on the hood of Trey's Jeep. "But STAT sent me a link for a Skype meeting. Said it was urgent."

"I hope so," Trevor said, coming over to join them. "The waitress was going to talk to the manager about letting us see some of the club's video footage. She's pretty sure that soul-sucker woman was in the club around the same time as Cordova."

Around lunch, STAT had finally come through with the identity of the desiccated body they'd found at the McCommas Bluff Landfill. Ramiro Cordova worked in the financial district as an investment analyst. Unlike the previous two victims, Cordova had only lived in the Dallas area for about a month or so. Trey guessed that was why it had taken STAT so long to come up with a name for the guy.

The four of them had spent most of the evening driving around the uptown club district, trying to find someone who might have seen Cordova. Trey and Connor had struck out, but it seemed that Trevor and Hale might have gotten lucky.

Since Connor was still busy setting up the Skype connection, Trey pulled out his phone to send a quick message to Samantha. He wanted to let her know that he was probably going to be late tonight and that it might be best if he met her at her place. Even if they didn't do anything more than fall asleep in each other's arms, that would be fine with him.

Trey immediately disregarded the handful of sports and news updates, homing in on the phone message from Samantha. The music in the last club they'd been in had been so loud he hadn't even noticed his phone buzzing. He could only assume she'd called to say she finished up at the institute and was heading out.

He didn't bother moving off to the side to play the message, since his pack mates would hear it anyway. Besides, it wasn't like he had anything to hide. One sniff at the preserve last night and all three of his teammates had known he and Samantha had slept together.

Trey listened as Samantha's soft tones filled his ear, once again a little stunned at how his body reacted to the mere sound of her voice. But then he forced himself to focus on her words, a little worried when she started talking about stumbling onto something big that she needed to talk to him about. The fact that she asked him to call the minute he got a chance had his heart rate spiking.

But when he called her back, the phone ended up going to her voicemail. "I got your message, but I guess you're busy with something." he said after the beep, telling himself there was nothing to worry about. If Samantha had been in trouble, she would have said so in the message. "I have no idea when I'm getting done tonight, so I was thinking about heading to your apartment later. I know we talked about you coming to my place instead, but that might have to wait. Call or text me to let me know you got this and that you're cool with me dropping by, even if it's late."

He almost screwed up and said the L-word right there at the end but bit his tongue in time. Samantha hadn't said it, so he needed to chill out and let this thing develop in its own time. She might feel the soul-mate connection happening, but he couldn't expect her to understand the feeling yet.

Shoving his phone back in his pocket, Trey turned his attention to Connor's laptop to see a woman with long, blue hair on the screen. Okay, that wasn't a look he expected from a covert federal organization.

"My name is Davina De Merci. I'm a consultant for STAT," she was saying. "Sorry for the short-notice call, but we finally got a hit on the creature that has been leaving those desiccated bodies out there and thought you'd want to know right away."

Trey almost laughed. "Having personally gotten my ass handed to me by this thing, I think I can answer for everyone when I say that yes, we'd like to know what we're up against."

Davina smiled. "If it helps, it was your accurate description of the creature that finally helped us identify her. If not for that, we'd still be looking."

"Well, since I can't help but see the creature's face every time I close my eyes, it's not like I'll ever be able to forget what she looks like," he said dryly. "So, what is this thing we're dealing with?"

"The creature is called a *vita lamia*, which in Latin is roughly translated as life vampire." Davina said, leaning in closer to her laptop camera. "They're believed to be even older than their traditional vampire cousins who survive on blood. They are also extremely rare, which is part of the reason it took me a bit to figure out what you're dealing with. A lot of smart people out there insist the vita lamia are nothing more than fairy tales."

When Trey and the other members of his pack stood there staring at the screen, Davina apparently figured out she was rambling and pulled up with an embarrassed expression.

"So, right...vita lamia," she picked up again. "As the name implies, they survive on the life force of other living entities. It doesn't necessarily have to be human life, but apparently, we taste the best and provide the most nutrients."

"Yay for humans, I guess," Connor said. "If these things suck the life out of their victims, why haven't we found more desiccated corpses like these last three?"

Davina shrugged. "Well, like I mentioned, these creatures are extremely rare. There are likely no more than two or three in the entire northern hemisphere. For another, according to the material I was able to find, most vitas survive by taking tiny amounts of life force through casual contact, like a handshake, a hug, or a kiss, even a light touch on the arm is enough. It's not dangerous, and the person being fed on never realizes it. In fact, they don't feel anything beyond a slight bit of exhaustion."

Trevor frowned. "If these creatures normally nibble instead of gorge themselves as a way to avoid detection, why is this one draining people dry? Is she trying to get herself noticed?"

"All I can assume is that this woman is either newly created or untrained," Davina said. "And before you ask, I don't know a thing about either of those subjects when it comes to a vita. It's also possible she's simply become addicted to the life force she consumes. This happens with regular vampires sometimes. They develop a bloodlust and can't stop themselves anymore."

"Okay, let's assume we're dealing with a vita with impulse control issues," Trey said. "How do we take her down? When I fought her, the wounds healed almost instantly. If vitas are related to traditional vampires, does that mean they have the same weakness? Will our werewolf life force be like acid to them?"

Davina shook her head. "I have no idea. But considering how completely different vitas and traditional vampires are, I don't think I'd wager my life on the idea that a werewolf's life force would be toxic to this one in the same way your blood is toxic to vampires. It's been my experience that most creatures are rather fond of their heads and their hearts. Go for those first, and if that doesn't work, good luck. Either way, let me know how this turns out. I'd love to be able to add more details to my library on these creatures."

It was Trey's turn to frown. "That's it? No other advice to give on how to deal with this creature that nearly killed me the first time it touched me?"

Davina gave him a small smile before shrugging. "If she nearly killed you the first time she touched you, then maybe next time, don't let her touch you."

Before Trey had a chance to say something snarky in reply, Davina reached out to turn off the connection, leaving the four of them standing there on the top level of the parking garage, feeling no better off than when they'd started.

———————————

"I'm sure I've seen the woman you're looking for around here several times," the cocktail waitress said while the manager and a member of the club's security staff shuffled through endless file folders on the computer, looking for video clips from the Sunday before last. "She only comes in on the weekends, usually late in the evening, close to last call. She's definitely a one-night stand kind of woman. I saw her dancing with Ramiro, and let me tell you, they were getting friendly real fast."

Trey and Connor had gone back to the club with Trevor and Hale, since the one they'd been at earlier had been a complete bust. The waitress Trevor had mentioned was still there and had introduced them to her manager. While she seemed extremely confident about seeing Cordova and their soul-sucker suspect, the manager did his best to lower expectations, pointing out that the club had thirty different security cameras. Even if Trey and the others only focused on the last hour or two of the night in question, that was still going to be a lot of video footage to go through.

Once they got to the right video files, the manager and security guy gave them a quick tutorial on how to operate the equipment, leaving shortly after that. There were only three chairs available in the security room, so Trevor and Hale took the first shift, sitting down with the cocktail waitress in front of the monitor, trying to jog her memory about where exactly she might have seen their suspect to give them a place to start.

Connor motioned Trey to the far side of the small room, the expression on his friend's face making it obvious he wanted to have some privacy. Of course, that only meant that the waitress wouldn't be able to hear them. Trevor and Hale could hear every word.

"Did you get a chance to talk to Samantha yet about the soul-mate thing?" Connor asked softly. "I mean, since you two have finally slept together, I thought maybe you'd told her. And gotten her to agree not to out the Pack."

Trey glanced at Trevor and Hale, who were trying way too hard to make it seem like they weren't eavesdropping. He shrugged. "I meant to talk to her about it afterward, but then you called telling me to get my ass to the Cedar Ridge Preserve. I haven't had a chance to talk to her since."

"But what about earlier today?" Connor frowned. "I thought you went to her office specifically to talk to her about being *The One*?"

Trey grimaced. "That was the plan, but then her boss walked in and the moment was gone. We're getting together later tonight, so I'm hoping it'll be the right time then."

Connor muttered a curse under his breath. "Are you serious? How many times have we seen this blow up in our pack mates' faces? There's never a right time for something like this, only the wrong time, which tends to be after everything goes to hell and Samantha is running away from you in terror or spilling every-thing she knows to anyone who will listen. You need to just come out and tell her the truth, Trey. Before it's too late."

Trey knew Connor was right. But his friend acted like all Trey had to do was to tell Samantha that they were soul mates and then *poof*, everything would be better. What if telling her that she was *The One* for him—and admitting he was a werewolf—was the thing that made it all go bad? Everything was going so good with Samantha right now, even with all the lies between them. Was it really so wrong to want to hold on to that feeling for a little while longer?

"That's her!" the waitress suddenly shouted, jumping up to point at one of the large computer monitors mounted on the wall. "That's the woman I saw with Ramiro."

Trey walked over to look at the monitor. There was no way in hell the waitress could have found their suspect so quickly, but he was glad for the interruption regardless. It would give him time to think if nothing else. But when he caught sight of the dark-haired woman in the middle of the paused video, he had to admit she definitely looked like the person in their police sketch, even if the image on the screen was a little blurry.

The waitress was chattering nonstop about being right until Hale nudged her out the door, thanking her for the help and promising to give her all the credit when they closed the case.

Trevor slowly moved the video forward frame by frame, trying to find a clearer shot of the woman. He found several other shots, including one where they could nearly see the woman's entire face. With his werewolf eyesight, it wasn't like he needed to move closer to see the image clearly, but Trey found himself doing it anyway, instinctively wanting to get the best look possible.

She looked familiar, though he couldn't place where he'd seen her. It was only when he pictured her with her hair pulled back away from her face and wearing a hell of a lot less makeup that it hit him.

"Holy crap, I know her," he murmured, leaning in even closer, as if that would help make the picture clearer. "She's the woman we met in Samantha's office. I'm sure of it. I don't remember her name, but she was one of the other assistant MEs Samantha works with."

His pack mates crowded around the monitor with him, looking at the woman from every angle.

"Nadia!" Hale said. "Her name was Nadia. I kind of thought she was hot in that cold-and-detached kind of way."

Trey looked at his friend in surprise.

"How is that possible?" Connor demanded. "If you're right and Nadia is the vita that attacked you in the park, wouldn't you have recognized her scent?"

Trey shrugged, realizing how little Davina had really given them concerning the creature they were facing. "All I can think is that she has a completely different scent when she's in her vita form."

"What do we do now?" Trevor asked.

"The only thing we can do," Trey said. "We confront Nadia and see what the hell happens."

CHAPTER 17

SAMANTHA STRUGGLED, SWIMMING THROUGH WATER SO THICK and dark it felt like molasses, straining to reach the surface before choking to death. But every time she seemed close to reaching the light, something would wrap itself around her body and drag her back down into the darkness again.

A little voice in the back of her mind whispered that this was just a bad dream, that if she relaxed and stopped fighting, she'd wake up fine and happy in the morning. But there was another part, one of pure instinct, that screamed out in warning, telling her that if she gave up now, she might never see the light of day again. So she fought with everything she had, clawing her way back to the light.

She jerked upright with a gasp, her heading pounding so hard that the edges of her vision began to gray out again. Having no desire to pass out, she kept her eyes closed and tried to breathe through the moment. Remaining calm became a bit difficult when she started remembering the string of events that had brought her here—wherever the hell *here* was.

It had been bad enough discovering Hugh was involved in the Butcher case. But finding out Louis had something to do with all of this crap as well before being held down and chloroformed? It was more than she could wrap her head around at the moment.

It was the sound of movement and a slamming door from somewhere above that pulled Samantha out of her slow-motion tailspin, bringing her back to the reality that she didn't have a clue where she was, who else might be in here, or what they planned to do with her.

She slowly opened her eyes, expecting her headache to worsen the second she did. But wherever she was being held was poorly lit, which helped calm the throbbing at her temples a bit. Black metal grating was the first thing she could make out when her eyes cleared, and all it took was a quick glance left and right to confirm she was in some kind of cell. Or a cage. She forced herself to focus on the details around her, rather than give in to the panic attack threatening to creep up and overwhelm her.

The cage was no more than six-foot square but had a ceiling that was high enough that at least it didn't feel too claustrophobic. There was a door in the grating directly ahead of her, closed with some kind of hasp and lock on the outside that she couldn't make out from where she sat on the rough concrete floor. Windowless stone walls behind and to her left made her think she was in a basement, which suggested this was an industrial building, since residential basements definitely weren't common in this part of Texas. But the heavy wood beams that crisscrossed the ceiling, with the antique-looking planks above that, suggested something not quite so industrial. Maybe a do-it-yourself basement? Constructed by her psycho boss as a place to lock up his kidnapping victims?

Deciding it didn't matter where she was, Samantha edged closer to the door, reaching out to give it a soft nudge, just to see what happened. It rattled a little in its frame but didn't give much. Taking a deep breath, she laced her fingers in the grating and use it to help her stand. Her knees shook a little, not sure they liked the idea of being vertical right then. She stood there holding on, breathing slowly, and waiting for the weakness to pass.

When she could finally managed to move, Samantha leaned forward and peeked through the openings in the grating, trying to see what was keeping the door locked. It took a bit of work, twisting her head this way and that, mashing her face right into the grating and pressing hard. But in the end, she got the idea that the only thing actually keeping her in was a bolt dropped through the locking mechanism of the latch. Not that knowing that helped any.

There was no way she'd ever be able to get her fingers far enough through the openings of the grating to reach the bolt. It might as well have been on the other side of the planet.

Turning her attention to where she might be, Samantha peered through the grating at the rest of the room, trying to see what was beyond her cage. There was a lot more stone and heavy wooden support columns. After catching a glimpse of large glass jars with human parts floating in them along with the stainless steel table and the trays of surgical equipment, her first impressions was that Louis had created his own twisted version of an autopsy lab down here. But then she saw the glass cylinders of thick neon-green liquid mounted to the wall, right next to a rack full of electrical gear. That's when she realized there was definitely something else going on.

The rack held dozens of exposed coils of copper wire, some running upward to fragile-looking ceramic electrodes, while others ran into the liquid-filled cylinders. Heavy black cables snaked all over the place, connecting everything together, ultimately, in a series of junction boxes along the far side of the steel table. What the bizarre arrangement was supposed to do was beyond her. It looked like nothing she'd ever seen in a hospital or ME's office.

The area directly opposite her cage was draped in shadows so heavy she had a hard time making out the large rectangular shape draped in dark plastic sheeting. But when she saw the half-dressed man standing to the left of the big box and caught sight of large glassy eyes staring at her, she jumped back so fast she almost fell on her butt.

It took a few second to realize the man wasn't really standing. Instead he was reclined back against a metal bed frame attached to the wall, held in place by massive steel bands across his chest, waist, forearms, and lower legs. Another bracket of lighter metal, covered with more of those heavy-duty cables she'd seen before, was strapped around his head, holding it in place. His whole body was completely motionless, so still she might have thought him dead if not for the slight rise and fall of his massive chest. It was beyond creepy.

That's when Sam figured out the man wasn't staring at her. Yes, his eyes were open, but they were glazed over and distant, like he was unconscious. That shouldn't have been possible. All she could think was that it had something to do with that thing around his head.

Moving closer to the door of her cage again, she gazed at the huge man. He was the guy she and Trey had assumed to be the Butcher. He was the one witnesses had seen near the homeless camp dumping those body parts. And he was the one who'd nearly caved in Trey's chest. But if this man was the Butcher and strong enough to take on someone's Trey's size, how had he ended up strapped to a table like this, nearly dead to the world by all appearances?

Deep, violent scars covered his chest and stomach, wrists, and upper arms, and circled his neck. If the monster of a man hadn't been wearing pants, something told her that she'd see more scars along his legs. What the hell had happened to this man to leave him scarred this badly?

Samantha ran her gaze down the man's arms to his huge hands, wondering for a moment if those were the ones that had held the chloroform cloth over her face. She dismissed that idea immediately. The hand that had covered her face had been rather small, almost dainty. Definitely not as big as this guy's. Had it been Hugh? But that didn't seem right, either, leaving her to wonder if there was yet another person involved in this nightmare with them.

She stared at the man's face, trying to remember where she'd seen him before, because there was no doubting he was familiar. The fading yellow bruising, likely from the fight he had with Trey, made her unsure, and for a moment she thought maybe she was wrong. Then it hit her.

"Kyson?" she shouted, her head spinning as she leaned into the door of her cage, putting her mouth right up to one of the openings in the grating. "Kyson, wake up!"

"I wouldn't shout like that," a soft voice said from out of the darkness to her right. "Rogi will come down here and you don't want that. He's not right in the head."

Samantha spun around in the direction of the woman's voice, peering into the heavy shadows that filled the cell beside hers. All she could make out was a ratty-looking mattress shoved into the far corner and a pile of rags sitting on top of it.

"Who's there?" she demanded, keeping her voice down this time, not wanting to attract Rogi's attention…whoever the hell that was. "Who are you?"

There was nothing but silence for a few moments, and then the pile of what she'd thought were rags moved, revealing a woman who couldn't have been much over five feet tall. As she moved closer, Samantha could see that her long, blond hair was unkempt and dirty, her face pale and exhausted looking.

Samantha gasped as she realized she'd seen the woman before. She'd been in the same photo with Kyson.

"Shaylee?" Samantha murmured, leaning against the grating separating her cell from the one beside it, hooking her fingers through the openings. "How did you get here?"

The woman gazed at her with eyes that seemed so much older than the rest of her. "Do I know you?"

Samantha shook her head. "We've never met, but I know Trey—Kyson's friend. I saw a picture of you and Kyson together."

"Trey knows where we are? He's coming to help us?"

The hope that lit up the young woman's face was heart wrenching to see because Samantha already knew her next words would crush that hope completely.

"No, Trey doesn't know we're here." She gave Shaylee a small smile. "I doubt he even knows I'm missing yet. On top of that, he thinks Kyson is dead. He won't be able to help us, but maybe Kyson can? If we can wake him up."

Just as she'd predicted, the glimmer of hope disappeared from the woman's eyes like it had never been there at all.

"Ky can't help us," Shaylee said sadly. "When he came back from taking out the body parts the other night, he was all slashed up. It was so bad I could see his rib bones showing through. The doctor shut him down to heal him. Ky can hear us talking right now, but he can't do anything to help us. He can't snap out of the trance he's in on his own. Only the doctor can wake him up."

Samantha knew she probably looked like an idiot standing there with her mouth hanging open, but there was so much to unpack after what Shaylee had just said. She needed a moment to process everything. Figuring out what to ask first was even more difficult.

"Shaylee, did Kyson kill himself?" she finally asked. Samantha knew how insane her next question was going to sound, but she needed to know the answer "Is that true, or did the doctor you mentioned make it look that way?"

Tears shone in Shaylee's blue eyes. "It's true. I saw his body right after the guy who lives in the room next to his found him. Ky was dead." She swallowed hard. "But then a week ago, I saw him getting into a truck near the Trinity River Audubon Center and… well, I completely lost it. I chased after him and they caught me and brought me here."

"They?" Samantha pressed, forcing down the curiosity that also wanted to know what the hell the Shaylee had been doing in the woods near Trinity River. She needed to focus on the important details first. Everything else could wait. "Who caught you?"

"Rogi…and Ky." Shaylee took a deep breath, letting it out with a shudder. "Ky didn't want to do it, but the doctor did something to him that makes it hard for him to do anything but what he's told. It didn't help that Rogi threatened to shoot me if Ky didn't grab me. He had no choice."

Samantha almost groaned out loud in frustration. What Shaylee was saying about Kyson killing himself couldn't be true. Somehow, Louis must have made it appear that way. Dead people didn't come back to life. But it seemed that every question she had generated four more. Once again, she had to force herself to focus on the important stuff first.

"Okay, so they brought you here," Samantha said. "Which prompts the question: Where are we?"

Shaylee shook her head. "I don't know for sure. I only got a quick look around before Rogi dragged me down here. The place is big and fancy, though. All stone. Like a castle."

Castle.

That pretty much confirmed they were in Louis's home and that it actually had a basement. It also confirmed Louis was the doctor Shaylee mentioned, not that she'd doubted that part. But was still being at Louis's home a good thing? If Trey found out she was missing and that she'd come to see her boss earlier, would he look for her here?

"I don't think I've ever heard the doctor's name, but he's older, with a lot of gray in his hair," Shaylee said, moving a little closer to the grating and lowering her voice like she was worried someone was eavesdropping. "Other than that, all I can really say about him is that he's effing insane. Even Rogi is terrified of him. I wasn't here when they brought Ky back to life, but I've seen what they do when they replace the parts of his body that are dying. The doctor straps Ky to that damn table, does the surgery, pumps him full of that green junk, and then electrocutes him. He's done it to him multiple times since I've been here, anytime he has to fix something or puts him under so he can study him. It's horrible."

The rational, scientific part of Samantha's mind wanted to rebel at all of this, to rant and rave that it was all impossible. But the truth was standing across the room strapped to an inclined rack, covered in scars that couldn't be ignored. Kyson *had* killed himself.

The man she and Trey had talked to at that motel had confirmed that and so had Shaylee. Yet he was obviously alive now. If being strapped to a table and used as a test subject could be called alive. Being *shut down* to heal the injuries he'd obviously gotten in his fight with Trey, to replace parts that were dying, should have been beyond the realm of possibility. But she supposed it paled in comparison to the fact that Louis had apparently raised Kyson from the dead to begin with.

"Shaylee, do you know why they've kept you here?" Samantha asked carefully.

She didn't want to be blunt about it, but while she understood that grabbing Shaylee and bringing her back here was simply about hiding their secret, she didn't understand why the woman was still alive. After everything she'd heard about Louis, it didn't seem like he was doing it out of the goodness of his heart. If the man even had a heart any longer.

"Ky has started to resist the doctor's orders. Rogi's, too." Shaylee sighed dejectedly. "But now that I'm here, all they have to do is threaten me and he'll do anything they want. He doesn't want them to hurt me."

The thought of the poor woman being used as leverage like that was almost enough to bring tears to Samantha's eyes. "But why is the doctor doing all of this? It seems like a lot of effort to go to just to have a chance to play God."

Shaylee started to answer, but then snapped her mouth shut at the sound of a door slamming nearby, immediately followed by the thud of heavy footsteps.

Samantha watched as a man slowly shambled toward them in the dimly lit basement, stopping halfway between the door of her cage and Shaylee's. He was short but stocky with wide shoulders that made his head look too small for his body. His face was brutish with thick, dark brows and deep-set, beady eyes.

The man stared at Shaylee for a long time. The way his dark

gaze wandered up and down the woman's body sent a shiver of dread down Samantha's spine. She was just wondering if she should say something when he suddenly darted forward, his large hand coming up to slam against the metal grating of Samantha's cage, making a loud noise and shaking the metal walls. She jumped, resisting the urge to take a step back.

"The doctor said he doesn't want the two of you talking," the man said gruffly, glaring at Sam. "So unless you want me to open this cage door and give you a reason to make noise, you'll be quiet."

His gaze ran down her body, taking in her silk blouse and dark slacks, leaving her skin feeling like it had been coated with dirty oil. She couldn't help stepping back a little then, a move that drew a short bark of laughter from the creep.

He continued to leer at her for another moment before finally turning and walking over to jab Kyson in the chest with his stubby finger, like he was checking to see if the big man was awake.

Shaylee threw herself at the door of her cage. "Stay away from him!"

The man turned to pin her with a look. "Or what?"

When Shaylee didn't answer, he laughed and left the way he'd come. A few seconds later, Samantha heard a door slam, then the sound of slowly fading footsteps.

"That's Rogi," Shaylee whispered softly from her side of the grating. "He carries the bodies, cuts the hands and heads off when the doctor doesn't want to do it, and cleans up the blood. He doesn't mess with me too much because the doctor needs me around to control Ky, but if I were you, I wouldn't make Rogi mad. He's not right in the head."

That thought sent another shiver down her spine, and she prayed Trey figured out what happened to her and where she was...sooner rather than later.

CHAPTER 18

"Still no answer?" Connor asked from beside Trey as he ended yet another call to Samantha without attempting to leave a message. He'd left her a dozen already, each more urgent than the last. She simply wasn't answering.

"No," he murmured before getting out of his truck and heading across the parking lot to her apartment complex, forcing himself not to run even as the muscles of his legs twitched and spasmed with the desire to put on more speed. It was almost one o'clock in the morning. If she wasn't home, he had no idea where she was.

The original plan had been for him and Connor to go to Nadia's place with Hale and Trevor and confront her. Trey knew it was an overly simplistic plan, bordering on naive and stupid. But until they knew for sure the woman was actually a life-sucking vampire and found a way to tie her more directly to the deaths of those three men, there wasn't much more they could do.

After trying over and over to reach Samantha most of the night without success, his pack mates had insisted they change the plan. While he and Connor were here checking on Samantha, Trevor and Hale were on their way to Nadia's place.

"Samantha's okay, Trey," Connor said as they took the stairs to Samantha's apartment. "She probably just put her phone on do not disturb so she could get some sleep. She's been running herself ragged on the Butcher case."

Trey wanted to believe his friend, and he appreciated what Connor was trying to do, but he knew for a fact that Samantha would never shut her phone off for the night in the middle of an investigation, and not when they'd made plans to get together this evening.

When they got to her apartment, Trey knocked hard enough to wake Samantha up, but not rouse every neighbor along this stretch of hallway. Before the sound faded, he knew it was a waste of time. There were a lot of heartbeats thumping gently within the limits of his hearing, but none of them were coming from her apartment.

At the sound of a door opening behind them, he turned to see Crystal standing there in a pair of pajamas with a bad case of bedhead.

"She hasn't come home yet." Crystal pushed her dark hair behind her ear, regarding them intently. "And since the two of you are here, I'm starting to think that means I should be worried."

"Samantha and I were supposed to meet up tonight, but then she sent me a text saying she had something important to talk to me about," Trey said. "She hasn't replied to my calls or texts."

"Hang on. I've got a key to her place," Crystal said, disappearing into her apartment.

A moment later, she hurried across the hallway to where they stood. Unlocking the door, she opened it and immediately charged in, leaving him and Connor to follow. Samantha's apartment was dark, and Crystal flicked the light switch before making a beeline for the bedrooms. Trey could have told her Samantha wasn't in the either of them.

"She must still be at the institute," Crystal said, coming out of the guest bedroom and carefully closing the door behind her. "She can sometimes get tunnel vision when she's buried in evidence."

Connor looked dubious. "If that's all it is, why wouldn't she answer her phone?"

Crystal was already heading back across the hall to her apartment. "She frequently leaves her phone in her office when she's in the lab, so she won't be disturbed. Or the battery might have died." She glanced at them over her shoulder. "Give me a minute to get dressed and we'll go find out one way or the other."

"You don't need to come with us," Trey said to her, catching the door to her place before it closed, watching as she raced off through another door into what he assumed was her bedroom. "Connor and I can head over and check. If her car is in the parking lot, we'll know she's there."

Crystal didn't answer. Thirty seconds later, she came running out of the bedroom dressed in jeans and a T-shirt, jumping in place as she pulled on a pair of tennis shoes.

"And what would you do then?" she asked, grabbing up her purse from the counter in the kitchen. "Bang on all the windows until she lets you in or kick in the door?"

Not really having an argument to that logic, Trey exchanged looks with Connor, then they both followed her down the hall.

Crystal led the way to the institute in her bright green Kia. They were halfway there when Trey's phone rang. He answered immediately with the pickup's hands-free system, praying it was Samantha calling him.

It wasn't.

"Nadia wasn't home," Trevor said without preamble. "A quick check of her place indicates she hasn't been there for a few days at least. But we did pick up that sweet scent you described. She's definitely the vita."

At least they were right about that much.

"We haven't found Samantha yet," Trey said. "We stopped by her place and are on our way to the institute with her friend, Crystal."

"Okay, let us know when you find her," Trevor said "We've already contacted STAT about Nadia. They're going to try to find her. In the meantime, Hale and I are heading back downtown. We figured Nadia might be looking for someone to replace the guy you stopped her from killing this past weekend."

Samantha's car was nowhere to be seen when they reached the institute, but he and Connor still went inside with Crystal anyway, hoping they'd find something that would tell them where she'd gone.

From how weak Samantha's scent was in her office, Trey could tell that it had been a few hours since his soul mate had been there. He watched curiously as Crystal logged on to Samantha's computer, flipping through what he guessed were autopsy records, if the photos of body parts were any indication.

"Samantha and I have each other's passwords, so we can proofread each other's reports," Crystal said without looking up. "This is the institute's forensic database. Everything entered into the files gets a time stamp put on it for evidence-tracking purposes. It will tell us exactly what Samantha was doing right up until the moment she left work. I'm hoping this gives us an idea of what she might have found and tell us where she might have gone."

He and Connor stood there, leaning over Crystal's shoulder, trying to make sense of the endless string of photographs and narrative pages. They all sort of blurred together for Trey, but something must have caught her attention because she kept going back and forth over the last three or four pictures of a tattooed arm and the forms that accompanied them that were mainly description.

"Did you find something?" he prompted as Crystal continued to look at the pictures.

"I don't know if I found anything, but I think Samantha did," Crystal murmured, still flipping through the gruesome shots of the amputated arm. "You might have noticed that the narrative pages after each of the photos were stuffed with descriptive details—weights, measurements, skin texture, bruising, etc. That's Samantha for you—she's a compulsive notetaker. But when you get to these last four photos, all photos of this arm with the tattoo, there are hardly any notes at all."

"Maybe she didn't notice anything worth writing about," Connor suggested.

Crystal shook her head. "That isn't Samantha's style. If there was nothing to note, she'd actually write *nothing to note*. I'm thinking she saw something in these last few pictures that made her stop what she was doing and log out of the system."

Trey was tempted to ask what Sam might have seen, but it was obvious it was something they were all missing. "So that's it? She took these pictures and then left right after that?"

Crystal clicked around Samantha's computer for a few seconds before shaking her head. "Actually, after logging off the computer in her lab, she came back here and logged into her desk PC to look through Tuesday's staff meeting files. She must have left right afterward."

That's why she'd called and left him a message. She'd seen something on the computer—or in the lab. But what?

They went back to the lab to look around, hoping there would be a clue there that'd tell them something important. While he and Connor looked around, Crystal called Louis to ask if he knew what Samantha had found and where she'd gone after leaving the institute.

Across the room, Trey could hear the panic in the man's voice when he heard Samantha was missing and possibly in danger. Crystal told her boss everything they'd discovered since getting to the institute, which admittedly wasn't very much.

While Trey hadn't expected the older man to know anything, his gut tightened when the chief medical examiner said he hadn't heard from Samantha.

"Louis is coming in to help me search the lab reports and see if we can find anything," Crystal said after she hung up.

That was good. They'd take any help they could get.

The search of Samantha's lab didn't turn up anything useful, and Trey was trying to figure out what to do next when Connor mentioned they'd passed Nadia's lab earlier. "Do you think we should take a look around in there?"

Trey seriously doubted they'd find anything that would connect Nadia to her vita lamia identity or where she might be hiding, but he supposed there was no harm in searching the place.

Crystal frowned. "What would be in Nadia's lab?"

Trey exchanged looks with Connor before turning his attention back to Crystal. "It's complicated. That said, could you unlock the door?"

Crystal hesitated for a moment, but then nodded. Thankfully, one key unlocked all the labs in this part of the building.

When they walked into Nadia's lab, Trey didn't get even a hint of the sweet and dusty scent he'd come to associate with the vita. Then again, there wasn't much of any scent, unless he counted blood and corpses. It was like Nadia didn't have much of a smell in her human form, which was strange as hell. For a moment, he wondered why he hadn't noticed that distinct lack of scent when he'd first met her.

Trey was still trying to figure that out when he smelled something all too familiar. The odor was like a chemical disinfectant, but with a flowery noted blended in. He froze for a moment before following his nose straight toward the sink on the far side of the room.

"You got something?" Connor asked.

Trey was too focused on the plastic pump bottle filled with pink foamy soap on the counter to answer. Picking it up, he gave it a big sniff and almost gagged. It was like someone had dumped a bottle of perfume into a container of bleach. This was definitely it.

He turned and held up the bottle, giving Crystal a questioning look. "What is this stuff?"

"It's a disinfecting body wash. It's normally used for cleaning patients prior to surgery, but Nadia uses it to wash her hands. She buys it directly from a vendor in France or someplace fancy like that. It's ungodly expensive, but she claims it's the only thing that gets the stench of dead bodies off her skin. She makes a big deal out of having a sensitive nose."

Trey stood there wondering how it was possible he hadn't smelled this scent on the woman in their previous encounters. It was damn strong. Again, all he could think was that it had something to do with her vita half. Maybe shifting back and forth from human to vita diminished her scent? That would certainly explain why Nadia barely had a scent as a human.

"What's the big deal about the body wash?" Crystal asked, looking back and forth from him to Connor.

Trey exchanged another glance with Connor before answering. "The scent has shown up on a couple of the body parts related to the Butcher case and at least one of the crime scenes."

Crystal gaped in disbelief.

Trey tensed, waiting for the avalanche of questions to start.

"I really want to ask how the hell you know something like that, but instead, I think I'm just going to file it under that *it's complicated* category you mentioned earlier and leave it at that," she said. "I'm going to wait for Louis in Samantha's lab. I'll call you if we find anything."

Connor waited for Crystal to leave before looking at him. "Do you really think Nadia is working with the Butcher?"

Trey ran that possibility through his mind. He'd been sure that the second person he'd seen in the woods the other night was a man. Maybe he'd been wrong. "I don't know. But what really has me scared right now is that if we figured out Nadia is involved with the Butcher, maybe Samantha did, too. What if that's what she wanted to tell me, and when I didn't answer, she went to confront Nadia herself?"

"Samantha wouldn't do anything that crazy," Connor said.

Trey could tell from the doubt in his pack mate's eyes that Connor wasn't as sure about that as he sounded. The truth was, they had no idea what was going on. Or even what to do next. All Trey knew for sure was that Samantha was out there somewhere completely on her own.

CHAPTER 19

IT WAS THE SOUND OF HUMMING AND SOFT FOOTSTEPS ON rough concrete that pulled Samantha out of her restless sleep. She forced herself to stay calm and not jump up like she had the first time. Instead, she opened her eyes slowly and tried to sneak a look around the basement without giving away the fact that she was awake.

The basement was lit up much brighter than it previously had been. Looking up, she saw lines of overhead fluorescents attached to the ceiling, painting the entire place in a harsh industrial glow. It made her feel like she was back in her autopsy lab at the institute.

Catching sight of a pair of leather dress shoes through the openings in the grating of her cage, she knew without lifting her gaze any higher that it was Louis. She'd recognize those waterproof wingtip oxfords of his anywhere. The man had been wearing them every day since she'd met him.

When Samantha realized Louis was standing in front of the rack Kyson was strapped to, she gave up all pretense of being asleep, pushing herself up on one hip so she could see better. A quick glance to the right showed Shaylee lying on her mattress in the corner of her cell, apparently still sleeping.

Louis pushed a large syringe of neon green goo—the same kind in the glass cylinder on the wall—into a heart catheter. The stuff must have been unusually thick because Louis's knuckles were turning white from the force he was applying to the plunger. As unsettling as it was to see him put green goo into the big man, it was even more disconcerting to see Kyson's open eyes stay flat and inexpressive, even though Shaylee had said he was aware of everything happening to him when he was like this.

"What are you doing to him?" Samantha demanded.

From the corner of her eye, she saw Shaylee jump a little, pushing herself up from her mattress. The woman looked around, terrified, and Samantha wondered if she'd just made their situation worse than it already was. As hard as it was to believe that could even be possible.

"I'm making him better," Louis replied, the words spoken so casually that she'd think he'd simply said it might rain today.

"What is that stuff doing to him?" Samantha pressed.

Getting up, she walked across the cage and leaned against the door. She pushed on the lock, even though she knew it wouldn't budge. She glanced Shaylee's way and saw the woman moving closer as well, her agonized expression making Samantha think she'd seen this kind of thing before.

Louis didn't answer at first, waiting until he had finished injecting the rest of the goo into the catheter and then moving over to scan a bank of monitors Samantha couldn't quite see. Only then did he turn and approach her cage, his face taking on that patient mentoring expression she'd become so used to over the past few years.

"Around three o'clock Wednesday morning, my test subject had a run-in with your boyfriend in the Cedar Ridge Preserve," Louis said, regarding her calmly. "You may not be aware of this, Samantha, but your boyfriend can be quite vicious when he wants to be. Even though my subject is an incredibly powerful man, I watched Officer Duncan literally tear him to shreds. From a scientific point of view, I must admit it was quite impressive."

Louis was about to say something else, but Samantha interrupted him, unable to stop herself. "You were there that night in the forest? You were dumping remains?"

Her boss scowled, though whether his displeasure was because she'd interrupted him or because she'd reminded him that he'd been out in the woods disposing of human body parts was difficult to say.

"Admittedly, it's a task Rogi normally handles," he said, lip curling like he was admitting to cleaning his own toilets instead of letting the person he'd hired to do it do it. "But after he got lazy the last time I sent him out and decided to dump the remains a mere hundred feet from a heavily populated homeless camp, I decided to step in and deal with the task myself. I'm not a fan of walking in the woods in the middle of the night, but then again, if I hadn't been there, I would never have seen the performance Officer Duncan put on. Again, it was unlike anything I've ever seen. Inhuman, one might say. Or supernatural at the very least."

After hearing her boss describe the way Trey had torn Kyson to shreds, it was difficult not falling for the bait and asking what Louis had seen. But no matter how much Samantha might have wanted to learn more about Trey and what the hell was going on with him, she knew now wasn't the right time. And Louis definitely wasn't the right person to be getting answers from.

"You can stop trying to distract me. It won't work," Samantha said softly, determined to put the spotlight right where it needed to be. "Trey had nothing to do with the bodies Hugh has been stealing for you from the ME's office. That's completely on you. Just like the immoral experiments you've been conducting."

She expected some kind of violent response, an impassioned defense of his actions. Instead, Louis simply turned his attention back to Kyson, humming as he examined the well-healed scars that crisscrossed the poor man's chest and stomach.

"Just to be clear," Louis said a little while later, apparently satisfied with whatever he found in his inspection of Kyson's injuries and glancing over his shoulder at her. "Hugh had nothing to do with acquiring those dead bodies for me. He didn't have anything to do with the living donors I've been forced to turn to lately, either." Her boss shrugged. "That said, Hugh will ultimately take the fall for everything when the time comes. Once I'm done with my work, the task force will receive an anonymous call and the police will have their *Butcher*. All of the necessary evidence, some of which you found, has already been put into place."

As stunned as she was to learn that Hugh was completely innocent in all of this, it was the part about living donors that caught and held Samantha's attention. But before she could say anything, Louis kept going, as if talking to himself.

"And as far as my experiments go, I really don't think you can call them immoral," he continued. "Technically, my test subject was dead when I started. And in accordance with Dallas County policy, unclaimed bodies left at the institute will be turned over to the medical and scientific communities for the betterment of mankind. I think discovering a process to resurrect the dead would certainly be considered the betterment of mankind, don't you?"

Samantha had already known where Louis was going with this. Everything Shaylee had told her earlier made his confession almost anticlimactic. Still, hearing Louis say the words and knowing that the man's moral compass was obviously broken beyond all recognition was hard to wrap her head around.

"I'd call you insane, but you're so far past that point that the word doesn't even begin to cover it," she said. "What gives you the right to play God like this?"

"God gave me the right!" Louis shouted as he spun around, his face twisted in a grimace that made him seem almost inhuman. Just like the things he'd been doing to Kyson. "When he stole my son from me, he gave me the right to do anything I deemed necessary."

Samantha stared at him through the grating. Her boss was even further gone than she'd imagined. But before she could point that out, Louis moved over to the big rectangular shape to Kyson's left, ripping off the fabric tarp that had been covering it with the flourish of a magician.

"Everything I've done is for my son," he said in a low voice as he leaned over the glass tank he'd exposed, his hands resting on the top, eyes locking on the body inside.

Even through the thick reddish fluid that filled the tank, Samantha was able to recognize the young man floating there. She'd seen a painting of him only hours before posed with his father and mother. Of course, the eighteen-year-old in the tank looked far from the smiling boy now. The vicious unhealed scars covering almost every inch of his body implied impossible pain and suffering.

"Oh, Louis," she whispered. "What have you done?"

Sagging against the grating of her cell, Samantha gazed at the hundreds of tubes and wires running into the boy's body. She knew without having to ask that the tank and liquid in it were somehow meant to keep the body from decaying. It was like he was in some kind of bizarre, suspended animation.

"What have I done?" Louis repeated, momentarily lifting his eyes to gaze at her before turning his attention back to his son. "I have found a way to create life where there was only death. And now that I have the answer to the systemic rejection issue that has been holding me in check, there's nothing to stop me from getting my son back."

Samantha didn't say anything. What the hell could she say? This was completely insane and yet it was happening all the same.

"I expected some problem with rejection of the donor parts, but I'll admit, it's been worse than I anticipated," Louis said in a conversational tone as he moved back over to Kyson and began to check the scars around the man's wrists. "I've had to replace the subject's hands, hearts, and lungs multiple times since I started this experiment weeks ago. It shouldn't be happening, considering the steps I took to completely remove and replace his existing immune system before I even resurrected him."

Replaced his existing immune system?

Samantha guessed that explained how Kyson was able to survive having blood in his body that was literally a stew of every type and rhesus factor there was. She was wondering how something like that was possible when noise from Shaylee's cell distracted her.

"I already told you why it's happening," Shaylee said, her voice soft. "The man I love doesn't want to live like this. Ky is making his body reject the parts you keep forcing on him, and he'll keep doing it until you stop and let him go."

Shaylee's words were so desolate that tears welled in Samantha's eyes. Louis, on the other hand, wasn't nearly as moved by them.

"And as I've already told you many times, the man strapped to the table over there isn't the Kyson you knew anymore. The voltage I dumped into him as part of the resurrection process wiped the majority of his mind. Even if he did know who he'd been before, he couldn't will his body to reject the new parts. Science doesn't work that way."

"Then why is it happening?" Samantha questioned even though she was having a hard time thinking about anything other than what Louis had said about dumping voltage into Kyson and wiping the majority of his mind. It called to mind visions of Mary Shelley's Dr. Frankenstein and the experiments he'd conducted on his monster. The similarities between that fiction story and this reality were impossible to ignore.

"Perhaps he is a poor choice of test subject," Louis said as Shaylee made a sound of disgust and walked toward the back of her cage, dropping back down onto her ratty mattress. "I selected him based on his military background and the types of injuries he'd sustained," he added, motioning at Kyson but refusing to address him by name—or as though he was anything remotely resembling a human being. "I had assumed that his trauma, which was so similar to my son's, would make him a perfect test subject. That if I could resolve his extreme physical issues, then my son's would be a cake walk. I even thought that having a subject who was already dealing with severe PTSD would help when it came time to deal with the same issues if they developed in my son. I never considered that he simply might be too broken to ever be a viable candidate."

That earned Louis another snort of disgust and disdain from Shaylee, which he ignored.

"At one point, I even considered terminating the subject and simply starting fresh with another one," Louis said, seeming to take great pleasure in the gasp that Shaylee let out at that. "The only thing that stopped me was my pride, I guess. I didn't want to admit I'd made a mistake in the first place. But now that I've stumbled over the solution to the entire problem, none of that matters anymore."

This was the second time Louis stated he'd found the answer to his problem. And by problem, she assumed he meant Kyson's continued rejection of the various parts Louis had forced on him.

"What solution did you happen to stumble over?" she asked.

"Your boyfriend, of course." Louis turned to give her a smile. "I'm sure you noticed how badly injured he was after fighting with my creation in the Cedar Ridge Preserve. I mean, practically every rib on his right side had been broken. Yet a mere few hours later, he walked into the institute with barely a bruise to show for it. You're an intelligent, observant woman. I'm sure you've noticed Officer Duncan possesses abnormally fast healing abilities. As well as quite a few other talents that suggest he's far more than he appears. I'm not sure exactly what he is, though I have no doubt I'll figure it out before I'm done."

Fear raced down her spine at Louis's words and the maniacal, almost gleeful, expression on his face. "What do you mean, before you're done?"

Before Louis could reply, the thumping of heavy footsteps interrupted him. She peered to the side to see Rogi coming into view. His eyes locked on Kyson for a moment before he turned to the doctor.

"Ah, Rogi. Perfect timing," Louis said. "I was just about to wake up the test subject so you can take him with you when you go do that thing I asked you to do."

Rogi didn't look thrilled at the prospect of whatever this task might be, but he nodded nonetheless, moving over to assist Louis as he began to route a series of black cables from the rack of electrical equipment on the far side of the room to the inclined table Kyson was strapped to.

"What are you doing to him?" Samantha yelled, banging on the metal grating of her cell. Beside her, Shaylee was doing the same to the door of her cage. Both Louis and Rogi ignored them. "What does Trey have to do with any of this?"

After messing with more of the black cables, connecting a few them to the shackles at Kyson's wrists and the one attached to his head, Louis finally turned and regarded her calmly. "As I was saying, your boyfriend seems to possess some kind of supernatural healing ability. I believe those abilities, properly harvested and refined, will stop the rejection issues I've been dealing with. Rogi and this large mountain of muscle will go get Officer Duncan and bring him back here."

"Ky will never help you hurt his best friend," Shaylee yelled, banging on the door of her cell again. "Trey is the only friend he's ever had."

Louis seemed shocked at the knowledge that Trey and Kyson knew each other but then passed it off with a shrug. "It's not like I'm going to give him a choice."

Before either Samantha or Shaylee could respond, Louis moved over to the rack of electrical gear and started flipping switches. The hum of electricity immediately filled the air, quickly followed by an odor that made her think of ionized air after a storm.

Kyson's eyes were still glassy and distant, but Samantha swore she could see the panic in them anyway. Shaylee began to cry as Louis continued flipping more switches, actually laughing a little as he put his hand on a big black lever near the side of the rack.

"For all the aggravation this subject has caused me, I have to give him one thing," Louis said, what could only be called an evil grin crossing his face as he looked over at Samantha. "He can handle a lot of pain."

As he flipped the big lever downward, the hairs on Samantha's arms were lifting and bolts of lightning filled the air around Kyson's body even as his back arched and a shout of absolutely terrifying pain was ripped from him.

It went on and on, long after the point when Samantha had slapped her hands over her ears in an attempt to keep out the tortured sounds. But even with the noises deadened somewhat, she could see Kyson writhing in pain as the man she used to respect watched him flail with a sick glint in his eyes.

When Louis finally pulled the heavy lever back up, the air had taken on a burnt smell, and Samantha had to force herself not to throw up. To her right, Shaylee was on her knees, sobbing at the display of horrible cruelty on the man she loved.

Samantha was stunned when Kyson stepped away from the table. His legs seemed surprisingly steady, considering he'd just been electrocuted. She found herself staring into his eyes, which were achingly *aware* now. Samantha couldn't look away, even as Louis informed Kyson that he would be going with Rogi to get his friend, Trey, and bring him back there.

"You *do* remember him, don't you?" Louis asked, moving closer to Kyson and gazing up into his eyes curiously. "Yes, I can see it. Somewhere in that burnt-out mind of yours, you still have a little piece of Officer Trey Duncan wedged in there. I suppose that's actually a good thing. It will help make sure you grab the right guy."

Kyson stared down at Louis for a long time, his face twitching, his shoulders tense. "Don't...want to," he finally said, each word sounded out slowly and carefully.

Louis seemed surprised that Kyson had spoken. But then his expression twisted, darkening with anger. He threw a glance at Rogi, who moved over to Shaylee's cage, one hand coming to rest on the latch. "Do you think I give a shit what you want? You'll do what I say, or I'll have Rogi go into that cage and hurt your pretty little girlfriend. Is that what you want?"

Samantha felt rage boil up inside her. If she could have somehow ripped the door of her cage off and killed Louis, she would have. But as it was, she wasn't getting through that door, and there wasn't a damn thing she could do to help Kyson...or Shaylee.

Kyson didn't say anything more. Instead, he slowly shook his head, then moved to follow Rogi toward the door at the far end of the basement. Just before they walked out, Louis caught their attention.

"Rogi, take some extra help with you," he said casually. "Something tells me that Officer Duncan is going to be rather difficult to bring down."

As Kyson and Rogi walked out, Samantha wanted to scream at them to stop, to leave Trey out of this, but she knew her words would be wasted. She only prayed Kyson and Rogi failed in the task Louis had given them, even if she was terrified of what that would mean for her and Shaylee.

CHAPTER 20

TREY STUMBLED TWICE AS HE SLOWLY WALKED UP THE LAST few steps in front of his apartment, nearly face-planting both times. His head was so fuzzy that doing math at this point was damn near impossible, but the best he could remember, he hadn't slept at all in the last forty-eight hours. And had maybe gotten four or five hours in the past three days. Smacking his face on the concrete before he could get to his place was a very real possibility.

The past six hours had been gut-wrenchingly brutal. While Connor had sat down with Crystal and Louis to go over Samantha's autopsy notes, trying to figure out what she'd learned right before leaving him that message, Trey had focused on finding Samantha and Nadia. With help from the rest of the Pack, STAT, and dozens of other DPD officers he knew well enough to call in a few favors, Trey had gone all out to find them.

He'd started with the traffic cameras around the institute, using them to track Samantha and Nadia after they'd each left work. Nadia had disappeared from camera view almost immediately, but Trey had been able to follow Samantha for almost fifteen miles until they'd lost her on Interstate 30 heading west toward Fort Worth. Since he had no idea where she might have been heading at that point, he'd tracked down her sister and talked to her, hoping Samantha might have told her something. But beyond freaking the poor woman out, he hadn't gotten anything useful from that conversation. Though it seemed pretty damn obvious Loralei was suspicious of him for some reason. If he wasn't so worried about Samantha, he would have been concerned that his soul mate had already spilled his pack's secrets to her sister. Right now, he simply didn't have time to think about it.

STAT had done their thing next, digging through the hours of tollbooth video from all over the Dallas/Fort Worth area, checking into Samantha's and Nadia's credit cards, even trying to ping the location of their cell phones. Nothing had worked. When Connor had called to tell him that they'd struck out with the autopsy records, Trey had been left with little choice but to drive around the city, hoping to get lucky.

By the time the sun had come up, he had been forced to accept that plan wasn't going to work. With no other avenues to explore, he'd finally headed back to his apartment before he fell asleep at the wheel. He prayed that a hot shower and a little food would clear his head enough to allow him to come up with another angle to approach this situation—because he was so scared for Samantha that he was about to lose his damn mind.

When he opened the door to his apartment, his nose was assaulted by multiple scents that had his body fighting to wake up. There was that overly sweet odor coming from inside even as the burnt electrical smell suddenly filled the hallway behind him.

Trey was reaching for his service-issued weapon when a ton of bricks slammed into his back, pinning his arms to his side and smashing him through the partially opened door of his apartment. His werewolf instincts responded faster than his sluggish human mind was in the mood for, claws and fangs extending, muscles shifting, to twist him around in midair so he landed on top of whoever had tackled him.

But the grunt of pain that exploded through the small apartment was all his. Shit. It felt like he'd landed on a frigging boulder. He knew without even being able to see him that he was dealing with the guy he'd fought with in the Cedar Ridge Preserve.

Trey moved to gain a little space, then slammed his head backward as hard as he could. He connected with something that crunched—the guy's nose most likely. But even though the sound told Trey he'd done some damage, the arms around his torso and arms didn't loosen a bit. If anything, they clamped down even harder. It was like this thing couldn't feel pain at all.

Movement to the side caught his eye. Trey jerked his head that way to see a short, stocky man who was all shoulders and arms swinging a baseball bat in his direction. He yanked aside just in time to keep the guy from smashing in his skull, the bat glancing off his temple and thudding hard into his shoulder. Stars exploded behind his eyes and Trey had to fight to keep his grip on consciousness as hard as he fought against the man holding him.

"He wants him alive you fool!" a female voice hissed as the arms around his chest loosened a little and the guy with the bat was suddenly jerked back out of Trey's sight and sent flying across the room. "He's no use if his head is bashed in."

"How are we supposed to get him out of here if we don't knock him out?" the man across the room muttered. "He's got frigging claws and fangs!"

There was a laugh and then Nadia Payne was in front of Trey, a vicious grin on her face. "Claws and fangs are overrated."

Before Trey had time to blink, she morphed from her human form to a bug-eyed vita lamia with a cackling laugh. From the grunt of shock that came out of the goon on the far side of the living room, the man with the baseball bat was clearly surprised to discover Nadia was a life-sucking vampire. He stopped wondering how much the stocky guy knew when the vita reached out her pale hands toward him. If she got her hands on him while he was trapped like this, he was done for.

He let his wolf instincts take over, shifting until he heard bones cracking as his whole body began to reshape itself. The noise must have startled the monstrously large man holding him because his grip loosened. Trey broke free with a savage growl, slashing his claws across the vita's face and shoving her away at the same time. He paused for half a second to make sure the guy with the bat was still standing on the far side of the living room, then he spun, reaching for his SIG, ready to put a bullet through the man who'd been holding him captive. But then he saw the guy's face and he froze.

"Kyson?"

Trey suddenly felt like he couldn't get enough air into his lungs as his eyes locked with the friend he thought was dead.

Trey was faintly aware of long, cold fingers wrapping around his neck from behind, but couldn't force himself to care—not until he felt his soul being ripped out through the icy contact. His inner wolf responded, snarling and telling him to twist around to defend himself. But before he could move, Kyson's huge hands came up and grabbed him again, holding him firm as the vita began to pull the life right out of him. Trey realized his groan of pain sounded a lot like that guy downtown had made right before Trey rescued him.

There was no one here to rescue Trey, though, and as every muscle in his body locked up in spasms of excruciating pain, there was no way in hell he was going to be able to rescue himself.

He felt like he was a battery being drained too fast. He went from exhausted to not caring about anything in the span of a few seconds. The last thing he saw before fading into darkness was Kyson gazing down at him with sad, sorrowful eyes, as if he didn't want to be part of this.

If that was true, then why was his best friend helping the vita lamia kill him?

———

Samantha leaned back against one of the stone walls of her cell, trying her hardest to tune out the constant drone of Louis's obnoxious voice. He was talking in the same tone she'd always identified as his mentoring voice, but now that she knew he was a certified whack-a-doodle, she decided she couldn't stand it. Of course, it didn't help that he'd spent the past two hours going on nonstop about how brilliant—if misunderstood—he was. During that time, she'd learned more about bringing dead people back to life than she ever wanted to know. The scary part of it was that Louis really *was* brilliant. Unfortunately, he was also bent as an old coat hanger.

"I first proposed my resurrection theory during my third-year rotation at Johns Hopkins," he murmured.

When he didn't say any more, Samantha looked up, curious despite herself. Louis was staring intently at a monitor on the wall, which was displaying an enlarged image from the electron microscope on the desk. From her angle, she couldn't see what he was so interested in, but it shut him up and that was good enough for her.

"My ideas were not well received," Louis continued, as if he hadn't just been silent for the past five minutes. "It was the primary reason my advisers steered me away from a more mainstream medical career. They thought my views were extremely unacceptable."

Samantha considered pointing out that those advisers had obviously been correct when a loud noise at the far end of the basement caught her attention. She jumped up, moving close to the door of her cage and wedging herself against it so she could see what was coming, fearing the worse. In the cage next to hers, Shaylee did the same.

Samantha's breath caught in her throat when she saw Kyson walking in with Trey's body slung over his shoulder, Rogi behind him. The big man moved across the basement, his face expressionless as he gently placed Trey on the stainless steel table over by the rack full of electrical gear. Her heart started thumping harder as Trey remained completely motionless on the table. There was blood running down the side of his head, soaking his hair and the collar of his shirt. Trey's skin was pale and sallow, like he was wiped out.

"What the hell did you do to him?" she shouted, banging the palm of her hand against the metal grating of her cage. "Is he alive?"

The three men ignored her, which only freaked her out even more. Kyson moved over to stand near the inclined table he'd been strapped to earlier, his eyes slanting momentarily toward Shaylee before staring straight ahead again. When Rogi came over and strapped him down on the rack a moment later, Kyson didn't resist at all.

Samantha didn't bother trying to get Kyson to tell her anything because she knew that would be useless. Instead, she focused all her attention on Trey, praying she would see his chest rising and falling. She was still holding her breath for such a sight when there was more movement over by the door. A moment later, Nadia strolled into the basement as if she were walking into the break room at the institute. She didn't bat an eye at the sight of Trey lying on the table bleeding, or the hulking Kyson strapped in place near the wall.

When the woman cupped Trey's jaw in one of her small, long-fingered hands and turned his head to the side to check the wound at his temple, Samantha started to hyperventilate a little. Her hand had been the one that had held the cloth to Samantha's mouth and nose and chloroformed her last night.

Hugh might not be involved in this mess, but Nadia sure as hell was. Crap. How was this even possible?

"What did you do to him?" Louis asked harshly, grabbing one of Trey's wrists to take his pulse, looking straight at Rogi the whole time. "If you've damaged him so much that I can't get any use from him, I will eviscerate you. And you'd better believe I will make sure you live long enough to experience every agonizing second of it."

Rogi turned a pale shade of green, shaking his head the entire time. "Okay, okay. I may have tapped him in the head with a base-ball bat, but I wouldn't have had to do it if the asshole hadn't spouted frigging fangs and claws. He damn near killed us."

Fangs and claws?

For the second time in the span of a few minutes, the air

seemed to freeze in Samantha's lungs. It only got worse as she listened to Rogi and Nadia go into detail as they told Louis about
what they'd seen. If the things they were describing didn't match
up so perfectly with the wounds she'd found at various SWAT
crime scenes over the past two years, Samantha wouldn't have
believed them. Strangely, Louis didn't seem surprised by anything
they told him, making her wonder exactly what he'd seen during
the fight between Trey and Kyson at the Cedar Ridge Preserve the
other night.

Louis glared at Nadia as he shoved a syringe into one of Trey's
forearms and drew blood. "I'm assuming you're responsible for his
unconscious condition. How long did you feed on him?"

Feed on him?

Samantha jerked her head up. She had no idea what Louis was
talking about, but she knew it couldn't be good.

"You knew?" Rogi demanded, his normally small beady eyes
wide in shock as he threw a terrified look in Nadia's direction.
"You knew she was…whatever the fuck she is, and you sent me
out with her anyway? What if she lost control and decided to feed
on me instead of him?"

Louis didn't say anything as he moved over to the counter and
began to use the blood he'd taken from Trey to prep slides for the
electron microscope.

Nadia laughed as she motioned toward a still unconscious
Trey. "Trust me, Rogi. There will never come a day when you have
to worry about me feeding on you instead of him. Why have cold
cuts when I could have wagyu beef?"

Rogi bristled at that even as Nadia turned and looked at Louis.
"And don't worry about how long I fed on him. Like I told you
before, Officer Duncan is extremely strong. I fed enough to render
him unconscious, but I have no doubt he'll wake up soon enough.
Probably a lot sooner than we'd like, too, so I suggest you complete your examination as quickly as possible. We don't want him

coming to before we're ready. Not unless you want me to feed on him again."

Samantha spent the next hour shouting questions at Louis and Nadia, receiving few if any answers in return. Her former boss was too intent on whatever he was doing to Trey and his blood, while her former coworker seemed far more interested in torturing Samantha about getting a taste of her man. It drove her crazy that she still had no idea what the whole "feeding" thing was about, but if she was picking up properly on the occasional comment, it seemed like Nadia was somehow able to absorb energy from Trey by touching him. Simply thinking something like that made Samantha feel like the world was tipping off its axis, but it was the only thing that made sense based on what she'd heard.

Samantha winced as Louis pulled a scalpel out and sliced open Trey's arm. The wound was deep and bloody, and she slammed herself against the door of her cage in an attempt to get free. It was useless, of course, but she couldn't stop trying to get to Trey. She was so freaked out she almost missed the awe in Louis's eyes when the wound stopped bleeding and began to scar over in seconds. She'd seen that same thing before, when Trey had cut his hand on the piece of broken coffee mug, but it was still too incredible to believe.

Muttering something to himself that sounded like, "Fascinating," Louis picked up a knife and stabbed Trey in the chest.

Samantha screamed. Even from where she stood, she knew Louis had deliberately missed Trey's heart, but that didn't make the agony of seeing the man she loved in pain any less, not even when that wound healed as easily and quickly as the one on his arm.

She was given a few moments of distraction when Nadia released Shaylee from her cage and handed her a plate of food. Samantha wondered for a second why they hadn't simply slid the tray into the cell with Shaylee until she saw the girl walk over and stand beside Kyson, straining up on her toes to slowly feed him bit by bit with her tiny hands. Samantha had no idea why, but seeing a man as gigantic as Kyson eat so carefully and gently from Shaylee's hand struck her as the most beautiful thing she'd ever seen. Even Rogi, who was standing a few feet away, leering at Shaylee, couldn't ruin the tender moment.

Samantha was so caught up in the scene, she barely realized Louis had stopped torturing Trey and come over to stand in front of her cage. She'd missed most of what he said until one word snapped her attention back to him.

"What did you just say?" she asked.

She was sure she'd heard wrong. Because there was no way even a psychopath like Louis would use that word in a serious conversation.

Louis's mouth twitched in amusement. "I said that it turns out your boyfriend is a werewolf. I must admit that when Nadia told me her suspicious, I wasn't sure I believed her. But the blood work confirms it. The man you've been going out with is definitely a werewolf."

Samantha stared, speechless. A person could only have so many bombs dropped on them before becoming numb to the sensation.

"You…you're…crazy," she finally forced out, unable to come up with anything more rational.

Louis's expression twisted into something that almost seemed like disappointment. "Please, Samantha. Are you really going to tell me this is a total surprise to you? I know you've been collecting evidence on the SWAT team for some time now. You've tried to do a good job covering up your interest, but it didn't escape my notice how you jumped up to take any call involving them. After spending so much time investigating them, I know you had to have picked up on all the strange things that happen around them. The torn-up bodies at the crime scenes, the silly coyote explanation that gets used over and over to cover it up, the way they go up against unbelievable odds and come out on top time after time. And the injuries they survive? That by itself screams supernatural. Are you going to seriously tell me that you haven't done your own DNA profile yet? Hell, for a time, I thought the only reason you were dating Officer Duncan was to get more conclusive evidence against them."

That last part hit a little too close to home, making her wince. "But…a werewolf?" she murmured, looking over at Trey still lying unmoving on the stainless-steel table. "That can't be true."

Louis merely smiled as he handed her a piece of paper. She recognized it immediately as a DNA profile sheet. It seemed his basement lab was very well stocked when it came to high-tech equipment.

"There's some kind of wolf DNA mixed in with your boy-friend's otherwise normal genetic material," Louis said calmly. "I can't tell you exactly what kind of wolf, not with the equipment I have here, but ultimately, it doesn't matter. Claws, fangs, extreme strength, and speed on top of rapid healing? It spells werewolf, whether you believe it or not."

Yes, it was insane. Samantha knew that. But so was bringing a dead person back to life, and Kyson was walking, talking proof of that. Maybe it was time to stop dismissing what was right in front of her face. With that thought in mind, she turned and moved to the back of her cage, dropping down to her thin uncomfortable mattress. Louis was saying something else, but she found it much easier to tune him out this time.

Samantha was still lost in thought when the door of her cage suddenly opened. She lifted her head to see Nadia and Rogi drag Trey's unconscious form in. It was all Samantha could do to get in the way so Trey wouldn't crash straight to the ground when the pair shoved him at her. Even then, her legs buckled under his weight, and they both ended up on the floor in a tangle of arms and legs.

She was attempting to get out from under Trey's heavy body without hurting him when a pair of big hands grabbed her. Samantha struggled against them, but Rogi was so much stronger than she was that it was useless. Before she could even think about stopping him, the jerk wrapped something hard and rough around her neck, metal clicking on metal as he tightened it. She struggled, kicking and punching at him, and when he took his hands off her, she thought maybe she'd won. Until she realized there was still something around her neck.

Her hands immediately started scrambling, desperately trying to figure out what Rogi had put on her and, more importantly, how to get it off.

"I wouldn't do that if I were you," Rogi said sharply.

Samantha looked up in time to see him and Nadia stepping out the door of her cage, closing it behind them. She was all set to ignore his dumbass advice until she saw the small black box in his big hand. But it was the evil expression on his ugly face that had her hands freezing on the edges of the stiff leather wrapped around her throat.

"Doc originally designed that shock collar to control his pet before he realized that threatening the girlfriend was way more effective at making the creature behave," Rogi said, motioning with his chin toward Kyson. "But unfortunately for you, the collar is still powered to take down a three-hundred-pound monster. It would probably kill a woman your size and all it would take is one push of this button. So keep your hands off the collar or I'll have to test it out just to see if I'm right."

Rogi walked away with a smile, tossing the remote box casually into the air, catching it with first one hand and then the other, seemingly thrilled at the prospect of getting to electrocute her to death.

"Don't worry about the collar," Nadia said as she leaned against the metal grating of the cage and regarded Samantha coolly. "It's not really for you. It's meant to keep your boyfriend under control until Louis gets around to figuring out exactly how he's going to use his werewolf blood and healing abilities to resolve this little transplant rejection issue he'd been dealing with. Can't have Officer Duncan going all werewolf on us the second he wakes up. I have no doubt that seeing you wearing a shock collar will keep him nice and tame."

Samantha began to panic at the thought of what Louis might do to Trey. She'd already accepted her former boss was a flat-out psychopath. His willingness to keep his dead son in a tank of red goo was a clear indication of that. She doubted there was anything he wouldn't do to Trey if he thought it would get his mad experiment to the next stage.

"Oh, don't look so glum," Nadia gloated with a laugh. "You should be grateful there are only two cages down here. At least that way you'll get a chance to have some quality private time with your boyfriend before Louis gives him back to me."

Samantha's blood ran cold. "What do you mean by that?" she asked, instinctively moving to put herself between Trey and the woman standing outside her cage. "What do you want with him?"

Nadia smiled so wide she looked like the Cheshire Cat. As Samantha watched, she leaned in closer, her eyes slowly changing, becoming larger and darker, causing tingles of fear to run up and down her spine.

"When Louis is done playing Dr. Frankenstein with your werewolf boyfriend, I'm going to suck every bit of life out of him until he's nothing but a dried-up, old husk."

As she spoke, Nadia's eyes turned completely black and her skin started to take on a pale, waxy color. But instead of being afraid, Samantha was on her feet, moving forward until both hands were pressed on the metal grating of her cage door.

"You'll have to go through me," she ground out.

She wasn't sure what she expected, but the peal of delighted laughter wasn't it.

"Yes, that's part of the plan as well," Nadia said, suddenly abnormally long fingers reaching out to tease the palms of Samantha's hands.

The effect of the slight contact was immediate, cold and tingly, like electricity running through her body and Samantha jerked away, earning yet another laugh from Nadia.

"Hope your boyfriend wakes up soon," she said. "Wouldn't want you two to waste this little private time I'm giving you."

As Nadia walked away, Samantha dropped back down beside Trey and pulled his head into her lap, gently tracing her fingers along his scruffy jaw, praying he *did* wake up soon. Even if she was terrified of what would happen when he did.

CHAPTER 21

As he slowly woke, Trey couldn't help thinking that maybe it was time to get a new mattress. Because this one was uncomfortable as hell. Like he was sleeping on a damn rock. The pillow was comfy, though. Not to mention smelled absolutely scrumptious.

His eyes fluttered open, confusion hitting him as he caught sight of his old friend Kyson strapped to some kind of rack across the room. Less than a second later, the memories came rushing back and Trey was up and charging the lightweight metal door of the cage, claws and fangs extending fast. There was no way in hell that grating would keep him from reaching his friend. Then he'd find that vita and deal with her once and for all.

"Stop!"

The words were so urgent that Trey's boots slid across the concrete as he pulled up short of the door. The scent that Trey had thought merely part of a dream turned out to be real and he spun around to see Samantha sitting on the floor, looking absolutely terrified but, thankfully, alive. The sight of her took his breath away.

He saw the heavy leather collar around her neck before he took a step in her direction, and the rage that filled him made a savage growl rumble up from deep in his chest. He reached out, intending to shred the damn offensive thing off her with a single swipe of his claws.

When she backed away from him with fear in her eyes, it was like a ton of bricks had been dropped into the bottom of his stomach. That was when he realized his fangs and claws were out and he'd partially shifted, and that in his anger, his eyes were glowing frigging neon yellow.

And Samantha could see it all.

Trey jerked his hands back, trying to force his fangs to retract so he could tell Samantha that he'd never hurt her. Then he'd tell her how sorry he was, that he should have told her that he was a werewolf earlier, and how he wasn't the monster she must certainly believe him to be.

Then he heard the soft buzzing coming from the collar and saw Samantha's body stiffen. Her face went deathly pale.

"You can't touch the collar," she hissed in a painful gasp.

Her eyes slid to the side and she looked into the room beyond. Trey followed her gaze, finding the stocky man from his apartment with the beady eyes and the wide shoulders standing outside the cage, a smile on his face and a little black box in his hand.

"That's right," the man said. "Don't touch the collar and don't touch the door. Or your girlfriend pays the price. Though I'm not too sure she'll want to be your girlfriend anymore. Not now that she knows what you are."

The man turned away from the cage, his finger brushing over the top of the little black box in his hand. Samantha immediately slumped sideways, her body relaxing and a sigh of relief slipping out. Trey was immediately at her side, catching her before she could collapse all the way to the floor. He threw a glare at the man across the room, making sure the asshole could see Trey's hands were nowhere near the collar.

Trey paused for a moment to take in his surroundings, confused and concerned in alternating degrees by the creepy medical equipment, the big vat of red goo with the heavily scarred teenager inside, a living, breathing Kyson strapped to a rack on the far side of the room, and an exhausted young woman on the floor next to him. He couldn't see her entire face, but Trey was almost certain the woman was the woman who had a thing for Kyson, Shaylee Bright. He couldn't fathom how she'd ended up here. Then again, he had no idea how any of them had ended up here.

Wherever *here* was.

It was only when he looked back at Samantha and where his hand was rubbing little circles in the middle of her back that Trey realized his claws were still extended. So were his fangs. He'd been so freaked out that he hadn't even considered shifting back.

"So you're a werewolf?" she said softly as she gazed up at him, not looking quite as freaked out as he expected her to be.

Still, the question caught him off guard so badly that all he could do was sit there and stare, head spinning as his mind tried to come up with something coherent to say. Finally, when nothing rational would come, he gave up and simply nodded, surprised when she didn't skitter to the far side of the cage.

"How long have you known?" he asked, finally getting himself under control enough to banish his fang and claws.

"I've known that you and your SWAT teammates were hiding something big from the rest of the world for about two years now." She gave him a small smile. "But the werewolf thing? Louis dropped that particular bomb on me a few hours ago, after his minions dragged your unconscious body into the room. I have to admit, it's a secret I would have rather learned from you. But if I'm being honest, I can't complain too much since I've been keeping a lot of secrets from you, too."

He'd suspected as much. But since he'd been hiding things, too, he couldn't hold it against her.

Trey sighed, knowing it was time for a full confession. Unfortunately, there were a few other things they needed to talk about first. He tugged Samantha closer, moving them back toward the crappy mattress near the wall, carefully pulling her into his lap. He watched out of the corner of his eye as the guy with the collar remote eyed them suspiciously. Trey kept his hands where the man could see them, not wanting to give him a reason to push the button on the remote. The thought of Samantha getting hurt because of him made him want to throw up.

"Look," he whispered softly. "I know we have a lot to talk about when it comes to the secrets we've been keeping from each other, but could you maybe bring me up to speed first? I'd really like to know who that man with the remote is, where we are, and how you ended up here. And if you happen to know how the hell Kyson is alive when we both saw the paperwork declaring him dead, that would be nice, too."

Trey thought she might complain, considering the fangs and claws he'd been flashing not thirty seconds ago. But all she did was throw a quick look at the dumbass with the remote for the collar, then leaned in closer. The move made it nearly impossible to miss how good she smelled. Damn, he couldn't believe he was thinking about how distracting her scent was at a time like this.

"That might be difficult since I barely understand it myself," she said softly. "For starters, the guy holding the remote is Rogi. He's basically the muscle who gets rid of the body parts and does anything else Louis tells him to do. And yeah, before you ask, Louis is the Butcher by the way. He stumbled across a way to resurrect the dead, starting with your friend, Kyson. But he only did that so he can perfect the process before trying it on his son, the kid floating in the tank full of red goo."

Trey opened his mouth to ask the first of dozens of questions, but she continued before he could.

"There's more," she said. "The resurrection process apparently didn't take, at least not completely. Kyson's body is slowly dying, part by part. Shaylee says it's because Kyson has no desire to live…at least not like this. Louis has been amputating parts off Kyson as they fail and replacing them with the pieces he's taken from his victims, some of whom he's been stealing from the institute's morgue. And oh yeah, he's been setting Hugh up to take the fall for all of this. When I stumbled across the trail and thought Hugh was the Butcher, I went to talk to Louis, not realizing he was involved. That's how I ended up down here. We're in the basement of Louis's Westover Hills home, by the way."

"Damn," Trey whispered, trying to wrap his head around everything Samantha had told him. "Louis is the Butcher? I never saw that coming. And resurrecting the dead? If Kyson wasn't right here in front of me looking like something out of a horror movie, I never would have believed it."

Samantha leaned into him, resting her head on his shoulder as well as she could considering the heavy collar around her neck. "Trust me, I get it. I've seen some of what Louis has done to Kyson and I'm still having a hard time dealing with it. It's a lot to take in."

"And Shaylee?" Trey asked, motioning toward where the woman still sat on the floor near Kyson, looking utterly exhausted. "How did she get involved in this?"

Samantha moved her face just enough to look over at the woman, sighing softly. "She had the bad luck to be living in the woods near the Trinity River body dump location and saw Kyson. Rogi grabbed her and they've been holding her as leverage against Kyson ever since. They've done a number on your friend, Trey. Louis claims he barely remembers anything about his old life, but he loves that woman with everything he has left."

He groaned. "This is so screwed up. Kyson's whole life has been one long uphill battle of pain and struggle, from his so-called family to the war, to the years he spent trying to recover from his injuries, and then being homeless. Even after death, it seems he still can't catch a break."

"Unfortunately, it probably isn't going to get much better anytime soon," Samantha said. "From what Nadia told me, Louis is planning on using your werewolf DNA to improve Kyson's healing abilities to stop his body from rejecting the transplants. After seeing Louis's methods, I'm guessing that means another round of painful experiments for Kyson."

Trey realized that answered one of the questions he hadn't gotten around to asking yet—why they hadn't killed him in the first place. He was about to ask how Louis had figured out what he was when it occurred to him that Samantha had mentioned Nadia. In all the craziness, he'd completely forgotten about the vita.

"How is Nadia involved with Louis?" he asked, sniffing around for the overly sweet smell he'd come to associate with the vita lamia and finding nothing. "We only picked up her connection to the Butcher case late last night, then spent the rest of the time looking for her. We thought she was the one who'd kidnapped you."

"You sound like you already know more about her than I do," Samantha said. "I didn't know she was involved in this at all until she walked in the door shortly after Rogi and Kyson brought you here. I'm not sure what it means, but she said something about *feeding* on you. She implied that when Louis is done with you, she gets to have you. In fact, she compared you to wagyu beef. And… um…you may not believe this, but her eyes changed and got all big and buggy when she threatened me earlier. I'm assuming Nadia's something like you, but different."

Trey couldn't help but laugh a little, even if the part about Nadia wanting to feed on him was totally disgusting. "Like me, Nadia is a supernatural. But that's the only thing we have in common. She's something called a vita lamia. It's a kind of vampire that feeds on a person's life force—their energy. So yeah, we're different."

He could practically hear the wheels turning in Samantha's head as she processed what he'd told her. He had to admit, she was taking all of this exceptionally well. Maybe he should have taken Connor's suggestion and told her what he was sooner.

"So, my coworker is a life-sucking vampire." Samantha pulled back to look at him. "And you're a werewolf."

The word hung in the air between them and Trey's heart stopped a little. This was the moment he'd been dreading and now that it was here, he felt like he couldn't breathe. He'd gone up against bad guys trying to kill him more times than he could count, but he'd never been as terrified as he was right now. If Samantha rejected him, he wasn't sure he'd be able to handle it.

Somewhere inside, his inner wolf howled.

"I know this is a lot to take in," he said softly. "But I promise you I'm not the monster you think I am."

Samantha recoiled, stiffening in his lap. "I don't think you're a monster. I could never think that!" She reached up to cup his jaw. "You're the kindest, sweetest, most gentle man I've ever met. You have something in your blood that makes you unique. That's all. It doesn't change the way I feel about you."

Gazing into her blue eyes right then, Trey believed every word she'd said. Just like that, the stranglehold of fear around him disappeared—if the sigh of contentment his inner wolf let out was any indication, it was as relieved as he was. There was still the subject of soul mates to talk about, but they could explore that later. At the moment, knowing she cared for him was enough.

He smiled. "If I didn't think that jackass with the remote would zap you, I'd kiss you right now."

Samantha grimaced, darting a glance in Rogi's direction. "Since we can't do that, why don't you tell me how you became a werewolf? Did you get attacked and bitten while crossing the Yorkshire moors of Northern England or something?"

"Yorkshire moors?" He lifted a brow. "That's oddly specific."

She gave him a sheepish look. "Sorry. *An American Werewolf in London* is the total sum of my knowledge on the subject of werewolves. If not England, then where?"

"Afghanistan," he said simply. "But I wasn't attacked and bitten. That isn't how it works. Some people have a gene in their DNA that turns on if they go through a stressful, traumatic situation. A switch is flipped, and poof, you get a werewolf."

"A gene. Of course. The ambush you and Kyson lived through?" she said, though it really wasn't a question. "The one where Kyson was so badly injured."

"Yeah."

She chewed on her lip for a moment. "What happened to you?"

The way she said the words made it sound like she really didn't want to know.

He swallowed hard. "I got shot multiple times in the back. If I didn't have the werewolf gene, I would have bled out."

Her blue eyes glistened with tears. "I for one thank God you do have it. If you didn't…" She shook her head, unable to finish.

"I know." He let out a heavy sigh. "I can't tell you how many times I've wondered how things would have been different if Kyson had turned into a werewolf that night instead of me. Would he have gotten this charmed life I live, while I ended up in a homeless shelter?"

Samantha reached up to cup his jaw in her hand again. "I won't pretend that I've ever had to deal with anything like what you and Kyson went through, and I won't claim to know him as well as you, but I can't believe your friend would want you to blame yourself for how his life turned out. You moved to Dallas simply to be close enough to help him. You did everything you could."

"And he ended up killing himself anyway," Trey said quietly, realizing how bizarre it was to say that when Kyson was alive and strapped to a table not twenty feet away. "Doesn't that mean I didn't do enough?"

"No." Samantha slid her hand down to rest it over his heart. "It means that life is complicated, and no matter how hard we try, sometimes it doesn't go the way we expect. Then again, maybe everything that's happening right now is life's way of giving you another chance to change the ending of the story."

They didn't talk for a long time after that, and as insane and dangerous as the situation might have been, it felt unbelievably good to have Samantha in his lap, her cheek resting against his shoulder.

"I've wanted to tell you the truth for a while now. About what I am," he said softly. "But every time I tried, something got in the way. I know that sounds like I'm making excuses but revealing a secret like this isn't easy. Especially when it's not only my life that would be affected if that information got out to the wrong people."

Samantha nodded her head against his shoulder. "I can understand that. But you have to believe I would never have told anyone about you or your teammates."

"I know that now," he murmured against her hair. "But you'll have to forgive me for being a little doubtful before, especially since I stumbled across all the stuff you have tacked to the walls of your guest room."

Pulling back from his chest, she looked up at him in alarm—and maybe a little embarrassment, too. "You went in there?"

He nodded. "That night after learning about Kyson. I came out of the bathroom and the door to the room was ajar. I'm not sure why I even looked, other than the fact that I know you've been interested in my pack and me for a while. It's obvious you've been spending a lot of your free time checking up on us. It would have been endearing if it wasn't so scary. I've never had a stalker before."

Samantha let out a little snort of laughter that brought another smile to his face, even in this screwed up situation.

"At first, I was simply curious," she admitted. "There were so many strange things going on around you and the SWAT team that I couldn't let it go. You might not know this about me yet, but I have a problem walking away from a good mystery. I guess at some point curiosity turned into obsession. I *had* to know what you were hiding."

That answer hurt worse than Trey could have ever imagined. "Is that why you used that favor to get me to ask you out on a date?" he asked, hating how vulnerable the question made him sound. "So you could get closer to me and my pack and learn more about us?"

The fact that she didn't respond right away was all the answer Trey needed, and he turned to look away as his heart—which was still fragile despite the fact that she'd accepted his werewolf side—fractured a little bit more.

"In the beginning, yeah, that was part of it." The words were so soft that he had a difficult time hearing them, even with his enhanced sense. "I realized I'd gathered as much information on you and your teammates as I could from a distance and figured that if I could get closer to you, I might learn more. When you and the other guys came by the institute, it just happened."

"So all that time we spent together—slept together—was just a way to get more information so you could solve a damn puzzle?" he growled, the pain of her betrayal stabbing him like a knife. "Was breaking that coffee mug in your kitchen really an accident or did you contrive that entire situation so you could get a sample of my blood?"

Samantha lifted her head with a gasp, but she didn't deny it. Before he realized what he was doing, he moved to set her aside on the mattress, instincts screaming at him to put some distance between them, even if the cage wasn't big enough to allow that.

But then he felt a gentle hand on his arm, stopping him. When he didn't bother to look at her, Samantha's other hand came up to capture his jaw and slowly turn his face so he didn't have a choice but to look at her.

"I'm not proud of it, but I started seeing you with mixed intentions," she admitted. "Yes, I wanted to learn your secrets, but I also felt myself drawn to you and I couldn't ignore the pull. Somehow, I thought I could both spy on you and steal your blood for a DNA sample while still being with you. But it all changed at some point. I know this is going to sound like a load of crap, but something happened after I started spending time with you. I found myself less concerned with your secrets and more interested in you. I know the idea of two people falling for each other this quickly is absurd, but that's what happened. I fell so hard and fast it took my breath away."

Trey's heart beat faster. Even though she didn't know it, Samantha was describing their soul-mate connection. Should he try to explain it to her? He had to admit he was hesitant. What if Sam decided she didn't like the idea of an outside force controlling her emotions?

"I'm more sorry that you can ever know for what I did to you. I wanted to come clean about everything and tell you how I felt," Samantha said, interrupting his thoughts. "But like you, every time I tried to say something, it seemed like events were conspiring against me. And then I got chloroformed and locked up in this cage before I had a chance to say I'm in love with you."

Samantha's heart began to thump wildly, echoing in his ears. She looked stunned, maybe even a little panicked, as if surprised by what she'd just said.

"I didn't mean for it to come out quite that abruptly," she said in a small voice. ·

Trey would have laughed if he didn't think she'd take it the wrong way. So, instead, he dipped his head a little, catching her eyes. "You don't have to try to explain this thing going on between us. I feel it. I'm in love with you, too. I have been for a long time. I was too scared to tell you how I feel because I was worried I'd chase you off."

He had a second to see the look of relief on Samantha's face, then she was leaning forward to kiss him, her lips soft and warm on his. He started to slip his tongue in for a taste when she suddenly tensed, her body going completely rigid as she let out a moan of pain.

Trey jerked back, snapping his head around to snarl at Rogi, even as he heard the hum coming from the collar around her neck. The ugly man had moved closer to the metal walls of their cage, the remote held higher in his hand.

"None of that now." The asshat grinned. "Can't have you biting your girlfriend and turning her into a werewolf like you. It might get in the way of what I plan to do with her when the doctor is done with you."

Rogi gave Samantha another twisted grin, and Trey felt her shiver. He decided then and there that when he made his move to get them out of here, he was going to have to pay careful attention to Rogi. Something told him the man would go after Samantha the first chance he got.

Not wanting to risk Sam getting zapped again, Trey sat back a little, so the jackass with the remote could clearly see they weren't up to anything. Rogi smirked and walked away again.

"How the hell are we going to get out of here?" Samantha whispered. "Rogi is watching us like a hawk, and it's only going to get worse when Louis and Nadia come down here again."

Trey shook his head. "I don't know yet. We'll have to play it by ear and be ready to make our move when the opportunity presents itself."

He wished he could tell her that his teammates would provide backup, but while they were almost certainly out looking for him and Samantha, he wasn't holding out much hope that they'd find them.

Samantha nodded, then glanced at Rogi with a worried look on her face. "What do we do until then?"

"We wait." Trey gave her a small smile. "We could talk some more. At least that doesn't get you shocked."

"Okay, what do you want to talk about?" Samantha asked, leaning back against the stone wall of their cell but staying close enough so her leg was touching his.

There were about a hundred things Trey wanted to talk to her about—soul mates topping the list—but perhaps he should ease into that one.

"Maybe you could tell me about that blood sample you took from me and whether I need to worry about it coming back to haunt me later?"

CHAPTER 22

SAMANTHA WIGGLED DEEPER INTO THE WARMTH AND comfort of Trey's big, strong arms holding her close, a fuzzy part of her mind realizing she'd never felt so content and protected in her life. She supposed that was what it meant to be with the man you loved.

She slowly came awake with that thought bouncing around in her head, and even though she remembered exactly where they were and how desperate their situation might be, she still couldn't stop a smile from crossing her face. She'd fallen in love in a week— with a werewolf.

Both of those things suggested there might be something seriously wrong with her. People in the real world didn't fall in love this fast. Then again, for all she knew, a week could be on the slow side when it came to werewolf relationships. The only thing that really mattered was that it felt righter than anything she'd ever experienced.

Samantha lay there pressed up against Trey's chest for a while, listening to his heart beat steady and strong under her, wondering if they could stay like this forever. Barely ten seconds later she got her answer in the form of shuffling footsteps and the sound of the basement door opening. Samantha pushed herself upright slowly, afraid Rogi might zap her again if she didn't. He'd done it twice so far, and she wasn't interested in going through that experience a third time.

The moment Samantha saw Louis and Nadia coming their way, her pulse began to race. Whatever her former boss had been planning was about to start. But as scared as she was for herself, Samantha realized the only thing she could think about right then was what they were planning to do to Trey. She'd just found him. Fate couldn't let her lose him already.

She would fight for him. Even with the collar around her neck and Rogi's hand on the remote, she wouldn't let them hurt him. She had no idea what she'd do—fighting wasn't exactly in her wheelhouse—but she'd damn well do something.

She tensed when Louis stopped in front of their cell, ready to attack the moment he opened the door. But after he simply stood there without saying or doing anything, his eyes appraising, Samantha had no choice but to take a deep breath and do her best to calm down. There wasn't any other choice.

"I have to wonder if even you have any idea how incredibly unique your DNA happens to be," Louis said to Trey, holding up a large test tube filled with a greenish liquid. It wasn't quite as vivid and bright as the stuff he'd injected in Kyson earlier, but it was definitely similar. "Your healing abilities alone could drive my research for the next decade. I mean, the levels of wound healing hyaluronic acid, Lysine, and exotic collagen synthesizers in your blood are like nothing I've ever seen before. And the number of platelets, thrombin, and fibrinogen your body created in response to the wounds I caused should be impossible. Though they would explain the clotting and near instantaneous scaring I witnessed. It makes me wonder what would happen if I slit your throat. Would your body heal the wound before you bled out?"

Samantha had already known her former boss was certifiably insane. He'd been experimenting on Kyson, causing unimaginable pain, as well as mutilating corpses from the institute and killing innocent people simply to harvest more parts for his research. She shouldn't be stunned anymore. But the casual way he'd mentioned cutting Trey's throat merely to see if he'd die of blood loss before he could heal was beyond evil.

Louis turned away, as if bored with the conversation, walking over to Kyson.

"Leave him alone," Trey said, the words coming out in a low growl even as he reached clawed hands for the metal grating of the cage door.

"Rogi," Louis said casually.

A fraction of a second later, every muscle in Samantha's body contracted at once and pain gripped her. She knew she was falling, even as a part of her mind curiously noted the violent tingles as the electricity from the collar vibrated through the fillings in her teeth.

Then, as fast as the attack came, it ended, and Samantha found herself in Trey's strong arms, knowing she would have been flat on the floor if he hadn't caught her. He murmured soft, soothing words, telling her to sit down for a moment, but she resisted. She needed to see what Louis was doing to Kyson. Legs trembling, she stood with Trey's help. Had Rogi hit her with the collar's full power? It terrified her to think that he hadn't.

By the time Samantha got herself back together, Louis was already injecting a huge syringe full of the greenish liquid into Kyson's arm. The big man lay there strapped to the inclined rack, showing very little interest in what Louis was doing to him. Instead, his attention was focused on Shaylee, where Nadia was holding her off to the side. Shaylee was crying softly, tears running down her cheeks. The fear on her face tore at Samantha's heart.

"No need to worry," Louis said absently, and for a moment, Samantha wasn't sure if he was talking to Shaylee or himself. "This new serum I'm injecting is a modification to the formula I've been using to slow the organ rejection issue. Then again, the modification involves the healing components I've extracted from the werewolf's blood, so truthfully, irreversible septic shock isn't out of the question. It probably won't happen, but I guess we'll have to wait and see."

Louis stepped back and waited, monitoring Kyson's vitals the whole time. After a few minutes, Louis must have decided his test subject wasn't going to die on him because he moved froward and got back to work.

Samantha had hoped that injecting the greenish liquid into Kyson's arm was the only thing Louis was going to do to him, but then he shoved Kyson's head back against the table and strapped that metal band around his forehead, and she knew this wasn't over.

"You don't have to do this," she yelled, pounding on the metal grating of her cage even as Trey threw her a confused, worried look.

"Actually, I do," Louis said. "The serum I injected requires a certain level of ionization to encourage DNA restructuring and protein bonding. But don't worry. If any adverse reaction to the injection was going to occur, it would almost certainly have happened already."

Trey almost lost it when Louis dropped that big black lever, electricity began to hum, and Kyson began to fight against the restraints in obvious pain. If Rogi hadn't been standing right there in front of the cage with that damn remote in his hand and a demented smile on his face, Samantha had no doubt Trey would have been through the door in seconds.

Having seen the electrocution process once already didn't make this time any easier. Every muscle in Kyson's huge body tightened so much Samantha was sure she could hear them tear. But even worse than that was seeing his teeth grind together in an effort to hold in the pain, either because he didn't want to give Louis the satisfaction or because he didn't want Shaylee to see him scream.

Samantha had no idea how long the torture lasted. It was probably only a few seconds, but it seemed like forever. Beside her, Trey let out a loud gasp when Louis flipped the lever, as if he'd been holding his breath the entire time. Which was entirely possible since she'd been doing exactly the same thing.

Louis immediately moved over and started checking Kyson's vitals and examining his body. But even from across the room, Sam could tell that something had happened. The horrible, thick scars around Kyson's wrists and upper arms were already visibly fading, become smoother. When Louis opened Kyson's shirt, she saw that the endless scars crisscrossing Kyson's chest and abs were likewise fading.

Samantha flinched when Louis picked up a scalpel and sliced Kyson open from the top of the sternum all the way down to his belt line. The amount of blood was extreme and Rogi almost zapped Samantha off her feet to keep Trey from ripping through the cage. As she reached out to grab his arm and steady herself, she caught the venomous yellow-gold glare he gave Rogi. Like he was planning to rip off his face and eat it. Even with the leverage the collar remote gave him, the goon still went pale.

She never thought of herself as a violent person, but she prayed Trey got the chance to make Rogi pay for his part in this before it was over.

By the time Samantha turned her attention back to Kyson, the long, nasty gash was completely sealed and quickly becoming harder to see. She leaned against the door of the cage to get a better look, but within seconds, realized that Kyson's wounds were healing even faster than Trey's had. Though how that was possible, she had no idea.

Minutes later, every scar on Kyson's body had faded to the point where it looked like they'd happened a lifetime ago. She doubted they would ever disappear completely, but they weren't nearly as horrible as they'd been before.

Louis was practically bouncing on his toes from the excitement as he continued to poke and prod Kyson. Clearly, he was intensely satisfied with the results of his experiment. Unfortunately, while she was thrilled Kyson seemed okay, she wasn't sure if the outcome would be as good for the rest of them.

"That went better than I could have ever hoped," Louis said, turning to look at her and Trey after checking Kyson's vitals one more time. "I'm sure I should wait to period of time to see if any long-term issues develop with the DNA transfer, but I'm impatient to move on to the next step."

Samantha felt a shiver of dread trickle down her spine at those words, realizing that her previous fear had definitely been warranted.

"Next step?" she asked softly, caught between wanting to know what Louis was planning and wishing she could remain blissfully unaware.

"Yes, the next step," Louis announced almost eagerly, moving closer to the door of their cage and looking at Trey in a way that had Samantha's stomach twisting itself into knots. "The one that involves resurrecting my son using my process at the same time I transfer a suitable portion of his very unique DNA into his body."

Samantha's stomach started doing cartwheels and barrel rolls then. A split second later, Nadia shoved Shaylee into the cage with her, pulling an unresisting Trey out at the same time. Rogi stood to the side, finger on the collar's remote the whole time, looking like he hoped Trey would try something so he'd have a reason to fry her.

As Louis strapped Trey down to the operating table, Samantha wanted Trey to struggle, to shove his way off the table in the center of the room and tear these killers apart. But at the same time, Samantha knew exactly why he wouldn't do that. He loved her and that meant he wouldn't do anything that might get her hurt, even if that meant giving up without a fight.

CHAPTER 23

"YOU MIGHT BE WONDERING WHY I'M NOT USING A SERUM based on your blood, like I did with your friend," Louis murmured, motioning casually at Kyson before carefully inserting a second catheter into Trey's femoral artery, then taping it down with multiple pieces of surgical tape.

The excessive amount of tape the doctor used worried Trey. It was like Louis expected him to jerk around all over the place on the freezing cold steel table at some point very soon.

"But my son has been dead for almost three years now, versus your friend, who'd only been deceased for a few hours before I resurrected him," Louis said, moving on from the catheter to the thick electrical cables he began to attach to the shackles holding Trey's wrist down to the table. "Even with the stasis gel I've maintained him in that whole time, the amount of healing he'll require during the process will be significantly greater. I believe transferring the blood straight from your body to his while subjecting you both to high levels of electrical ionization will be the most effective way to overcome the existing cellular damage he's already sustained."

Trey let most of that go in one ear and out the other, so he wouldn't freak out about the prospects of being subjected to those *high levels of electrical ionization*. Instead, he used the doctor's rambling distraction to focus on his right arm, tensing the muscles until he felt the metal shackle around his wrist start to dig into his skin a bit. It hurt, but at the same time, he could already sense the cuff beginning to give. If he really tried, he could rip his way out of the shackles, along with the leather straps across his chest, hips, and thighs. It would be painful, and probably bloody, but he could do it. One look at Rogi standing off to the side of the basement, however, and the way the a-hole was fingering the remote in his hand, practically salivating at the chance to hurt Samantha, convinced him that tearing himself loose right now wasn't the best idea. At least not yet.

He glanced Samantha's way to see her standing at the door of her cage, looking terrified. Shaylee was beside her, eyes flitting back and forth between him and Kyson.

His friend seemed almost an afterthought now that Louis had finished experimenting on him. They'd left him strapped to the inclined rack, but even if they hadn't, it didn't seem like it mattered. Kyson simply stood there, eyes mostly vacant. He'd gazed at Shaylee for a while after Nadia had tossed her in the cage with Samantha, but then he'd shut down. Like there was no one home anymore. It was hard as hell seeing him like that. Trey knew he should be thrilled his best friend was alive. But truthfully, he wasn't sure how much of the man he knew was still in there.

Was this the life Kyson would have wanted?

Was this even a life at all?

Even with those thoughts bouncing around in his head, Trey was worried about what Louis was planning to do with his friend. Was the son of a bitch inhuman enough to kill Kyson now that he'd gotten what he wanted out of him? Trey worried the answer was yes and that there wasn't enough of his friend left to even fight back when the time came. The blankness in his eyes suggested he'd completely given up.

Trey subconsciously strained against the shackles again, only to feel the sensation of something crawling across his skin. He looked over to see Nadia staring at him, her eyes larger than they should have been for a normal human but still smaller than they would have been if she'd gone fully vita. A smile curving her lips, she walked over to stand beside the table he was shackled to and leaned down to put her face close to his.

"I know what you're thinking," she whispered in his ear as

Louis moved over to attach cables and catheters to his son. "And it won't work. You're not going to get off this table under your own power. And when the doctor is done with you, I'll get whatever is left. Trust me, I will take my time with you. You're not the first werewolf I've fed on, but you are the first alpha, and I won't waste the pleasure I'll get from consuming you by rushing it."

"Hope you choke," Trey said.

Nadia let out a soft laugh and walked away, leaving Louis to take her place alongside the table. By the time the doctor was done with him, there were so many needles, wires, and cables attached, all of them taped and retaped, that it all started to feel kind of over-the-top. Had it been this complicated when he'd resurrected Kyson?

To distract himself, Trey spent the time darting his gaze around the room, assessing the threats and trying to come up with a plan. He wasn't worried about the doctor himself, other than the fact that he might be able to order Kyson to attack him. But with his best friend strapped securely to the rack in the corner, that wasn't too much of a concern. That meant Trey could leave the doctor for last once he made his move. Rogi also wasn't much a threat either, other than the remote he had in his hand. That thing could kill Samantha, so Rogi would have to go first.

That left Nadia, the soul-sucking vampire. She was the only one who could stand toe-to-toe with a werewolf. She'd already shown that. Trey knew that no matter what happened, he couldn't let her get her hands on his bare skin. She'd suck the life out of him before he could even put up a fight.

He expected some kind of big announcement before something happened, but Louis simply stated they were about to start the "DNA transfer" and then the doctor flipped the big lever on the wall.

The pain as his body jerked and spasmed on the table was so unreal, Trey was sure he was going to die. He watched in horror as his blood began to flow through the endless number of tubes toward the kid in the glass tank, swearing he could feel his entire body being drained. A second later, electricity began to ripple across the surface of the red goo, and the teenager started to thrash around in the thick liquid. His mouth opened and Trey could hear screams even through the fluids and the glass casing.

The pain continued to climb higher and higher, until it seemed like his bones would shatter from the stress of his body fighting against the restraints. He knew that at any second, those bones would fly into pieces, tearing through his skin like shrapnel from a grenade. But even worse than the pain in his bones was the agony screaming through his skull. It was like church bells smashing around in there.

"I might have failed to mention that the transfer process is probably going to kill you," Louis said in a nonchalant tone as he watched his son splashing around in his tank of red goo. "Or at least leave you without all your faculties."

Trey could hear Samantha shouting and slamming her hands against the metal grating of her cage, pleading with Louis to stop. Shaylee was shouting, too, but at Kyson, begging him to do something. Even Nadia was complaining, saying the whole thing was taking too long. Apparently, she was impatient and wanted dinner.

Trey found it nearly impossible to focus on anything going on around him. The pain was ripping though his head like razor wire, shredding his mind to pieces. When his bones finally started to crack, he was sure it was the electricity killing him, and he berated himself for not doing something sooner. Now, Samantha would be left on her own with no way to protect herself.

"He's alive!" Louis shouted, stepping closer to the glass tank as his son fought his way to the surface of the goo, screaming and thrashing around even harder. "It's working!"

Trey ignored the doctor's announcement as he realized that the cracking sounds signified something drastically different than he'd thought. Something that had only happened to him twice in his entire life, both times under the guidance of someone in the Pack who knew what the hell they were doing.

Holy crap.

He was going through a full shift while being electrocuted to death.

Just as he felt the unnatural and itchy sensation of fur pushing its way through his skin, there was a horrendous roar of anger from the side, immediately followed by the shrieking of tearing metal. Barely able to control his body, Trey somehow managed to flop his head to the side in time to see Kyson jerking himself away from the rack holding him, eyes full of anger as he launched himself forward only to be met halfway across the room by Nadia in her fully transformed vita lamia form.

It was almost comical seeing the much smaller, almost frail-looking vita preparing to fight the mountain of a man that was Kyson. His friend easily outweighed her by at least a hundred and fifty pounds. Then the pale-skinned creature backhanded Kyson across the room, bouncing him off the metal rack he'd broken loose from, and Trey realized the fight might be as lopsided as he'd thought, but in the opposite direction.

Trey continued his shift, the process made more complicated by the shackles and straps confining him to the table. A wide-eyed Rogi came running toward him, remote in hand. Skidding to a stop beside the table, he grabbed a scalpel from the tray and stabbed Trey in the chest over and over with the blade.

"Stop it!" Louis shouted. "You'll ruin the resurrection process!"

Rogi ignored him. Apparently, he couldn't give a shit about the boy and his resurrection.

So distracted in his desire to stab Trey, Rogi seemed to have forgotten the remote in his hand. Trey wasn't complaining. The razor-sharp scalpel struck multiple times and hurt like hell, even though the agony of the electrical current was still rippling through him.

Once the shift had gone far enough, Trey was able to get a paw loose from one of the shackles. That freed him up enough to lunge forward. Rogi assumed Trey was going for his neck and threw up his hands to defend himself. Not going to turn down the target Rogi gave him, Trey sank his mostly formed fangs into the man's left arm. The resulting crunch and cry of pain was intensely satisfying—almost as good as watching the remote hit the floor and bounce away.

With Rogi slashing away at him, Samantha and Shaylee shouting in the background, and Kyson fighting with Nadia, it was damn near impossible to stay calm enough to focus on finishing the shift. Taking wolf form had never come easily for Trey, which was why he'd only done it with his pack mates around to help. Listening to your own bones shatter and then knit back together in a completely different shape was terrifying. Getting through it meant relaxing and letting it happen. And no, he wasn't exactly relaxed right now.

He was still fighting both the restraints and Rogi, barely avoiding a scalpel blade in the eye, when Louis showed up. The doctor threw his weight on top of Trey, trying to get his paw back under the shackle while attempting to reattach the catheters that were somehow still stuck in Trey's now partially shifted leg.

"Jamison could die if the resurrection process isn't finished properly," Louis ground out as if he thought that would keep Trey from trying to save himself.

Trey planted his free paw in the doctor's chest and shoved him away, propelling him halfway across the basement and bouncing the man off the glass case holding his struggling son. Jamison reached out and grabbed at his father, electricity continuing to sparkle across his goo-covered skin. Louis successfully shook off his son's grip, making the glass tank rock. The liquid inside sloshed dangerously as Jamison grabbed onto his father's lab coat.

Louis's knees gave way and he collapsed to the floor, dragging his son out of the tank, red liquid splashing everywhere. Jamison's cries of pain as he hit the floor made Trey's stomach twist into knots. But for reasons Trey didn't even attempt to understand, Jamison quickly jumped up and began to fight against his father, punching him.

Kyson suddenly came flying over the table, almost crushing Rogi in the process. Kyson bounced and slid across the floor, but immediately jumped to his feet, throwing himself right back into the fight with the vita. The battle was pure violence and rage, hisses and shouts filling the air and reverberating off the stone walls of the basement. Kyson and Nadia were both covered in blood, but they both healed as fast as the other tore them apart. Several times, he saw Nadia try to get her hands on his friend, probably to try to suck the life from his body. But every time she got that close, Kyson smashed the creature aside with one of his fists.

Trey was so worried about Kyson that he missed Rogi charging at him again. Trey didn't even have a chance to move before the jackass slammed the scalpel into Trey's chest, wedging the thin blade between two of his ribs before it snapped off. The pain was beyond description, but at least it gave him something to focus on besides the insanity all around him.

He used that focus to complete the shift, sliding out from under the leather straps before tumbling off the table and onto the concrete floor. The fall ripped out the catheters and remaining electrodes, ending those sources of pain at least. He was on his four paws immediately, off balance and unsteady, weak from blood loss, the electric shocks, and lack of practice. He looked around to figure out if he should help Kyson, try to free Samantha and Shaylee, or take down Rogi.

Kyson seemed to be holding his own, and even as much as Trey's instincts screamed at him to go to his soul mate, he knew he'd never get through the lock of the cage in his present form. It was the sight of Rogi scrambling for the remote, obviously realizing it was the only thing that would keep him safe from Trey's fangs and claws, that ultimately made the decision for him.

He launched himself at the man, reaching Rogi just as he found the remote under a bench full of surgery equipment. Trey dragged him out by his left leg, chomping down on his hand with the remote before he could push the button. Rogi dropped it with another whimper, the plastic device shattering into half a dozen pieces on impact with the floor.

Rogi jerked away, ignoring his damaged arm, and grabbed up the first weapon he could reach—a long surgical drill bit at least six inches. He plunged it into Trey's shoulder. Rogi didn't pause to see the results of his handiwork but, instead, turned and ran for the door at the end of the basement and the stairs beyond, shoving his way between Louis and Jamison in his effort to get way.

Louis stumbled backward, aided by a shove from his son, who barely seemed to be acting human at this point. The wounds that had been covering the kid's body were only partially healed, but it was difficult to make out the fresh blood from all the red goo drying on his skin. But it was Jamison's eyes—spread wide and filled with hatred and pain—that caught Trey's attention. Hatred and pain that were aimed straight at his father.

Louis sailed through the air, falling into the rack of electrical gear along the back wall. His eyes widened as sparks erupted all around him. A split second later, he exploded in flames. Louis screamed, scrambling away to escape the pain, but he fell to his knees in front of the tank that had recently held his dead son. The fire spread quickly upon coming into contact with the red goo and the tank exploded, sending glass everywhere. Flames leaped up Jamison's legs, sending him rolling across the concrete to the far wall, wailing in even greater pain than he had before.

Trey's fur began to curl from the intense heat, and it struck him then how insane it was for Louis to have preserved his son in a vat of flammable liquid for almost three years.

Smoke filled the basement, flames racing up the heavy wooden columns and across the ceiling. Kyson roared in, his friend's eyes filled with panic. Since getting burned in Afghanistan, Kyson had been deathly afraid of fire. Now that fear had left him paralyzed, cringing back against the wall even as the vita charged at him again.

Once more ignoring the instincts screaming at him to go to Samantha, Trey leaped, putting himself between his friend and the pale creature. Nadia hissed and came at him. They met in a fury of snarls and growls, fangs and claws.

The vita threw herself on Trey's back, trying to latch her hands around his thick neck. He felt the slight tremor as she tried to pull the life out of him like she'd done back in his apartment, but his thick fur kept the creature from getting close enough to his skin to do it right. He slung her off his back, lunging forward to close his jaws around her forearm, crushing down until he heard the crunch of bones. The flavor of her blood was bitter and nasty, making him want to gag. She slashed his face open, freeing herself, then taking a quick step back.

They circled each other, the vicious wound on her arm healing within seconds. Fire was eating into the ceiling beam and planks like a living thing, smoke quickly filling the basement. As he and the vita danced around each other, he heard Samantha and Shaylee coughing and calling out for Kyson to help them. A quick glance in his friend's direction showed that was a useless hope. Kyson was hunkered down against the nearest wall, eyes wide with terror and locked on the flames around him.

Trey knew he didn't have much time. If it were just him, he could have handled the smoke and flames for a while. Kyson probably could have, too. But Samantha and Shaylee? No way.

He was about to launch himself at the vita again when the creature let out a shriek that practically shook the walls of the basement. A second later, Nadia spread her arms wide and the space around her was filled with an enormous pair of frigging wings.

Pale gray and leathery, they were wide enough to nearly touch each wall and had sharp, curved claws at the very tips and another set midway along the upper side.

Vitas had wings. Like a frigging bat! Why hadn't that "expert" at STAT known that? Of all the things to leave out, it had to be the wings?

The creature charged him, wings buffeting the air like a hurricane, roiling the smoke, flames, and loose pieces of lab equipment into a swirling storm of chaos. Heat scorched some of his fur away, blistering his skin. Then she was on him, wings and claws working together to savage him, slicing into him and ripping hunks of fur and flesh right off his bones.

He howled but ignored the pain, fire, and smoke—even the fear that his soul mate would die any second if he didn't get her out of here—and attacked. He lunged forward and latched his jaws on the vita's throat, twisting and jerking as savagely as he could. The inky fluid pouring out of the wound nearly drowned him, but he didn't let go, continuing to yank and tear at the screeching creature. They rolled around on the floor, Nadia trying to yank him off her and Trey doing his best to rip out her throat.

She got her hands on his blistered skin, where the fur had been burned off and the agony of his life being ripped out of him felt worse than the electricity the doctor had dumped into him earlier. He felt himself weakening even as the vita began to get stronger. Trey swore he could feel the creature's throat healing under his fangs even as he continued to twist his head back and forth, digging them in deeper and deeper.

Trey's vision began to blur, and he knew he was close to passing out.

Suddenly, there was a loud roar above him, followed by a bloodcurdling scream. The vita fought to get away, apparently unconcerned about the fangs Trey had buried into her neck. He chomped down as hard as he could, figuring he'd do as much damage as possible in his last few seconds. The vita only struggled harder then, until one last savage yank pulled her away from Trey's hold, leaving most of her throat behind.

The life-sucking sensation disappeared immediately, and Trey shoved himself upright, woozy but ready to attack again. Then he saw the vita lying dead on the concrete floor, head almost completely separated from its body, and Kyson holding a bloody pair of floppy leathery wings in his trembling hands. Kyson didn't seem bothered by the smoke that was scorching Trey's lungs. Instead, he stood there staring at Trey in his wolf form.

Trey had no idea how long he and Kyson stood there, but it felt like forever as his friend gazed down at him with one emotion after the next crossing his features. Confusion, fear, suspicious—they were all there. But the one that worried Trey the most was the anger. It was bubbling right there below the surface, waiting for the slightest provocation to come roaring out.

Trey would have said something to calm his friend, but that clearly wasn't an option at the moment. And he sure as hell couldn't attempt a shift back into his human shape, not until he knew whether Kyson was done ripping things apart.

It was the sound of screaming and coughing that shattered the stalemate, and Trey looked over to see Samantha and Shaylee kneeling close to the floor, trying to find breathable air as they attempted to get either of their attention.

Trey ran to the door of the cage, avoiding the pieces of burning wood falling from the ceiling, reaching for the hasp only to discover yet again that he didn't have frigging hands. He considered tearing at the hasp with his jaws or physically smashing his way through the metal grating with his claws and the weight of his body. But at the last second, he turned and looked at Kyson, with eyes that he prayed communicated what he needed his friend to do.

Kyson hadn't moved at all since Trey had turned away, his attention locked now on the fire raging all around them, his whole body shaking in fear. Seeing the terror in those eyes and knowing where it came from tore Trey's heart out. And there wasn't a damn thing he could do to help the man.

Then a soft voice intruded into the madness.

At first, Trey thought he was the only one who could possibly have heard those words in the cacophony of raging fire, creaking wood, and exploding medical equipment. But Kyson's head immediately snapped away from the fire over his head, coming to rest on the young woman in the cage.

"Ky, I need your help," Shaylee said softly, calmly, like she was talking to a wounded animal. "I need you to open the door."

Kyson stared at Shaylee, his features relaxing and his gaze softening. But then a plank cracked above them, showering them all with flaming embers and a rush of heat, and the terror came roaring right back as Kyson's whole body tensed. His friend was seconds from losing it.

"Ky," Shaylee called out, a little louder this time. "I know you're scared of the fire and that, right now, all you want to do is run and hide. But I need you. Your friends need you."

Trey realized he was holding his breath as Kyson began to look back and forth between him, Samantha, and Shaylee, clearly unsure of what to do in the face of so much fear and confusion. But then his gaze locked on Shaylee's and he was moving, heading straight for the cage. Trey had almost forgotten how fast the man could move. He was almost a blur as he closed the distance between him and the cage.

Samantha and Shaylee pointed desperately at the hasp on the outside of their prison, but Kyson ignored them, reaching out and wrapping his fingers in the framework of the door itself. With a single heave and a screech of tearing metal, the whole side of the cage gave way. He kept yanking until the grating came loose, then he was slinging the whole section of metal across the basement. Shaylee was up off the floor in a flash, rushing into Kyson's arms, murmuring calming words to him even as she began to cough violently in the thick acrid smoke.

"We have to get out of here before we suffocate!" Samantha yelled, running out of the cage and over to Trey, laying her hand on his shoulder. "The ceiling could collapse any moment."

He froze at the feel of her warm hand against his fur, subconsciously leaning against her hip as her fingers weaved themselves into its thickness and tugged gently. It was hard to put into words how amazing it felt. But he forced himself to put those thoughts out of his head. Samantha was right: they needed to get the hell out of here.

Trey moved toward the far end of the basement, and the stairs he knew were in that direction. Samantha was right beside him, but he'd barely gone ten feet through the heavy smoke and falling firebrands before he realized Kyson and Shaylee weren't following.

Stopping, he swung his head around to look over his shoulder. Shaylee was trying to get Kyson to follow them, tugging on his hand and encouraging him, but his eyes were locked on the burning ceiling again and he wasn't moving an inch. Shaylee wasn't big enough to get him going, and her words were obviously having no effect.

Trey ran back to help but quickly realized there wasn't a whole hell of a lot he could do, short of clamping his fangs down on one of his friend's hands and trying to physically drag him out. Which was likely just going to piss Kyson off. Or freak him out.

Doubting they had time for this, but not knowing what else to do, Trey tried to calm down enough to reverse the werewolf shift and regain his human form. As he expected, it took longer than he'd hoped, but it helped when Samantha came over and knelt by his side, running her fingers through the fur of his shoulders and down his back. It was enough to help him forget the fire and smoke raging around them and the fact that his soul mate was choosing to stay down here with him instead of attempting to save her own life.

The pain of his bones cracking and reshaping was just as horrendous in this direction as it was in the other, and it was damn near impossible to ignore all the smoke pouring into his lungs as he gasped for air. But after another minute or so, Trey found himself lying naked on the concrete floor, the burns he'd gotten earlier in wolf form appearing along his back and sides. Huge pieces of the ceiling were falling all around them now, and the heat of the flames made every breath feel like his last. Samantha and Shaylee looked like they weren't going to last more than a few more seconds.

Ignoring the curious way Kyson was staring at him, Trey shoved himself upright and ran toward his friend, grabbing one of his hands. He would have liked to try to talk his friend through this calmly, but there simply wasn't time. "Kyson, we're leaving. Now!"

Then he yanked his friend's hand so hard Kyson almost tumbled off his feet. But when he kept pulling, Kyson didn't resist. Samantha and Shaylee moved to join them.

They had to dodge several pieces of burning wood as they made their way to the stairs, along with an entire section of one of the massive support beams. Right before they made it to the door out of the basement, he couldn't help looking back at the bodies they were leaving behind. The vita was lying limp and torn over by the cages, the doctor's corpse burnt and curled into a ball in the midst of the broken glass from the vat his son had been suspended in. But when Trey glanced at the wall where Jamison had rolled earlier, he was surprised to find that the body wasn't there.

Every instinct screamed at him to stop and find the kid, that something was wrong. But with the place falling apart all around them, he simply couldn't. Samantha and Shaylee were barely able move as it was. He had to get them out of here.

They were halfway up the fire-filled staircase when Shaylee collapsed, though whether it was from smoke inhalation or exhaustion, Trey didn't know.

"I got her," Kyson called out as he reached down and scooped her up in his arms without even slowing. "Keep going!"

Trey had no idea which way to go when they reached the top of the stairs and stepped out into the middle of ornate open-air atrium, suits of armor everywhere and burning staircases curving up to the upper levels. He wasn't sure how it was possible, but the fire seemed worse up here than it had been in the basement. This place wasn't going to last long.

He was sniffing the air, hoping it would lead him to the nearest exit, when a completely unexpected scent hit his nose.

Trey spun in time to see Rogi standing there holding a large bore hunting rifle. In that split second before the man pulled the trigger, all Trey had time to do was take one step to put himself between Samantha and the weapon. Then he flew backward like a train had just smashed into his chest.

CHAPTER 24

SAMANTHA WAS SO FOCUSED ON THE FIRE RAPIDLY CLIMBING the walls around her that she didn't even see Rogi until he stepped out of Louis's study with the big rifle in his hand. She opened her mouth to scream, but the warning never had a chance to make it out before Rogi pulled the trigger. The resultant boom vibrated through her chest like thunder, then Trey was flying past her, smashing into one of the suits of armor along the wall, the bullet going right through the middle of his chest.

Her scream made its way out then, even as Rogi turned the barrel of the rifle toward Kyson, his hands quickly working the bolt atop the weapon, loading another round in the chamber in a fluid motion as if he'd done it a thousand times before.

With Shaylee in his arms, there was little Kyson could do to avoid the shot beyond twisting awkwardly to the side in a desperate attempt to protect the woman he cared for. Samantha heard the gunshot, saw a line of red slicing across Kyson's back from shoulder to shoulder, watched the blood start to flow. Trey's friend stumbled forward as some distant part of Samantha's mind realized Rogi was working the bolt of the rifle again, undoubtedly preparing to put another round into Trey or Kyson, finishing whichever one he deemed the biggest threat first.

Samantha would be damned if she'd let that happen.

She spun around and grabbed for the first thing within reach, almost shocked when she realized it was the hilt of an antique sword resting in the hands of another suit of armor. The weight of the weapon shocked her. It was far heavier than she'd expected. It also seemed to somehow be attached to the armor. But there was so much adrenaline pumping through Samantha right then that she didn't have a problem jerking the weapon free and lifting it. She ended up holding it more like a spear than a sword as she turned and charged toward Rogi with a savage yell.

Rogi was so focused on putting another bullet into Kyson's back that he didn't see Samantha coming at him until the last second. He whirled around, swinging the barrel of the rifle in her direction. She didn't bother trying to slow down, knowing it was too late for that. The rifle went off just as she shoved the pointy end of the sword into his side right below the ribs.

Time seeming to slow as she realized the blade had gone nearly all the way through man's body. Blood trickled down Rogi's lip, shock on his face. Then the rifle dropped to the floor with a clatter, Rogi slowly tumbling backward, his weight dragging the sword from her hands.

It struck her then that she'd killed someone. Samantha knew she should feel something, but as the flames continued to climb higher and higher around them, nothing came. And she didn't have time to worry about that. Instead, she kicked Rogi's rifle away from the body—just in case—then turned and ran toward Trey.

From the corner of her eye, she caught sight of Kyson standing up, Shaylee still protected in his arms. The wound across his back was already closed and healing fast, but he'd be left with yet another scar on top of everything else he'd been forced to live with.

It wasn't fair.

No matter how worried she was about Kyson, all that disappeared the second she reached Trey where he lay tangled among the crushed pieces of antique armor he'd landed on, a huge pool of blood splattered all across his chest. Her doctor's training immediately told her there was no way he could still be alive even as she watched him pushing himself upright.

"Is it safe for you to be moving?" Samantha asked as she dropped to his side and slipped one arm behind his back to help him sit up.

A quick glance at his chest revealed a ragged hole the size of her little finger to the right of his heart. It was bleeding, but not nearly as much as it should have been. And obviously not as much as it had been only a few seconds ago, considering all the blood running down his chest. Her instincts were screaming in confusion, caught between wanting him to stay still to avoid injuring himself worse and dragging him out of there right this second before the place burned down around them.

"Do we have a choice?" he asked, using her arm to help him stand, motioning toward the fire that was consuming the second and third floor like a living thing.

Trey was right. Staying here for even a few more seconds could mean the difference between living and dying.

Ignoring how pale his face had become now that he was upright, Samantha slipped her shoulder under one of his arms and did the best she could to help him in the direction of the front door, Kyson right on their heels, Shaylee still unconscious in his arms.

Just before they slipped out of the atrium entryway, Samantha looked back, catching sight of Rogi's body lying there with the sword still sticking out of him. She knew that was going to be an image that stayed with her for a long, long time.

It was dark outside, and Samantha didn't have a clue where they were going, but none of them stopped moving until they were a good hundred feet from the home. Even at that distance, she could feel the heat on her skin, and she turned to see that flames were already shooting up high into the sky. She supposed they didn't need to find a phone to call for help. No way in hell someone hadn't seen the fire already.

They crashed to the ground in a section of perfectly manicured grass. Samantha gently helped Trey lie back on the ground, immediately moving to take a look at that terrifying wound in his chest. But he waved her away.

"I'm fine. Check on Shaylee."

Samantha hesitated for a moment, then reluctantly nodded. Turning, she saw Kyson sitting on the grass, still holding Shaylee in his arms, his blue eyes glassy and scared, his expression making her think of a little kid holding an injured puppy.

Samantha moved closer to check the girl's heart rate and respiration, but Shaylee was already coming around, coughing violently as she gasped for fresh air. Kyson pulled her close to his enormous chest, rocking the girl back and forth, making soft calming sounds that seemed so out of place coming from a man his size.

The moment Shaylee stopped coughing, she reached up and threw her arms around Kyson, dragging his head down to hers and kissing the hell out of him. Kyson seemed a little surprised at first, but then kissed her back. It was so damn sweet that Samantha had to bite her lip to keep from saying *aw*. Trey's big hand closed around hers, and she glanced over to see him smiling, clearly as affected by Kyson and Shaylee's moment as she was.

"I'm okay," Shaylee whispered, her resting her forehead against Kyson's. "You got us out in time. You saved me. You saved all of us."

Samantha was still a little amazed at how this evening had ultimately turned out. Yes, they'd been imprisoned by a complete psychopath, tortured, experimented on, almost burned alive, and then shot, but they were all alive…and together.

She turned back to Trey, finally able to get a look at the wound in his chest. It took a second to realize it wasn't even bleeding anymore. In fact, there was already soft pink scar tissue starting to fill in the void.

"Rogi shot you through the lung with a high-powered rifle," she whispered. "How can you possibly be okay?"

Reaching out, she traced her fingertips over the area, her medical training telling her it wasn't possible. Without questioning why she hadn't thought about it earlier, she checked Trey's back for an exit wound. Sure enough, there was one, the hole on this side worse than the one in the front. But while it was obvious that a lot of blood had poured down his back in the beginning, the thumb-size hole was closed up now. She sat back on her heels again.

"Is it because it wasn't a silver bullet?" she asked.

"Nah, silver has nothing to do with it," he said softly. "I'm alive because the bullet missed my heart. That's what it takes to take to kill a werewolf—severe damage to the heart or head. With the bullet passing clean through, I healed in minutes. If any of the bullet had been left inside, it would have been worse. In fact, the small piece of scalpel blade Rogi left in me hurts worse than the gunshot wound ever did. That's going to have to come out at some point."

Samantha was more than a little rattled about the casual way he talked about werewolves dying, never wanting him to even think those words. But she pushed those thoughts aside, leaning in closer and trying to find anything that looked like a cut made by something thin and sharp like a scalpel. But other than the dried blood and endless scraps and abrasions from his fight with Nadia, she didn't see anything obvious.

"You won't find it that way," he said. "The skin has already closed up."

He cupped her face in a gentle hand, lifting her chin. That was the moment she remembered quite clearly that Trey was as naked as the day he was born.

"The moment an ambulance gets here, I'll have them take you straight to the hospital," she murmured, trying to stay focused on the pain Trey had to be feeling and not how much she wanted to kiss him. "A few X-rays to pinpoint exactly where it is, and they'll have it out in no time flat."

Trey leaned in and snagged a quick kiss, which turned into one that wasn't so quick. Fortunately, Kyson and Shaylee were too busy with their own tender moment to pay any attention.

"Don't worry about getting me to the hospital," Trey said softly. "In fact, we don't even need an ambulance. All we need is a pocketknife and a pair of pliers, and you can dig the fragment out yourself."

She waited for him to say he was kidding, but when he continued to look at her, she realized he was deadly serious. "Oh, hell no. I'm not cutting into you with a pocketknife. I'm not cutting into you at all. Remember, I'm the doctor who chose to work with dead people because the living ones scare me too much."

The sound of sirens in the distance interrupted whatever Trey might have been about to say, and while the expression on his face suggested he hadn't given up on that stupid idea, it was Kyson jerking upright suddenly, his face displaying pure panic, that grabbed all her attention.

"Ky, what's wrong?" Shaylee asked, her voice betraying her own alarm as she tried to keep her grip on his arms even as he attempted to set her back down on the grass. "What are you doing?"

Kyson scrambled to his feet, his head snapping left and right in the dark, like he was trying to pinpoint exactly where the sirens were coming from and how far away they might be.

"I have to go," he announced, his breath starting to come faster. "The cops will know I was out there when the doctor and Rogi dumped those body parts. All I ever did was carry the pieces, but with the doctor and Rogi dead, you know they'll be looking for someone to pin all of this on. They'll lock me in a cage just like the doctor did in his basement. I can't live like that. Not again!"

Kyson was hyperventilating by the time he finished, and Samantha knew he was seconds from running, even if Shaylee was holding on to his arm like it was a life jacket. It occurred to Samantha then that Kyson was speaking normally, though she didn't know if it was thanks to Trey's werewolf blood coursing through his veins or the knowledge that he was finally free of Louis and his torture.

"Then I'm going with you," Shaylee said, clearly about to lose control herself, tears starting to roll down her face. "I just got you back. I'm not giving you up!"

Kyson shook his head, trying to pull his arm out of Shaylee's grasp. "No! They'll be coming after me. I'll have to go on the run forever. Mexico, maybe South America. I won't let you ruin your life to be with me. You deserve better than that."

Samantha thought Shaylee might smack him, and she wouldn't have blamed the woman if she did. God save all women from men and their grand frigging sacrifices.

"You both deserve better," Trey said firmly, tugging Samantha with him as he stood and moved closer to his friend. "Kyson, if you run now, you'll be running for the rest of your life. But it doesn't have to be that way."

Kyson looked off into the darkness for a moment, his whole body tensing as the sirens got closer and closer, before he finally turned his attention on Trey. Samantha could see hope in his eyes warring with instincts that were almost certainly telling him to run. "What else can I do?"

"You can stay," Trey said simply, reaching out to put a hand on his friend's shoulder. "The cops will understand that you were a victim in all of this, just like Shaylee."

Kyson thought that over for all of a second before he shook his head and pointed at the faded lines crisscrossing his chest and stomach. "You know the cops will never believe that. They'll take one look at me and all these scars and decide that I'm exactly the kind of psychopath who would kill all those people. I look like a monster. It will be easy to believe I am one."

Shaylee was crying even harder now, but Trey simply squeezed Kyson's shoulder and shook his head.

"The only people who know what happened in that basement are the four of us," Trey said. "Once that fire in there is out, there won't be anything left to go on but what we tell them. When the cops start asking the questions, you're going to let Samantha and me do the talking, okay? We're going to tell them that Louis Russo was a complete whack job who thought he

could bring his dead son back to life by using parts he was getting from the bodies he stole from the morgue and the people
he killed. Nadia Payne was helping him cover it up at the institute, and Rogi was the one who helped get rid of the bodies. You
and Shaylee were simply his next victims, people Louis grabbed
to experiment on."

Kyson still seemed doubtful and he glanced toward the night
sky that was already being lit up by all the approaching emergency
vehicles. When he turned to Trey again, he looked like he was
scared and he didn't know what to do.

"Buddy, if you really want to run, I'll help you," Trey said, his
voice low and rough. "You *and* Shaylee. But if you stay, I swear I
can make the cops and everyone else believe what I just told you.
I'm begging you to trust me, Kyson. Please. I won't let you down."

Kyson looked down at Samantha. "Why would you lie for us,
too? You don't even know us."

Samantha smiled and reached out to take his hand in one of
hers and Shaylee's in the other. "I don't know you two as well as I
want to yet, but I know Trey. And for him, I'd say anything I have
to. You two have gone through enough already."

Kyson glanced questioningly at Shaylee, who was nodding
urgently, her free hand latching on to his. "Okay, we'll let you do
the talking," he said, finally agreeing. "But what happens after
that? Shaylee and I can't go back to living in the homeless camps.
I couldn't get a job before. You really think anyone is going to hire
me now, looking like I do?"

"I'll find a place where you and Shaylee can stay," Trey said
softly. "A place you and Shaylee can start over, with nobody looking
at any scars. I don't know where yet, but I'll find a place, I promise."

Kyson took a deep breath, then nodded. Reaching out, he
pulled Trey and Samantha close, hugging them both. The move
brought tears to Samantha's eyes. Another minute and she was
going to start crying like a baby.

"Okay, I'm trusting you," Kyson said, pulling away. "But I do have a question."

"What's that, big guy?" Trey asked, his eyes a little misty, too.

"How are you going to explain why you're naked?"

Trey exchanged looks with Samantha, then shrugged. "I have no idea."

CHAPTER 25

"IS CONNOR ACTUALLY HAVING A CONVERSATION WITH THAT cat?" Samantha asked as she watched the black cat sitting atop one of the tables near the line of grills, nodding her head knowingly as the SWAT cop said something. Though whether the man was talking to the cat or the steaks and burgers he was busy flipping, she wasn't sure.

"Kat is probably telling him exactly how she wants her burger cooked," Trevor said casually as he munched on a chip covered in salsa.

Samantha was sure Trevor was kidding, but when several other people around the picnic table with them made sounds of agreement, she wondered if maybe talking cats weren't as bizarre as they sounded. Truthfully, she didn't know anymore. Discovering that werewolves, life-sucking vampires, and reanimated corpses were all real had a way of messing with a person's fundamental understanding of the universe.

Deciding to set the topic aside for the time being, Samantha turned her attention to the rest of the people hanging out at the SWAT compound for today's cookout. Trey and a few other members of his pack were playing volleyball with a bunch of teenagers, goofing off more than playing any serious kind of game. People stood around the sand-filled court watching the game with one eye and the handful of young children chasing after a collection of excited and very happy dogs with the other. She was still trying to learn everyone's name and accepted that it might take a while, but they already felt like family. The moment was rendered all the more surreal by the fact that at least half the people around the compound were werewolves and many of the others were friends, family, and mates of the aforementioned werewolves. And yes, she was still getting used to the whole "mate" thing. She was the mate of a real-life werewolf!

It was hard not shaking her head. It had only been three weeks since Louis's home had burnt to the ground, putting an end to the Butcher case and changing her life forever.

She and Trey had no problem selling their version of reality to the detective in charge of the task force. Yeah, Chief Leclair had been there too, looking more than a little dubious for some reason, but with no physical evidence to prove them wrong because the fire in the basement had burned so hot there hadn't even been anything left of the bodies, there'd been little choice but to believe their admittedly outlandish story.

As for the vacant position of chief medical examiner, they'd already offered her the job. She'd been thrilled—even if she wasn't looking forward to all the political stuff that came with the title—and had immediately accepted, much to Hugh's consternation.

"How was your trip to Alaska?" Bree Harlow asked, dragging Samantha's attention back to the other people around her at the table. "Diego mentioned it was the second time you and Trey went up there in three weeks."

Samantha smiled. She and Bree had struck up an easy friendship the moment they'd met. Bree was almost as new to the Pack as Samantha, meeting her mate, Diego, earlier in the summer. While it was incredibly easy to talk to Trey about anything, it was still nice to connect with someone experiencing the same stuff she was. It helped when Bree admitted she'd fallen for her werewolf in less than a week and now couldn't imagine living without him. It made her whirlwind romance with Trey seem more normal, if that was possible.

"It was wonderful," Samantha said, thinking of the long weekend she and Trey had spent together up there. "The weather in Homer is perfect this time of the year. Of course, that only made coming back to our hundred-degree heat here in Dallas that much worse."

"Are your friends getting settled in okay?" Bree asked, sipping her iced tea.

Everyone in the extended Pack was at least somewhat aware of the situation with Kyson and Shaylee, though she doubted Trey had told any of them all the details. It had taken a few days for Samantha and Trey to come up with a new place for Kyson and Shaylee to live where they could get a completely new start. When the idea of letting them use her grandparents' place up in Homer had first popped into her head, Samantha had almost dismissed it immediately. Who the hell would want to run away and hide in the middle nowhere in a place you had to wear long sleeves year-round?

But it turned out that the answer was obvious. Kyson most definitely would. And Shaylee would go anywhere the man she loved would be happy.

It hadn't been all that difficult to get the two of them up there and settled into the big home. The hard part had been convincing the army and the VA that Kyson wasn't dead. But after getting through the military bureaucracy—there was even a damn form for resurrecting a person erroneously deemed deceased—the rest had been a piece of cake. True, her parents weren't thrilled when they learned she'd given the place to someone they thought of as a stranger, but she wasn't too concerned about that.

"They're doing well," Samantha said, looking over at the volleyball court to see Trey lifting up a little boy so he could whack the ball over the net. The endearing image made her suddenly wonder what their own kids would look like. That out-of-nowhere thought had her suspecting falling in love wasn't the only thing that happened fast when it came to werewolves.

"Shaylee already has my grandparents' house looking more like a home than it has in forever," Samantha added. "And Kyson is getting more involved in the running of the wilderness tourism business every day. I think being in a place like Homer suits him. And Trey even found a VA-certified PTSD therapist in Anchorage who makes house calls. Kyson has seen her twice already. He doesn't like talking about everything that happened to him, but he's doing it. That's all that matters."

She and Bree continued to talk about what life in Homer would be like for Kyson and Shaylee, with some of the other people around the table occasionally asking questions. Samantha couldn't help noticing that none of those questions or comments came from Trevor or any of the other werewolves. In fact, it seemed like none of them were even paying attention to the conversation. They all seemed lost in their own thoughts, expressions pensive.

It wasn't difficult for Samantha to guess why they were so quiet. She and Trey had spent hours talking about the subject last night. Zane and his mate, Alyssa, had gone down to San Antonio to investigate some kind of ritualistic murders about three weeks ago and hadn't been heard from since. Samantha still didn't know a thing about this STAT organization that Alyssa worked for, but according to Trey, they dealt with things that went bump in the night. It was shocking to believe anything could have gone wrong, considering Zane was a werewolf, but it was obvious the SWAT team was worried. Despite everyone having fun at the cookout today, Samantha could feel the tension in the air.

Samantha was talking to Bree about her teenage son—who was also a werewolf—when Connor announced the food was ready. The volleyball was on the ground two seconds later as everyone made a beeline for the grills. She got up from the table with Bree and the others, ready to get in the line with Trey, when her phone rang. She considered ignoring it, but then realized it could be the office, which was working understaffed at the moment, and pulled out her phone to at least check and see who it was. She frowned when she saw her sister's name on the screen.

The urge to stuff the phone back in the pocket of her shorts was hard to resist, especially since she had very little doubt as to why Loralei was calling. Out the corner of her eye, she saw Trey glancing her way with concern clear on his face. No doubt he was picking up on the tension in her muscles, her slightly elevated heart rate, and the way her scent changed when she was anxious. She really wasn't clear on everything he could do in that regard. It would probably take a while to pick up on everything.

She gave him a small smile and a nod, then thumbed the green button on her phone. "Loralei, hey."

"Hey," her sister said. "How was your trip to Homer? Did your friends get moved into Grandma and Grandpa's house?"

"They did," Samantha said. "It's nice to see the place being used as a home again."

"Yeah, it is. I think Grandma and Grandpa would approve, by the way."

"Me, too."

Samantha glanced at Trey to see him loading two plates full of food over by the grill. Even as Trey fixed a burger for her, he kept looking her way every few seconds. She smiled again and waved at him.

"Well, while you and Trey were up in Homer, I checked on the progress of those samples you gave me a few weeks ago, figuring you'd be eager for more info on them, but they weren't there," Loralei said. "The results I'd already collected are gone, too."

Samantha didn't say anything. She'd wanted to slip into her sister's lab the day after they'd all escaped from Louis's demented lab, but she and Trey had been too busy getting ready for the first trip up to Homer with Kyson and Shaylee, so they'd waited until they'd gotten back. It turned out that Trey was exceptionally good at breaking and entering. Knowing all of her sister's computer passwords had helped, too. Within minutes, they'd taken every-thing Loralei had come up with.

She and Trey had quickly flipped through the results detailing what kind of prehistoric wolf DNA was blended so perfectly with his and the parts of his DNA strand that were no longer human at all. It was exactly the kind of stuff Louis would have drooled over.

It was also the kind of stuff she'd spent two years looking for.

And they'd burned it all. Every single piece of it.

"Don't worry about the samples," she told her sister. "Don't worry about any of it. In fact, I want you to act like it never happened, okay?"

Loralei was quiet for a moment. "You broke into the lab and took everything, didn't you?" she asked incredulously. "You know how crazy that is, right? What you've uncovered could change the world. Hell, it could make you famous."

"You're right. It would make me famous. Probably rich, too," Samantha replied. "But it would also destroy the life of someone I love. So I'm begging you, Loralei, let this go. For me, please let it go."

There was more silence, then a heavy sigh. "Okay, I'll let it go."

Samantha released the breath she hadn't known she'd been holding. "Thanks. You don't know how much I appreciate this."

"You're my sister. You know I'd do anything for you," Loralei said. "But are you ever going to explain to me what this is all about?"

"Someday," Samantha said. But only if Trey felt comfortable sharing his secret with her sister.

Telling Loralei she'd call her later, Samantha put her phone away, then headed over to join Trey at the table, at the space he'd saved for her in front of an overloaded plate of food. There was no way she could eat that much. Of course, she'd already learned that Trey was always up for eating anything she couldn't.

"Everything okay?" Trey asked as she sat down beside him.

She smiled and nodded, leaning her shoulder into his, picking up her cheeseburger and taking a bite. It was juicy and perfectly cooked. Connor definitely knew his way around a grill.

She was so relaxed and comfortable among the Pack that she didn't realize someone had asked her a question until she glanced up from her plate to see everyone at the table regarding her expectantly.

Oh crap. What did I miss?

"What?" she asked to the table in general, not even sure who'd been talking to her.

Beside her, Trey looked a little panicked. Hopefully, it wasn't anything embarrassing.

On the other side of the table, Hale gave her a knowing smile, like he thought she was trying to come up with a way to delay answering. "I asked what you thought about being *The One*? You never talk about it."

From the corner of her eye, she caught Trey making a shushing motion in Hale's direction with his hand.

"The one what?" she asked.

The whole table went silent. Everyone at the two tables closest to theirs went just as quiet. It was like Samantha had cast aspersions on the Super Bowl lineage of the Dallas Cowboys. That was when she realized they weren't staring at her but Trey. And some of his pack mates—Trevor and Hale in particular—looked kind of pissed.

"You haven't told her?" Connor demanded, his voice flat but his expression making it clear he was stunned. "Are you frigging kidding me? You've had weeks!"

Samantha looked from Trey to Connor and back again. Damn, she hated being on the outside of anything that everyone else obviously knew about.

"Tell me what?" she asked.

No one answered. Not even Trey. She was one the verge of getting a little annoyed when Trey stood up so quickly that he practically flipped over the bench she and everyone else was sitting on.

"We need to talk," he said, his voice calm but edged with

tension. Reaching down, he took her hand, urging her up from the bench. "Let's take a walk."

She fell into step beside him as he walked toward the far end of the compound. It was obvious that he wanted a little privacy and that scared the hell out her. Whatever he had to say must be bad, especially if he hadn't wanted to tell her.

Samantha was practically hyperventilating by the time they reached the far end of the compound's obstacle course, tears gathering at the corner of her eyes. Everything was so good between them. She couldn't bear the thought of anything messing that up.

"We're soul mates," he said softly, turning to look at her. "Being *The One* means that you're the one person in the world who I'm supposed to be with. The only one who can ever accept me for what I am."

Soul mates? Things like soul mates belonged in romance books and fairy tales. But then she remembered there weren't supposed to be werewolves, vampires, and monsters. Look how wrong she'd been about that.

Her head suddenly started to spin. After everything she'd learned over the past few weeks, hearing they were soul mates still threw her for loop. She couldn't help it. The implications were... scary.

"What are you saying?" she asked, all too aware that every werewolf at the compound could listen in on their conversation if they wanted to. "That the two of us were destined to be together from the day we met? That we didn't even have a say in the matter? That everything we've done—falling in love with each other and moving in together—wasn't our choice?"

"It's not like that," Trey said softly, taking her free hand in his other one. "Fate—or whatever you want to call it—may have put us together, but there's nothing predestined about it. We could have ignored what was right in front of us." His mouth quirked. "And considering the fact that we danced around each other for almost two years, I think it's safe to say we both did our best to screw up what fate was trying to do. If you chose to walk away from me after you found out I was a werewolf, there would have been nothing stopping you. Even after I said I love you."

The thought of walking away from him made her feel light-headed and she found herself tightening her grip on his hands a little. Maybe that was what it meant to be *The One*. But did that truly matter? Trey loved her and she loved him. *That* was the important thing.

"How long have you known that I'm your soul mate?" she asked.

"I've been attracted to you since the first time I saw you at that first crime scene," Trey admitted, smiling a little, like he was replaying a happy memory. "But it wasn't until our first date, when I realized your scent had become impossible to resist, that I knew you were *The One* for me."

"My scent?" she repeated, caught off guard and more than a little curious. "What do I smell like?"

Smiling, he bent his head to bury his nose in her neck and breathe deeply. "Cherry blossoms and spring air after a light rain," he whispered against her skin.

Yeah, that worked for her. There was no denying she loved him and wanted to spend the rest of her life with him.

"If you knew all the way back then, why didn't you tell me?" she said.

Trey suddenly looked like a little boy who'd been caught throwing his baseball through a neighbor's window. It was impossible to stay mad at a guy who looked like that.

"I was already nervous about telling you I'm a werewolf because I was worried about how you'd react. If I dropped the whole soul-mate thing on you at the same time, I was pretty sure you'd run for the hills. Which I didn't want since I was falling in love with you at the time."

Ah, damn. This guy was good. "And after I knew you were a werewolf? Why didn't you tell me then? Say, during that first flight up to Alaska."

Trey looked so chagrined, he was damn close to blushing. It was adorable!

"I tried, but by that point, the lie—if only one of omission—had taken on a life of its own. And every day that passed made it that much harder to bring it up. I kept falling more in love with you and becoming more terrified you'd bail when you finally learned the truth. I had no idea how to climb out of the hole I'd dug for myself."

She wrapped her arms around his neck, dragging him down for a long, languorous kiss. On the other side of the compound, she heard cheering and clapping.

"That's it, right?" she asked when they came up for air. "That's the last secret you're keeping from me?"

He nodded and kissed her again. "No more secrets. Promise."

They were met with more applause and cheers when they got back to the picnic tables, which made her and Trey both laugh. They'd just sat down when the back door of the admin building opened and the SWAT team commander, Gage Dixon, strode out.

Trey and every other werewolf in the Pack tensed in the blink of an eye. Samantha wondered what was up until she saw the look on Gage's face. The SWAT commander had always struck her as a formidable guy—she guessed being the alpha of a pack of alpha werewolves required that—but right now, he seemed even more intense than usual.

"I just got off the phone with Nathan McKay," Gage said as he sat down beside his wife at the other end of the table. "He's as concerned as we are that none of us have heard from Zane and Alyssa, so we've decided to do something about it. Mike, Connor, Trevor, Hale, and Diego—I want you to go to San Antonio and find out what's going on."

"When do we leave?" was the only thing Mike said even as Diego leaned over and whispered something in Bree's ear. She looked scared as hell, and Samantha thanked God that Gage hadn't asked Trey to go with them. Even Kat the cat looked upset.

"First thing in the morning," Gage said. "I need to push through some paperwork and make it look like you'll be taking part in a joint training operation with the SWAT team in San Antonio."

As she and Trey were walking hand in hand to his truck after the cookout wound down, he was rather quiet and she wondered aloud if it was because he wanted to go with Connor and his other pack mates. But Trey shook his head.

"Mike and the other guys know what they're doing. If they need any help from us, they'll ask." He flashed her a smile. "Until then, I thought we could go home and finish moving the rest of my stuff into your place. I've technically been there for a week and a half and haven't unpacked a single box."

Samantha laughed. "Works for me. Though I doubt we'll get much unpacking done if past experience is anything to go by."

Every time they started, they ended up in bed. Or on the couch. Or in the shower. Even up against the wall. Not that she was complaining.

Samantha spotted Bree and Diego heading to their vehicle with her teenage son, and she ran over to catch them before they left, telling Bree to call if she needed anything.

"Your packmates are going to be okay, right?" Samantha asked Trey. "They'll be able to handle anything they run up against?"

Trey nodded as he helped her into the passenger seat of his truck. "Definitely. And if they run into trouble, they'll call us in for backup."

He must have picked up on her heart starting to beat a little faster at that announcement because he stepped forward and kissed her, long and slow, on the mouth. "But we're not going to worry about that right now. Let's go home and unpack my stuff."

Samantha smiled and kissed him back, more than ready to head home with her soul mate.

Keep reading for a sneak peek of the
next book in Paige Tyler's thrilling STAT:
Special Threat Assessment Team series

TRUE WOLF

Caleb seemed content to let Brielle take the lead on their late-night stroll, falling into step beside her as she turned left on the main road outside the pub and headed that way, not familiar enough with the city to have any particular destination in mind. He didn't say anything as they wandered, but simply walked beside her as she took in the sights along the brightly lit streets.

She realized she'd picked a good part of the city to explore as she caught sight of the beautiful Odessa Opera and Ballet Theater. The ornate Neo-Baroque architecture of the circular building made her wish it was open so they could go inside and explore, but since it wasn't, she contented herself by taking photos of the exterior. From there, they wandered past Vorontsov Palace, where they stopped again so she could take more photos, once more wishing they were taking this little sightseeing walk during the day so she'd be able to see even more of the historical landmarks.

When they reached the top of the impressive Potemkin Stairs fifteen minutes later, they both stopped again, this time on the bridge, and gazed out at the shimmering expanse of the Black Sea beyond. Brielle was so caught up in the lights of the city sparkling off the water that she didn't realize Caleb had spoken until she felt him looking at her.

"What?" she said, glancing at him.

"I asked how old were you when you first realized you could

borrow other people's abilities by touching them?" he said patiently, as if realizing she'd been lost in thought.

She turned to gaze out at the water, a smile curving her lips. "Remember that family friend I told you about? The one who let me work in his grocery store."

"Uh-huh."

"Well, one night he was doing the store's inventory when his wife called and told him she needed him at home. I knew he was stressed about getting the inventory done, but I couldn't offer to help because I didn't even know how to use the computer program. He was in such a hurry that he almost left without his coat and when I handed it to him, my hand brushed his and all of a sudden, I *knew* how to do the inventory. I finished the whole thing in a few hours, which surprised the heck out of him. Especially since I could barely remember how to even start the program the next day."

"That must have freaked you out," he murmured as they slowly started walking down the broad stairs.

"Not really." She stuck her hands in the pockets of her coat. "I wasn't even fifteen years old at the time and so focused on everything going on in my life that this one weird moment barely registered on my radar. It wasn't until a year or so later, after the same scenario played over and over with different people, that I finally figured out what was happening. And yeah, at that point, it did freak me out."

"Did Julian ever figure out what you could do?" Caleb asked, pausing with her on one of the steps to watch a big cruise ship sail into the harbor. "I mean at some point before you helped him escape from that Turkish prison."

She nodded, standing close enough to Caleb that she could feel the heat his big body generated in the cold night air. "Julian can be a bit slow sometimes—and since I'm his sister, I'm allowed to say that—but he noticed after I slipped up and borrowed someone's martial arts skills to fend off a mugger as were walking home. After that, he wanted me to use my abilities all the time, while I went out of my way never to use them."

"Why don't you like to use your abilities?" he asked as they started walking again. Whereas before she'd been warm and toasty, the temperature must have dropped five degrees when he put a couple feet between them. "I would have thought they'd come in handy considering how things were so difficult for you at that point in your life."

"You sound like my brother." She sighed. "He always wanted me to use my abilities to take advantage of people. He saw it as nothing more than a way to make money and was jealous that I had these abilities when he didn't. Whenever I refused to use them the way he wanted, we'd end up arguing." She swallowed hard at the memory. "I can't tell you how many times I thought my abilities would be the thing that finally pushed us apart."

Caleb moved a little closer, his shoulder so near her arm that she could feel his warmth again. "Would using your abilities to make your lives easier have been so bad?"

She shrugged as they continued down the steps. "It's hard to explain, but I never felt right about using my abilities for something so cheap. It made me feel like I was misusing it."

Brielle expected Caleb to laugh at her and call her silly like Julian had done so many times. Instead, he grinned.

"I'm impressed," he said. "It's definitely not the way I would have handled the situation had I been in your shoes. If I had gotten your gift at that age, I probably would have used it to rob a bank or something. The fact that you resisted the urge to go the super villain route says a lot about you."

She laughed. She had to admit it was nice to hear Caleb say something like that. She'd certainly never gotten praise like that from Julian. "You should probably refrain from being too impressed. Because while I didn't ever want to use my abilities, that doesn't mean I never did. Mostly because my brother had his own unique ways of forcing my hand."

"What do you mean?" Caleb asked as they reached the wide street at the base of the stairs and started across. "Because I gotta tell you, that sounded a little ominous."

She couldn't help but laugh again. "Sorry, I didn't mean for it to come out like that. It's just that Julian has always been good at getting into trouble and usually left it up to me to find a way to get him out of it. Unfortunately, that usually meant I had to use my abilities, whether it was finding ways to get money to bail him out of jail or fighting to keep someone from killing him. Once I even had to break into a jewelry store to return the stuff he'd stolen before they realized it was missing. And yeah, there was other stuff, too. Sometimes, it scares me to think about how many times I broke the law for my brother."

Brielle wasn't ashamed of what she'd had to do for Julian, but that didn't keep her from looking away into the darkness out on the water, wishing she hadn't been quite so honest with her criminal confession. Did Caleb honestly need to know about the jewelry store thing?

He stopped and put his hand on her sleeve, gently turning her to look at him. "Before you start worrying that I'm going to judge you for your wayward youth, I should probably let you know that I have more than a passing knowledge of what it's like to be on the wrong side of the law. And for reasons not nearly as noble as saving a sibling's ass."

She gazed up at him, wondering if he was making that stuff up to make her feel better. Then she thought about the way she'd seen him fight, both on this mission and the previous one, and how he'd always seemed on the ragged edge of control or well beyond it.

"Yeah, I can see you having problems with the police." She smiled. "You definitely have that proverbial bad boy vibe going on."

Most guys would have preened at least a little at that description. In her experience, men liked to think of themselves as dangerous. Caleb didn't seem to notice the label. Probably because he really *was* dangerous.

"I'd like to be able to blame my inner omega for all the trouble I've gotten myself into over the years," he said casually, taking her hand and guiding her out onto one of the concrete piers leading out into the bay. "But since I've been getting into trouble since I was old enough to walk—and the werewolf thing didn't happen until much later—I guess I can't use that as an excuse."

They stopped halfway down the pier to lean against the metal railing and look out over the dark water. Brielle wanted to ask Caleb about his formative years and where he'd grown up. She got the feeling he'd gotten into as much trouble as Julian. And yet, he had ended up completely different than her brother. Then again, Caleb was different from any man she'd ever met.

"If you got in so much trouble, how did you end up working for STAT?" she asked, moving closer to him, telling herself it was the heat rolling off him in waves that she was seeking. "I mean, I'm sure they wouldn't have recruited you if they thought you were that much of a troublemaker."

He snorted as he leaned in a little closer to her, still gazing down at the soft waves lapping the base of the pier. "I think you're giving them a little too much credit. STAT was so eager to get their hands on another werewolf, they simply ignored my background, figuring that was Jake's problem to deal with."

"Even if you're right about the people at the top seeing you as nothing more than a means to an end, what does any of that matter when it's obvious your teammates couldn't care less about your past?" she asked, looking over and capturing his eyes. "You guys are closer than Julian and I have ever been. Or ever will be. He might be my brother, but in all the ways that matter, I'm on my own. I can only dream of what it's like to be part of something bigger, knowing you've got someone on your side."

Caleb regarded her silently for a long moment, his face unreadable. "I meant what I said earlier when I told Ethan that you're part of the team. After what you did for all of us in Siberia, I know Forrest and the rest of my teammates think of you like that, too."

She let out a little laugh. "That's a nice thought, but somehow I doubt it's that easy. They all know I only agreed to work with STAT to find my brother. Doing one thing right isn't going to outweigh that fact. People don't trust that quickly."

"I would normally be the first to agree with you since I'm not big on the whole trust thing myself," Caleb murmured. "But when it comes to my team—my *pack*—I think you'll find it's easier than you think. You risked your life for them. That's all they're going to care about. So, give them a chance, okay? Like you said, they accepted me, even with all my baggage. If you let them, they'll be there for you, too."

Brielle didn't know what to say. Suddenly, she found herself blinking to keep the tears from welling in her eyes. Where had these emotions come from? Was she so needy for acceptance that merely thinking about being part of the STAT team was enough to make her cry?

Sadly, the answer to that question seemed to be yes.

She and Caleb stood there, gazing out at the passing ships and chatting about some of that baggage he'd mentioned earlier. Unfortunately, beyond getting him to admit to having been in jail more than once, she couldn't get anything else out of him. If she didn't know better, she would think he didn't want to make himself look bad in her eyes. Which was hilarious. He was amazing. Nothing he could say would change that.

"Why hasn't there ever been anyone else?" he asked quietly. "I mean, you've mentioned several times that it's just been you and Julian. Why aren't you with a guy?"

The question was so blunt that all Brielle could do was stare at him with her mouth open.

Caleb held up his hands apologetically. "I didn't mean that the way it came out. I just meant that you're a beautiful woman. I find it hard to believe there haven't been men interested in spending time with you."

Brielle felt a burst of warmth and happiness swirling up inside her chest at his words, and suddenly, she wasn't upset by his choice of words. The fact that she was reacting so strongly to him calling her beautiful struck her as both silly and juvenile. What was she, a sixteen-year-old going gaga over the latest boy band singer?

"I tried a few times," she said, brushing her hair back when the breeze coming in from the water tossed it playfully around her face and forcing herself to answer his question instead of thinking about the way his casual compliment made her feel. "I dated a few guys, but it never went anywhere. Having a brother around who was constantly getting into trouble certainly didn't help. What about you? Do you have anyone waiting for you back home when you return from saving the world?"

He let out a snort of amusement that quickly turned into a laugh. "I'm an omega. By definition, I'm a loner. Like you, I've dated, but it never seemed to work out. I've never had a connection with anyone."

Brielle gazed up at him. Why did it bother her so much that this amazing man hadn't found someone to share his life with? For some reason, it seemed like such a waste.

"Maybe you simply haven't found the right woman yet," she murmured, fighting the urge to reach up and caress his chiseled jaw. She wanted to do it so badly, she could almost feel his scruff under her fingers.

"Or maybe I have," Caleb said, bending his head to touch his lips to hers.

He kissed her slowly, tentatively, like he wanted to give her a chance to pull away if she wanted to. She didn't pull away—or want to. Instead, she reached up and buried her fingers in his shaggy hair, pulling him down and opening her mouth to invite him in, desperate to let him to know how much she wanted this.

ACKNOWLEDGMENTS

I hope you had as much fun reading Samantha and Trey's story as I had writing it! If you read the previous books in the SWAT: Special Wolf Alpha Team Series, then you know Samantha and Trey have been flirting with each other for a while. It took some time to finally get them together, but I think it was worth the wait! And a big shout out to Mary Shelley and her story, *Frankenstein*, for inspiring Kyson's character.

This whole series wouldn't be possible without some very incredible people. In addition to another big thank-you to my hubby for all his help with the action scenes and military and tactical jargon, thanks to my fantastic agent, Courtney Miller-Callihan, and editors at Sourcebooks (who are always a phone call, text, or email away whenever I need something), and all the other amazing people at Sourcebooks, including my fantastic publicist and the crazy-talented art department. The covers they make for me are seriously drool-worthy!

Because I could never leave out my readers, a huge thank-you to everyone who reads my books and Snoopy Dances right along with me with every new release. That includes the fantastic people on my amazing Review Team, as well my assistant, Janet. You rock!

I also want to give a big thank-you to the men, women, and working dogs who protect and serve in police departments everywhere, as well as their families.

And a very special shout-out to our favorite restaurant, P.F. Chang's, where hubby and I bat story lines back and forth and come up with all of our best ideas, as well as a thank-you to our fantastic waiter-turned-manager, Andrew, who makes sure our order is ready the moment we walk in the door!

Hope you enjoy the next book in the SWAT: Special Wolf Alpha Team series coming soon from Sourcebooks and look forward to reading the rest of the series as much as I look forward to sharing it with you. Also, don't forget to look for my new series from Sourcebooks, STAT: Special Threat Assessment Team, a spin-off from SWAT!

If you love a man in uniform as much as I do, make sure you check out X-OPS, my other action-packed paranormal/romantic-suspense series from Sourcebooks.

Happy Reading!

ABOUT THE AUTHOR

Paige Tyler is a *New York Times* and *USA Today* bestselling author of action-packed romantic suspense, romantic thrillers, and paranormal romance. Paige writes books about hunky alpha males and the kick-butt heroines they fall in love with. She lives with her very own military hero (also known as her husband) and their adorable dog on the beautiful Florida coast. Visit her at paigetylertheauthor.com.

WOLF UNDER FIRE

New from *New York Times* and *USA Today* bestselling
author Paige Tyler is the action-packed, international
series STAT: Special Threat Assessment Team

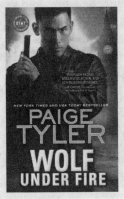

Supernatural creatures are no longer keeping their existence secret from
humans, causing panic around the globe. To monitor and, when necessary, take down dangerous supernatural offenders, a joint international
task force has been established: the Special Threat Assessment Team.

STAT agent Jestina Ridley has been teamed with former Navy SEAL
and alpha werewolf Jake Huang. Jes doesn't trust werewolves. But if
they're going to survive, she'll need Jake's help.

**"Unputdownable... Whiplash pacing, breathless
action, and scintillating romance."**
—K. J. Howe, international bestselling author

For more info about Sourcebooks's books and authors, visit:
sourcebooks.com

BIG BAD WOLF

First in an action-packed new paranormal romantic suspense series from award-winning author Suleikha Snyder

Joe Peluso has blood on his hands, and he's more than willing to pay the price for the lives he's taken. He knows that shifters like him deserve the worst. Darkness. Pain. Solitude. But lawyer and psychologist Neha Ahluwalia is determined to help the dangerous wolf shifter craft a solid defense…even if she can't defend her own obsession in the process. When Joe's trial is torn apart in a blaze of bullets, Neha only knows that she'll do anything to defend Joe…even if that means protecting him from himself.

"*Big Bad Wolf* is a perfect urban fantasy for the times: clever, romantic, heroic, and filled with hope for a better future. Suleikha Snyder has crafted an amazing world."
—Award-winning author Alisha Rai

SEASON OF THE WOLF

NIGHT OF THE BILLIONAIRE WOLF

USA Today bestselling author Terry Spear brings you a shifter world like no other

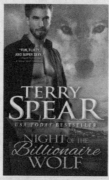

Lexi Summerfield built her business from the ground up. But with great wealth comes great responsibility, and some drawbacks she could never have anticipated. Lexi never knows who she can trust... And for good reason—the paparazzi are dogging her, and so is someone else with evil intent.

When Lexi meets bodyguard and gray wolf shifter Ryder Gallagher on the hiking trails, she breaks her own rules about getting involved. But secrets have a way of surfacing. And with the danger around Lexi escalating, Ryder will do whatever it takes to stay by her side...

"Fun, flirty, and super sexy."
—*Fresh Fiction* for *A Silver Wolf Christmas*

For more info about Sourcebooks's books and authors, visit:
sourcebooks.com

A WOLF AFTER
MY OWN HEART

Escape into this hot and delicious shifter romance
from bestselling author MaryJanice Davidson

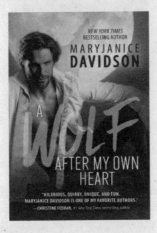

Oz Adway is a rare breed: an accountant who wants to get dirty. He's a
werewolf working for the Interspecies Placement Agency, and when
opportunity arises, he jumps at the chance to help find a runaway orphan
bear cub. Piece of cake, right? Unfortunately, the young bear has taken
refuge with clueless "ordinary" human Lila Kai, who is determined to
figure out what the heck is going on, regardless of the escalating threats to
her safety and Oz's distracting hotness...

**"Hilarious, quirky, unique, and fun. MaryJanice
Davidson is one of my favorite authors."**
—Christine Feehan, #1 *New York Times* bestselling author

For more info about Sourcebooks's books and authors, visit:
sourcebooks.com

FIERCE COWBOY WOLF

Ranchers by day, wolf shifters by night. Don't miss the thrilling Seven Range Shifters series from acclaimed author Kait Ballenger

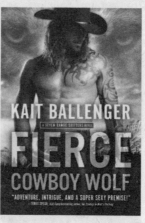

"ADVENTURE, INTRIGUE, AND A SUPER SEXY PREMISE!"
—TERRY SPEAR, *USA Today* bestselling author, *Her Cowboy in Wolf's Clothing*

Sierra Cavanaugh has worked her whole life to become the first female elite warrior in Grey Wolf history. With her nomination finally put forward, she needs the pack council's approval, and they insist she must find herself a mate.

Packmaster Maverick Grey was reconciled to spending the rest of his life alone. But he needs the elite warrior vacancy filled—and fast. If Sierra needs a mate, this is his chance to claim her.

For these two rivals, the only thing more dangerous than fighting the enemy at their backs is battling the war of seduction building between them...

**"Kait Ballenger is a
treasure you don't want to miss."**
—Gena Showalter, *New York Times* bestselling author

For more info about Sourcebooks's books and authors, visit:
sourcebooks.com

A WOLF IN DUKE'S CLOTHING

A delicious mix of Regency romance and shapeshifting adventure in an exciting new series from author Susanna Allen

Alfred Blakesley, Duke of Lowell, has long been an enigma. No one dares to give a man of his status the cut direct, but there's simply something not quite right about him. What would the society ladies say if they learned the truth—that the Duke of Lowell is a wolf shifter and the leader of a pack facing extinction if he doesn't find his true love? So now he's on the hunt…for a wife.

"Sparkling wit, scrumptious chemistry, and characters who will go straight to your heart!"
—Grace Burrowes, *New York Times* and
USA Today bestselling author

Also by Paige Tyler